THE FIRST KISS

By the Author

McCall

London

Innis Harbor

The First Kiss

Wild Wales

Laying of Hands

Return to McCall

Visit us at www.boldstrokesbooks.com

THE FIRST KISS

by

Patricia Evans

2024

ISBN 13: 978-1-63679-775-5

This Trade Paperback Original Is Published By
Bold Strokes Books, Inc.
P.O. Box 249
Valley Falls, NY 12185

First Edition: October 2024

Credits
Editor: Stacia Seaman
Production Design: Stacia Seaman
Cover Design by Tammy Seidick

THE FIRST KISS

Chapter One

Parker Haven wound her way through the streets, the early spring rain lifting the earthy scent of the wet cobblestones to her nose as she turned to avoid the crush of bodies coming toward her. The back streets of Salerno were always crowded, but this morning there was a throng of people pressing through the back alleys like a rush of rainwater through a parched valley. She stayed close to the brick wall of the alley around the front corner of the building and then into Pavé, her favorite café and the only place that felt like home.

The building that housed it was narrow and several stories tall, typical of the Italian architecture from the late seventeenth century. The café was tiny, with a timber-framed doorway, crumbling brick-and-plaster walls, and tables adorned with chipped saucers containing brown sugar cubes for coffee. The warmth of the wood-fired ovens behind the counter enveloped her as she sank down into a chair at her favorite table near the wall and pulled a stack of files from her bag.

Parker made it to the café most mornings from the military base where she was stationed and always placed the same order of rye toast, butter, and black coffee. This time, the spare breakfast was placed dangerously close to her usual stack of paperwork, which more than once had slid off the table and fluttered dramatically to the floor.

This morning the owner, a plump older woman in a faded linen apron, set Parker's coffee on the table and waited until she looked up. Her accent made even English sound like Italian.

"You will eat today?"

Parker looked up and smiled. "I never eat much in the morning, Giada. You know that."

Giada Cavalii shook her head, crumpling and smoothing her apron in one motion as she walked back to the kitchen.

Parker had been in southern Italy for the better part of a year, stationed at the North Atlantic Treaty Organization camp just outside of Salerno. A military organization, NATO was made up of representatives from thirty-two North American and European countries, and she'd been brought in as a gender perspective chief to deal specifically with women's issues arising from conflict or immigration. Military service ran in her family; her grandmother had been an army nurse during World War II, and her father had fought in the Korean War. She'd been the only person in her family to choose a military career, since her brother Wes and his husband had instead started a business in their hometown in Alabama.

Parker had just finished her toast when Giada set a small dish of scrambled eggs on her table with a raised eyebrow just as the brass bell above the entrance clanged against the glass door. A young woman hurried in as they looked on, the scent of rain following her as she passed Parker's table on the way to the counter, shrugging off her coat as she walked. She was slender, with full lips and thick hair that moved across her shoulders like dark water as she slipped behind the counter.

"Ma," she said with a glance in Giada's direction as she tied an apron low around her hips. "There's a thousand people out there already, and they're all headed in this direction."

"And that is why your sister should be here, Alessia," Giada said. "The music festival is the start of the season, and I need to be in the kitchen."

"What, she still hasn't shown up?" Alessia said, pulling her hair up into a bun as she looked out the window. "She has to come in today. I haven't been here since I bought the winery, and I don't have a clue about this new espresso machine. She knows that."

A group of tourists pushed through the door as she spoke and started to line up in front of the counter, studying the menu painted in black onto the plaster wall behind the glass bakery cases. Parker heard Alessia mutter something in Italian under her breath as she walked over to the slick chrome-and-copper espresso machine, approaching as if it were a shadowed cougar in the wild. Giada left the register hurriedly to hand her the first few espresso orders.

"Just go back to the front, I've got this," Alessia said, staring at the stainless steel pitcher of milk spitting back at her as she steamed it into foam. "It can't be that much different than your last one."

Parker went back to her stack of paperwork, but after a few minutes she saw Alessia toss the stack of orders down on the counter and rub her temples.

"Ma," she called toward the register, tucking a stray lock of glossy hair back into her bun. "Did you know Lexie was planning to show up today, or were you just hoping?"

Giada just shook her head as she made change for a German tourist, then hurriedly dropped a sausage roll into a white paper bag and handed it over the counter. The line was quickly expanding into a crush of humanity that filled all the available standing room in the tiny café, with several more people forming a line that extended out the door and wrapped around the outside wall.

Parker was considering taking her work back to her office on the base when a piercing scream ricocheted against the walls, causing every head to turn in the direction of the espresso machine. Giada rushed over to find Alessia unsuccessfully dodging a flailing hose spurting water in every direction.

"Holy Mary Mother of God," she said, making an unsuccessful attempt to capture the hose. "What did you do to it, Alessia?"

She finally managed to grab the hose, still flailing about like a medieval sea creature, and put it back into place as her daughter wrung the water from her white button-down shirt, now transparent and clinging to her skin.

"I didn't do anything, it just attacked me."

Giada glanced back at the growing line of customers pressed against the counter, all leaning in for a better look at the drama. Alessia took a handful of white towels from under the counter and disappeared around the corner into the kitchen just as the hose took flight again and water shot up over the bakery case, narrowly missing the next customer in line. Parker reached Giada just as she ducked to avoid the stream of water and managed to grab the hose. She attached it to the intake valve at the back of the espresso machine and looked over her shoulder, still holding the connection tightly in place.

"Giada," she said. "This hose should have a little metal clamp on the end that tightens on the valve. It keeps the hose from slipping off when the water pressure builds."

"When my husband put it together last week, he gave me a little box of"—Giada furrowed her brows, apparently struggling to find the correct word in English—"more parts."

"Spare parts?"

She nodded as she rummaged around in the drawer underneath the machine and handed Parker a rumpled cardboard box full of random screws and clamps. Parker chose the one she needed and tightened it onto the back of the hose as Alessia walked back up to the counter, tying the front of her still-damp shirt at her waist. She looked Parker up and down, taking in her military uniform, then turned to her mother.

"Why is he here?"

Parker held her eyes until Alessia realized her mistake.

"Alessia, this is Captain Parker Haven. *She* eats breakfast here every morning," Giada said, turning to Parker. "And this is my youngest daughter, Alessia, who was not raised to be so rude."

Parker was used to being mistaken for a man, especially in Italy where fashion tended to lean toward classically feminine. She'd always been muscular and fit with broad shoulders, and US Army regulations required her to wear her blond, shoulder-length hair pulled back tightly under her uniform cap. Except for the softness in her eyes, she'd always had an androgynous edge to her look.

Giada handed Alessia another crumpled stack of orders from her apron pocket.

"Start from the top with this cappuccino. I'm going back to the counter."

"You can't be serious," Alessia said, her voice rising in panic as her mother walked away. "I still have no idea how to work this stupid machine."

By the time she turned back, Parker had started a shot of espresso and was steaming a pitcher of milk. When it reached the right temperature, she poured the espresso into the white porcelain cup and topped it with foam. Parker tamped down the espresso grounds in the wand to start another shot, then glanced over at her and nodded at the cup still on the counter.

"You may want to deliver that before it gets cold."

"Wait," Alessia said, staring at the cappuccino. "How did you know how to do that?"

Parker winked as she wiped the foam from the tip of the steam wand. "That's classified information, ma'am."

She looked up just in time to see Alessia roll her eyes as she handed the cup to the customer across the counter. Her shirt was still damp enough to see through, revealing a slice of tawny skin just above her jeans. Parker made herself look away as she turned back around.

"I'd love to help you here, but the orders are written in Italian," Parker said, sifting through the stack of discarded orders. "Either that or I just can't read your mother's writing."

"It's probably the latter, but you don't have to stay." Alessia held her hand out. "I can take it from here."

Parker paused, but then nodded toward the tables and handed them over. "I'll be right over there if you get snowed under."

Alessia tipped her head to the side. "If…what?"

"If you get snowed under." Parker washed her hands in the prep sink. "It means if you get too busy and need a hand."

"This may come as a surprise," Alessia said, adding to the stack of cups warming on top of the espresso machine, "but not every woman is waiting to be rescued by random Americans in uniform."

"Understood," Parker said with a smile as she put down the hand towel and edged past the customers on the way back to her table. She had three days of paperwork to finish, and after a while she was able to tune out the crowd enough to make progress. When she finally looked up after about an hour, she found Alessia standing at her table in an apron streaked with chocolate powder and espresso grounds, not quite meeting her eyes. When she spoke, Parker noticed her accent was softer at the edges than her mother's, although still distinctly Italian.

"Okay," she said. "It is…snowing."

Parker tried not to smile as she gathered her things and followed her back behind the counter, stowing them out of the way and rolling up her sleeves. Alessia nodded to the massive stack of orders, toppled over in defeat and spread out across the counter.

"I don't usually work here. My sister is supposed to be doing this, but she's done a disappearing act. And I don't know how to make them…look like you did."

An impatient group of customers waited on the other side of the pickup counter, clearly willing someone to get to work on their drinks.

"Okay," Parker said, glancing over at the crowd. "How old are these orders?"

"All within the last ten minutes."

"Then let's get all the espressos out first. They take the least time." She looked over Alessia's shoulders at the throng of people waiting. "How many of you ordered a single espresso?"

Seven hands went up and Parker started the shots. She pushed several buttons on the machine and packed the next espresso wands while they brewed. They were done in under a minute, and she poured them quickly into cups. Parker looked up again at the crowd and held up two fingers.

"And how many of you ordered a double?"

Four more hands went up, and within just a few minutes those customers had also left with their drinks, leaving a much smaller and more manageable group still waiting. Parker heard Alessia let out a slow breath beside her.

"Okay," Parker said. "Do you think you can keep the espresso shots brewing while I steam milk and pour?"

Alessia nodded, pushing up the sleeves of her shirt. Her face was flushed, and her dark eyes flashed with unexpected flecks of gold in the light. Her face was bare except for perfect dark brows and a slick of red lipstick. She bit her lower lip as she looked up at Parker.

"And you'll have to tell me what the drinks are." Parker smiled, catching just a flash of a smile in return. "I just checked again, but it seems I still can't read Italian."

They worked side by side until the crowds coming through the door finally started to slow, a full hour after the café usually closed in the early afternoon. Alessia wiped the counter as Parker lined up the last few drinks.

"So how did you know how to do all this?" Alessia handed a cappuccino to a sleek American blonde who dumped three packets of sweetener into it before she dropped the empty packets on the counter and walked away. "And if you tell me it's classified again, I'll hit you with this towel."

Parker smiled over her shoulder as she turned up the steam until the milk she was foaming reached the perfect density.

"My brother Wes owns the only coffee shop in Red Cove, Alabama, so they're constantly busy. It's not the first time I've been pulled in to help." She rinsed the last of the wet grounds off her hands in the old ceramic sink and dried her hands with a towel as she leaned against it. "He pretty much considers me free labor."

They watched as Giada finally flipped the sign on the door and hurried to the back, pulling Parker into a hug and kissing both her cheeks.

"You come to dinner tonight, no?" She looked at her daughter, who raised an eyebrow but said nothing. "Alessia will let you in the café door at seven and bring you upstairs."

"Ma," she said, untying her apron and shaking her head. "You know I can't. I'm leaving now to break down those barrels at the winery."

Giada waited, arms folded across her chest, until Alessia sighed and muttered to Parker not to be late, then walked out the door and disappeared into the crowded street, still wearing her coffee-stained apron.

❖

Parker stopped on the way back to the café later that evening and picked up a bottle of wine. It felt strange to be wearing civilian clothes; after being stationed at NATO for nearly a year, it was the first time she'd worn something other than her uniform. At the last moment, she'd chosen her gray trousers, a slim black leather belt, and glossy wingtips, with a short-sleeved Cuban button-down. She'd almost forgotten how her hair looked when it wasn't slicked back under her cap. The wind picked up the airy edges of it to remind her, touching it to her face as she walked.

She rounded the corner of the alley and saw Alessia through the glass leaning against the counter, looking at her watch. She was barefoot, in a navy dress with white polka dots that buttoned up the front, with dark, wild waves of hair around her face that she pushed behind her ear just as Parker knocked. Alessia jumped, startled, then unlocked the door.

"What?" Parker said as she came in. "Were you expecting some other random American to show up at your door?"

"I didn't recognize you," she said, locking the door behind Parker. "I guess I was expecting the uniform."

Her eyes met Parker's as she took the bottle of wine. "Thank you for this. I'll be sure to give it to my mother."

She paused, then clicked the light switch beside her to look more closely at the parchment label on the bottle.

"Mourvèdre?" She glanced up at Parker. "No one drinks mourvèdre."

"I do," Parker said. "And you're right, it's not for everyone. But I love it."

Alessia's fingertip traced the label as she met Parker's eyes again. It was a moment before she spoke.

"What do you love about it?"

"The intensity," Parker said, searching for the right words to describe it. "Or maybe 'contrast' is a better word. It starts floral, like violets, but turns harsh at the back of your throat, like swallowing ash."

Alessia switched off the light and motioned for Parker to follow. "I've never heard anyone describe it that way." She crossed the café floor and had reached the door that led upstairs before Parker heard her speak without looking back, her words as soft as air. "But maybe they should."

They climbed what looked like an endless stone spiral staircase until they reached a narrow landing with tall windows that overlooked the sea, warmed by the last of the setting sun. Alessia opened a heavy hand-carved pine door adorned with a handful of fresh lavender and led them into the bright yellow kitchen. The air was warm with the scent of simmering butter and white wine, and Giada was fussing over a sink full of mussels on ice, muttering to herself in Italian. Parker leaned in to Alessia, catching the faint scent of bergamot on her skin as she spoke.

"What did she say?"

Alessia shook her head as she watched her mother. "Evidently my father buried the wire brush she uses to clean the mussels underneath them when he dumped them into the sink."

Giada looked up suddenly and smiled at Parker, coming over to clasp her face with icy hands and kiss both cheeks.

"Benvenuta! You save the café today," she said, her smile as wide as her face. "So I cook for you tonight."

Parker stepped up to the sink, plunged her hand to the bottom, and moved the ice aside until the wire brush scraped the tips of her fingers. She pulled it out of the sink and handed it to Giada, who shook her head and looked in her daughter's direction.

"Now, why your father not do that?" She picked up a mussel and scrubbed it with the brush, nodding toward the patio door. "You will set the table? The wine is there already."

Alessia headed for the door just past the kitchen and motioned for Parker to follow. Parker watched the navy evening sky open up above them as they stepped out onto a rooftop patio. A long, natural wood table was set with an assortment of mismatched chairs and benches, and a row of ivory candles occupied the center. Moss had grown between the wide, uneven stones that made up the floor, brilliant green and dense as velvet.

"There's wine at the end of the table," Alessia said, glancing up as she lit the first candle. "You can open one of the whites while I get these candles going."

Parker chose a bottle from the ice-filled zinc bucket and poured, setting the glasses out along the tabletop. The sky had deepened into dense violet blue, and the faintest dusting of stars was visible just beyond the last of the terra-cotta rooftops.

"This is beautiful," Parker said, handing Alessia her glass. "How long has your family lived here?"

"My father's from Greece, but my mother's family has lived here for over two hundred years."

She flipped a switch on the outside wall, and countless golden café bulbs lit up the dusk, strung in long rows overhead from the roof of the house to the ivy-covered stone barrier wall. Alessia took a sip from her glass and looked out to the darkening sea in the distance.

"I've eaten dinner on this roof for as long as I can remember. My mother expects me every Sunday whether I want to be here or not."

"Well," Parker said, watching the light strings sway slightly in the breeze, "I love it. Thanks for inviting me."

"I didn't invite you." Alessia's eyes were still on the choppy, white-capped surface of the water. It was a moment before she spoke again. "My mother did."

There was nothing to say in response to that, so Parker swirled the honey-colored wine in her glass and took a sip. It was very light, dry, almost grassy.

"I've actually never liked pinot grigio, but this is nice."

Alessia took Parker's glass and brought it to her nose, closing her eyes before she spoke.

"You still don't," she said, handing the glass back to her. "It's sauvignon blanc."

Parker walked back to the wine she'd opened; she'd intended to open the pinot grigio, but had mistaken it for a sauvignon blanc from Argentina. She looked up to see Alessia smile for the first time that evening as a salt breeze swept over the patio, taking the candle flames with it. Alessia pulled a book of matches out of her pocket and struck two that refused to light. The third match blazed to life, but the last of the breeze took it out as well.

Parker walked back and stepped between Alessia and the wind. She held her breath as she took the matches from her, not willing to take in the delicate warmth of her skin again. The match flared suddenly and Alessia lit the candles, then stepped back and tossed the spent match over the edge of the patio to the street below. She glanced at Parker then looked away, her fingers tracing the frayed edge of the matchbook before she slipped it back into her pocket.

"I know I've been rude today. I guess I've just had enough arrogant Americans to last a lifetime."

"Well, damn," Parker said, smiling and meeting her eyes as she finally looked up. "I guess I'm out of luck. That's my best quality."

Alessia laughed despite herself as Giada stepped out onto the patio carrying a steaming platter of mussels.

"Alessia, the bread?" she said, out of breath as she set the platter in the middle of the table and wiped her hands on her apron. "It is in too long."

Giada rearranged the candles so they sat at each end of the table and slid the steaming platter to the center of it as Alessia disappeared into the kitchen and returned with the bread, a golden-brown loaf wrapped in a white cloth with a knife sticking straight up in the center.

"Alessia!" Giada said as she pulled it out and set it back on the cutting board. "Why you always do this? Is so aggressive."

Alessia smiled. "I know, I know, respect the bread." She pulled her mother into a hug and kissed her cheek. "I just wanted to hear you say it again."

Giada smiled and brushed a stray lock of hair out of Alessia's face, then returned to the kitchen, reemerging with a small ceramic bowl of butter. Parker poured Giada a glass of wine and handed it to her as Alessia glanced toward the house.

"Where's Da?"

"Your father?" Giada said, smoothing her white cloth napkin onto her lap. "Who knows? He's been closing up the shop for an hour now."

"What?" Parker said, sure Alessia had locked the door behind them when they'd headed upstairs. "The café?"

"No," Alessia said, spotting her father through the kitchen window on his way out to the patio. "He has the jewelry shop to the right of the café, Ravello Goldsmiths."

Parker had seen it beside the café, typically Italian in style with expansive windows framed by shiny black shutters and gold lettering across the antique door. The jewelry in the windows was displayed on deep green velvet, the sun glinting across the polished gold and gemstones.

They all heard sudden pounding footsteps as Alessia's father threw open the door and stopped in his tracks.

"So," he said in a booming voice that seemed to bounce off the stone walls. "I finally meet this American?"

Parker stood and extended her hand as he approached the table, but he drew Parker into a hug, kissing both cheeks as he clapped a firm hand on her shoulder.

"Parker," Alessia said as she stood. "This is my father, Salvatore Cavalii."

"It's a pleasure to meet you, sir," Parker said as they both sat back down. "You have a beautiful home. I've never seen anything like it."

Alessia poured the wine into a glass and handed it to her father, who took an enthusiastic swig and nodded his approval. A vaguely familiar Italian opera drifted in from the door Salvatore had left open, and seagulls called and glided overhead. The streets and alleys below had grown quieter as darkness fell, just enough for faint sounds of the ocean to drift in with the breeze.

"So what is it you do here?" Salvatore said, shrugging his jacket off and draping it over the back in his chair. "You're with the American military?"

Parker nodded and set her glass on the table. "Yes, sir," she said. "I'm an officer in the US Army, stationed at NATO."

Giada placed a large sprig of fresh rosemary at the bottom of each of their dishes, then ladled mussels and white wine broth over their shoulders as they spoke, the shells clattering into clay bowls glazed a faded white.

"What's your rank?"

"Salvatore!" Giada paused and shot her husband a look, a ladle of steaming broth still in her hand.

"No, it's okay," Parker said, smiling. "It's a fair question."

Giada gave her husband a look and topped each dish with a torn hunk of flaky white baguette.

"I'm a captain, sir. I'm a detective with the MP in the States, but I'm on special assignment here at NATO."

Giada sat and spooned broth over the mussels in her own bowl. "What is...the MP?"

Alessia spoke without looking up. "It stands for Military Police, Ma."

Parker glanced in her direction, surprised that she'd answered a question most non-military Americans wouldn't know. Salvatore dunked his bread in the savory broth and looked up at Parker.

"And how long are you here?"

"My deployment is for eighteen months, so I'll be here for a while yet."

Fragrant steam rose from Parker's bowl as she pried the first mussel from its shell, bringing with it the warm, rich scent of garlic, butter, and wine, with fresh shallot and parsley scattered throughout. Parker was familiar with mussels, but the intensity of the flavors in this dish surprised her. It was briny, like sharp seawater, but warmed and softened by the wine.

"Alessia," Salvatore said, tearing a chunk from his baguette and dunking it in his dish. "What wine is this?"

"The one we're drinking now is a sauvignon blanc from Argentina, but the wine I actually brought for the mussels is a steel-cask chardonnay from the Willamette Valley in Oregon."

Giada smiled and glanced from her daughter to Parker. "We are very proud of Alessia," she said. "She is a wine genius."

Alessia gave her mother a look and attempted to change the subject, but Salvatore swiftly intercepted, lifting his wineglass for emphasis.

"This is true," he said. "Since she was a little girl, she's always seen the world through her nose."

He tossed a handful of empty mussel shells over his shoulder to the stone floor, and the seagulls descended immediately, searching for unretrieved bits of meat, expertly kicking aside the shells. Alessia and her mother looked up at each other, both raising an identical eyebrow at Salvatore.

"When I was little, my sister and I used to toss the shells to the gulls," Alessia explained. "And it seems my father has never tired of it, although it's less than charming when a grown man is doing it."

"I don't know about that," Parker said with a wink in Salvatore's direction. "The gulls seem to love it."

She dunked a piece of bread into her bowl and looked over at Alessia.

"Actually," she said, "I think I need to know more about you being a wine genius."

"What," Giada said, glancing at her daughter. "I say wrong? You are a...wine master?"

Alessia whispered something in Italian and squeezed her hand as she looked over at Parker.

"I'm a sommelier, and I work as a wine consultant." She refilled her mother's wineglass, handed it back to her, and took a sip from her own. "It's no big deal."

"It's a huge deal," Salvatore cut in, his attention now diverted from the gulls and placed firmly on his daughter. "She's being modest. She's a Master Sommelier, one of only about two hundred in the world."

"And only twenty-six of those are women," Giada said, beaming at her daughter. "We are very proud."

Giada scooped the last of the mussels into Parker's dish as Salvatore refilled the half-empty wineglasses and opened the next bottle. The lights overhead glittered on the surface of the light gold wine slowly sinking into the glass, illuminating it against the black expanse of sky. The crash of waves against the beach in the distance had grown suddenly louder, as if the cover of darkness had emboldened it.

Salvatore placed another piece of bread on top of Parker's dish and then his own. "So," he said, buttering his bread and topping it with a flourish of flaked sea salt. "What do you think of our beautiful country? Is it the first time you've seen it?"

"It is," Parker said, dropping an empty shell in the dish beside her plate. "And I love it. The food, it's…" She paused, searching for the word. "Beautiful. Not at all like what I'm used to."

"How so?" Alessia turned to look at Parker.

"It's hard to describe," Parker said, pausing to choose her words carefully. "More thoughtful, maybe."

"And how would you describe food in America?" Alessia asked, her eyes still on Parker.

"Don't get me wrong, there are great restaurants," Parker said, her words slowed by thought. "But they're mostly in major cities." She paused, glancing down the table at Alessia. "But it's a whole different world. The pace of everyday life is faster there. Most people don't have time to sit and eat together."

"In Italy, food is life," Salvatore said, wiping his mouth with his napkin and setting it squarely in the center of his plate. "Nothing is more important than eating with your family."

"Take my advice: Get out now while you can." Alessia smiled as she stood and gathered the empty dishes with Giada. "He's about to explain his theories on food as a form of edible art."

Salvatore winked at Parker as he stood and took the dishes from Alessia and motioned for her to sit, then followed his wife into the kitchen, pulling her into an impromptu dance as the last dramatic strains of the opera drifted out to the rooftop. Giada laughed and pretended to resist as they fell perfectly into step, framed in the golden light by the kitchen windows.

Alessia stood and reached over to the opposite end of the table for the bottle of mourvèdre, her hair brushing across Parker's shoulder. She nodded toward the kitchen as she cut the foil, which Parker took to mean they'd need new glasses, so she retrieved two clean crystal glasses and set them on the table as Alessia pulled the cork from the bottle.

"Are you trying to get me drunk?"

"Well, you're an American, so that wouldn't be hard." Alessia poured a taste into each. "But I'm actually curious to taste this violet ash you were talking about."

"So you get me to describe the wine, then tell me you're a Master Sommelier?" Parker raised an eyebrow. "That doesn't seem fair."

Parker caught a flash of a smile as Alessia handed her a glass.

"Well," Alessia said, "if fair is a prerequisite, you're drinking with the wrong girl."

She swirled the wine in her glass and watched it move, her eyes locked onto the glass. They were dark like wet earth, with lashes that brushed her cheeks when she closed her eyes to taste the wine. She covered her mouth and nose with the glass, then drew a slow breath and tipped it to her lips. The wind lifted her hair and brushed it against her cheek as she lowered the glass, eyes still closed.

"So, what do you taste?"

"Not the violets," she said, opening her eyes. "When are you getting that?"

"You mean when do I taste it?"

"Yes. Violet is nuanced, so you'll have to guide me there."

Parker smiled, raising an eyebrow.

"And if you ever tell anyone I just said that, I'll have you killed."

"No promises," Parker said, lifting her glass to her lips as Alessia shot her a look.

"What are you doing?"

"Tasting the wine," she said, smiling. "I thought you might have picked up on that one."

Alessia took the glass out of Parker's hand and set it back on the table, then went back to her own and swirled it, the dark currant tint thinning as it spun, transmuting into a slick of ruby. Parker reached again for her own glass.

"Don't touch that glass," Alessia said, her eyes locked onto the wine as it slowed and intensified back into a deep currant hue. "I'll tell you when you can taste it."

Parker smiled, leaning back in her seat. "Yes, ma'am."

CHAPTER TWO

The next day was Sunday and the café was closed, but Alessia let herself in and locked the door behind her, checking twice to make sure the sign was turned. She'd seen on the news earlier that traffic was expected to be at an all-time high in the evening because of some celebrity appearance at the art festival closing ceremonies, which was enough to convince her mother not to open. She didn't always open the café on a Sunday anyway, and this was certainly one to skip.

She clicked on the overhead lights, which fell in warm rivulets of gold and shadow against the crumbling brick-and-mortar walls. Even in the chill of an early summer morning, the air held the scent of baguette and the bitter remnants of espresso. Alessia shrugged off her jacket and bag onto the counter, pulling an Orangina out of the display fridge and popping the top. She'd only stopped by to pick up the deposit from the safe and drop it at the bank, but when she saw the register out of the corner of her eye, it was clear that someone had already been there. The drawer was open, and the clip on the stack of twenty-euro notes was left up, with a crumpled note on top of the bills. Alessia picked it up and leaned against the counter. Her sister had finally decided to show up.

I took 80, it said in Lexie's feminine handwriting. *Sorry.*

Alessia counted the drawer and dropped the deposit into the green zippered bank bag, adding four twenty-euro notes from her wallet. Her mother had unsurprisingly retained far more patience for Lexie than Alessia had over the years. A recent family gathering had ended in disaster, and Lexie had disappeared for the last few months. To Alessia that was a luxury, but Giada had lit a candle in the cathedral every morning since she'd seen her, her head covered by a scarf, whispering prayers as silent as the rosary beads tangled into her fingers. Alessia took her to early mass so she wouldn't have to go alone, their footsteps sharp repeating echoes on the stone cathedral floor as they crossed themselves and slid silently into the back pew. The secret Alessia kept from her mother played silently on a black-and-white movie reel in her mind every morning as she entered the church. She felt the weight of it settling onto her shoulders and pushing her daily to her knees, forcing her to whisper empty prayers for her sister's safe return.

A taxi horn blared suddenly outside, and Alessia looked up to see a dense crush of shoulders scraping the windows of the café as they passed. That morning she'd wedged her car into the only spot she could find at the end of the street, but she knew that there was no way she'd be able to get to it if she left it there much longer. She shrugged her coat back on as she reached into the pastry case for a lemon biscuit and dropped it into her bag with the bank deposit as she headed back to the door, keys in hand.

It was difficult to press the door open with her shoulder against the foot traffic, even using all her weight, but she managed to squeeze out and quickly lock the door behind her. Almost instantly she was swept into the crush of bodies and shoved around the corner into the alleyway that rapidly filled behind her. People were shouting from every direction, and as she looked back toward the street, she felt her bag slip from her shoulder. She reached for it just as another person pushed past her, sending her to her knees, the gravel cutting into the palms of her hands as she landed. She slipped her arm through the strap and tried to stand, only to feel her cheek collide with a knee, knocking her sideways into the alley wall. Alessia sank against the blur of collision, cobblestones grating in slow motion under the heels of her hands and then against her forehead as she was pitched forward. She squeezed her eyes shut against the blood rushing into her mouth and fought the arm she sensed suddenly underneath her ribs, lifting her to her feet.

"Alessia," Parker whispered hard and hot against her ear. "Don't move. Keep your back against the wall."

The noise was deafening, closing the space tighter around them. Parker braced her elbows against the stone wall on either side of Alessia's head, creating a strong square of space around her. Alessia wrapped her hands around Parker's shoulders, forehead sinking slowly into her chest. Time seemed to stop as she drew a slow breath. She felt the rough canvas of Parker's uniform jacket under her fingertips, and every muscle in her arms and shoulders tensed as Parker held the space she'd created against the jostling crowd. The shouts around them seemed to fade in and out, and she felt the slow warmth of Parker's breath against her forehead as she focused on the ground beneath her feet, desperate for an anchor.

Gradually the crowd moved out of the alley and onto the main street, but as Parker finally stepped back, Alessia still felt the world swirling around them.

"This cut on your head is going to need to be cleaned," Parker said, one hand on her shoulder, the other gingerly touching her forehead. "How are you feeling?"

Alessia opened her eyes to see Parker staring at her intently, then felt Parker's hand slide strong around her back. "Let's go back to the café," she said. "You look like you might pass out."

Alessia shook her head and stepped away. "No, I'm fine, I just want to go home."

Parker looked again toward the café.

"No, sorry, my home." Alessia shook her head slightly to clear her vision. "My car is parked on the street down there." She gestured toward the bright sunlight at the end of the alley, then closed her eyes against it. "I just need to find it."

Parker lifted Alessia's chin with her finger, examining the swelling near her temple. "You look like you've taken a couple of blows to the head. There's no way I'm letting you drive like this."

"I appreciate you stepping in back there, Captain," Alessia said. "But I'm fine." She started to walk around Parker, but her legs crumpled and suddenly the ground was rushing toward her again.

"Well, that's clearly bullshit," Parker said, sweeping her off the ground and into her arms. "So it looks like you're stuck with me."

Shards of gravel still stuck to her face scraped her skin when she ran her hand over her cheek as they walked, and the sunlight made her suddenly nauseous when they finally stepped out onto the street. Parker asked which car was hers as she lowered her to her feet.

"It's the yellow Citroën on the corner, two cars up." Alessia nodded in its direction, brushing the last of the dirt from her bag and sliding it back on her shoulder. "I live just past the edge of town, so I'll be fine. It's not even a kilometer from here."

Parker smiled, squinting into the sun at seagulls calling above their heads.

"You have two options," she said, her voice kinder than her words. "I can drive you home, or I can get you a taxi and you can leave your car here."

Alessia felt sudden tears sting her eyes. Her face ached, she just wanted to get home, and handing over her keys suddenly seemed like the only option. She handed them to Parker, then pulled them back suddenly.

"Wait, can you even drive a stick?"

Parker laughed out loud, opening the door for Alessia and leaning against it, her eyes dark and warm, softened suddenly by crinkles at the edges. "What do you think?"

Parker shut the door and walked around to her own side of the car, pulling out into traffic toward the deep gold path of the afternoon sun. Alessia closed her eyes and leaned her head back against the seat. The world had stopped spinning, but now she had a massive headache and a questionable American driving her car, which was arguably even worse.

"Where do I turn?"

"In about a hundred meters you'll get to a roundabout. Just take the first right and you'll see the signs."

Alessia opened her eyes long enough to see Parker glance in her direction, then shift into third as she neared the roundabout. The sun glinted off the windshield in the shape of a dagger, and she closed her eyes again.

"I'm assuming you mean the sign for the Toscano Winery?" Parker turned onto a narrow road bordered on both sides by gnarled trees, branches reaching toward the road and hung low with plump green olives.

Alessia nodded, reaching over to Parker and pulling the military cap off her head and onto her own, trying to position it just right to shade her eyes from the sun.

"I'm pretty sure you're not authorized to wear that, ma'am."

Parker looked over at her and winked, which she ignored and sank farther down in her seat.

"The sun just seems brighter than it needs to be." Alessia spread her fingers against the cold glass of the window and leaned back in her seat. "Believe me, I have no desire to keep it."

The road wound up a hill until it suddenly opened to a circular gravel drive. Parker cut the engine in front of an immense but crumbling stone winery draped in ivy, topped by a timber beam and expansive glass third story that looked out over the sheer edge of a cliff. Fields of ripening grapes sloped out in undulating waves on either side like rumpled green velvet as the sun sank just lower than the slate roof, taking the harsh glare of light with it.

"Holy shit," Parker said, her eyes fixed on the horizon beyond the edge of the cliff into the canyon below. "This is where you live?"

"Don't be impressed." Alessia opened the door and stood carefully, markedly sorer than she'd expected to be. "When I bought it, it was falling down around me. I got it a few months ago at an auction, and I'm just now getting it to where it needs to be."

"I'm not sure it would look as romantic if it was perfect," Parker said, stepping out and shutting the door behind her. "Did you add the top level?"

"I did." Alessia glanced over at her as she handed back her cap and twisted her hair into a soft bun at the nape of her neck. "The former owners started the renovations, then sold the property to move back to Paris. It seems it was a little more actual work than they'd expected."

"American or French?"

"Good guess," Alessia said with a sudden smile, taking the keys from Parker. "They were French. Although it'd be far more satisfying right now to say they were American."

They stepped out of the car and Alessia walked toward the door, then shaded her eyes and looked back at Parker, who had stopped at the hood of the car and leaned against it.

"How are you getting back to town?"

"I'm walking," Parker said, glancing back at the road. "But not until I see that you make it inside."

Alessia turned the house key in the lock and looked down at the sleeves of Parker's jacket. They were torn at the elbows from bracing against the rough stone of the alleyway, the edges stained with dried blood.

"You should come in and let me look at your…" She paused and looked down, trying to remember the word she needed.

"Elbows. My elbows are fine," Parker said. "But thank you."

"Bullshit. Which is what I believe is exactly what you said to me."

Parker stood her ground, smiling.

"What?" Alessia said.

"Are you saying you want me to come in?"

"I'm saying I'd like to make sure your elbows are okay, which is hard to do unless you're inside."

Parker walked to the door, taking the keys when she noticed Alessia's hands shaking.

"I can open the door," Alessia said. "I'm fine."

"I know you can open the door," Parker said, turning the key. "But I need to be back on base before tomorrow, so I'm going to do it for you this once."

The door swung open to a massive great room, with a glittering chandelier made from California chardonnay bottles suspended from the second-floor ceiling that scattered pale gold light across the scarred timber floors.

"Seriously?" Parker said, closing the door behind them and handing the keys back to her. "Wine bottles from California? How did you end up with those?"

"I drank them. I happen to be a fan of Napa Valley chard. I can't help what I like," Alessia said, climbing the short, curved stairs that led from the entryway to the great room. "Believe me, I've tried."

Parker followed her up the stairs and took in the enormous great room around her. A massive fireplace made of whitewashed antique brick, crumbling at the edges, took up the left wall. Two couches covered in smoky tweed framed each side, with a split wine barrel on a base serving as a coffee table. A sheet of thick glass the color of woodsmoke sat across the open top, with books stacked and scattered across the surface beside a forgotten espresso cup and saucer.

The hearth was made of Italian clay tiles, and the brick walls curved upward from there to create an organic fireplace opening about five feet across, more charming than lopsided, as if someone had sketched it into the background. Deep, whitewashed sunken spaces on either side were haphazardly filled with rough-cut firewood.

Alessia hung her bag on the hook by the stairs and headed to the kitchen on the right of the great room. A red enamel stove with shiny chrome accents dominated the space, surrounded by unfinished cedar slab countertops. Alessia pulled a bottle of wine from the shelf above them and spoke without looking back.

"Would you like a drink?"

"That depends. What are we drinking?" Parker said. "I'm not sure I trust you after that Napa Valley confession."

Alessia twisted the opener and pulled the corkscrew smoothly from the bottle, turning to set it on the island between them and reaching up to the rack above them, dangling with crystal glasses.

"Cute," she said, nodding toward the black leather stools at the island as she dug in a drawer on the other side of the island. "Now sit down."

Parker slid onto one of the stools and carefully draped her jacket across another, although the sleeves were ripped into ragged edges at the elbows from the alley wall, so it would have to be replaced anyway. She suddenly felt bare in just her khaki T-shirt and camo uniform pants.

Alessia washed her hands, then pushed a glass of deep ruby wine across the island and joined her on the other side. She sat on the stool next to Parker and opened a small wooden box. Her fingers brushed Parker's knee as she guided it between hers and reached for her arm. A smile flashed when Parker flinched.

"I'm assuming you're going to let me clean that?"

They both looked at the cuts crisscrossing her elbow and forearm.

"You assume wrong," Parker smiled, lowering her arm. "I'm fine."

"Don't make me call bullshit again."

Alessia's smile was more of a challenge than anything else, and with that hanging in the air, there was no other choice. Parker extended her arm.

She selected a cotton pad from the box and soaked it with

a clear liquid from a small black bottle, then pressed it onto the bloodiest part of her skin.

"Jesus." Parker shifted in her chair. "Is there a razor blade in that cotton ball?"

"It's just alcohol, soldier," Alessia said, her eyes glinting with the sun as it beamed through the window that looked out over what seemed to be the edge of the world. "What…can't take it?"

Alessia lifted the cotton to find that the scrape was a significant cut about two inches long. "Actually," she said, rewetting a new pad and holding it against the skin, "I didn't realize it was as deep as this is. There's no way it will heal well unless the edges stay together for a few days." She looked up at Parker. "I'm assuming the Army has people for this? Will you take care of this on base?"

"They do, but believe me, they have more important things to handle than a cut. It will be fine."

Alessia pilfered through the box, pulling out a sterile needle in a case and packet of sutures. She handed Parker a wineglass and waited until she drank before she went back to cleaning the cut. Parker watched as if it were happening to someone else until Alessia stopped and glanced at the wine, sitting back slightly in her chair.

"Yes, ma'am," Parker said, picking her glass back up. "But it's not that bad."

"I know you didn't get to be a captain without seeing something worse than this, but this is my house, and you drink when I tell you to drink."

She looked up for a second and winked, which was just charming enough to get a hesitant Parker to let her continue. Alessia pulled on latex gloves and worked quickly and steadily, gently pressing the edges of the wound together and suturing from the outside in.

"Breathe."

Parker looked at her and released the breath she was holding. Alessia took a deep breath and held it until Parker followed suit, their eyes locked together.

"Just breathe through it. We're two stitches in, so the worst is over."

"I'm okay for the moment," Parker said, running her free hand through her hair. "But I may need to swap this wine for whiskey."

"You need to hold still or all you'll get is some syrupy California moscato," Alessia said, glancing up. "Which, I can tell by the look of you, you'd hate."

Parker laughed despite herself and watched her work. Alessia's fingers were quick and sure, and she had yet to hesitate, even when a bright patch of blood seeped from the closure and dripped onto the white gauze she'd laid under Parker's arm.

"You're a little too good at this not to have a medical background," Parker said, examining her neat row of stitches. "This is clearly not your first rodeo."

Alessia tied off the end of the suture at the outside edge of the cut and started in the other direction to finish closing the wound, then lifted her head to look at Parker.

"Drink."

"Yes, ma'am."

Parker's eyes strayed from the needle to the neckline of the faded denim of her shirt. It was creased and streaked with dust from the alley. Three tiny brass snaps had come unfastened, exposing the lace of her bra, the same translucent umber tone as her skin, as if it had slowly melted onto the curve of her breast.

"Tell me," Alessia said. "What is a rodeo?"

Parker watched her tie off the final stitch, then disinfect the wound again and bandage it before she remembered to answer. "What?"

"Nothing." Alessia leaned back on her stool and pulled off the latex gloves. "You're done." She looked up as she snapped her shirt back together. "You're not subtle, you know."

"I wasn't trying to be."

Parker met her eyes until Alessia glanced behind her at the sun setting like falling fire, framed by three floor-to-ceiling windows that faced west over the cliffs below. Parker walked over and looked down into the darkening canyon below. The building extended just beyond the lip of the cliff, making it seem as if the room was framed only by sky, extended over the edge of the world. The sun had just started to set in a pink-copper blaze beyond the mountains in the distance, and a hawk swooped suddenly just past the glass and up toward the roof, as if to underscore the point.

Parker turned to face Alessia. "So why this place?"

She didn't answer, but poured whiskey into two cut glass

tumblers and walked over to the windows, handing one to Parker and staring at the dusky shadows falling over the mountains.

"I fell in love with it." The light from the setting sun pierced the whiskey as she tipped it to her mouth. "I wanted to be alone, and this is as close as it gets."

Parker watched as her eyes fell and decided not to ask the question that hung thick in the air. She drew a long swig before she handed her glass back to Alessia and walked back to the kitchen, pausing to lift her jacket and cap from the barstool and turn back toward the windows.

"Thank you," she said, holding Alessia's eyes. "I enjoyed this."

The scarred oak door shut quietly behind her as she left and started the walk back into town.

❖

"Where the hell have you been all day?"

Parker's roommate switched off her laptop and turned to face Parker as she came in and hung her cap on the wall hook beside the door. Petra Heinoen seemed to be always smaller than her uniform, with a quick smile and warm brown eyes. The barracks on base were constructed of stacked steel shipping containers, with each container housing two or more soldiers. NATO was an international base with military personnel from dozens of countries, so there was never a shortage of noise, always amplified by the thin sheet metal walls and lack of insulation. Petra, a ballistics specialist from Romania, had been initially assigned to share a room with Mirabelle Grace, a Disney enthusiast from Macon, Georgia, which proved to be a bit more than she could handle. She'd showed up at Parker's door one morning with a detailed plan to kill her roommate if she had to spend one more night listening to the *Pocahontas* soundtrack and told Parker she could either help her hide the body or let her move in.

Petra stood and held out her hand to take the jacket Parker shrugged off.

"And what the hell happened to your jacket?"

Not much got by Petra.

"It's a long story."

"Well, condense that down to two minutes because we're late for dinner."

Parker chose another jacket from the closet. "You're genuinely worried you're going to miss the fried chicken, aren't you?"

"Yes," Petra said, without a hint of a smile. "I waited all week for American chicken night."

"Okay," Parker said, sliding the jacket on and sweeping her hair back into a regulation bun at the nape of her neck. "You know that festival in Salerno this weekend?"

"Yes," she said, slipping her cap onto her head and grabbing her coat off the wall. "I was going to go into town today, but I heard it was mobbed."

"You heard right." Parker slid her cap back on her head and grabbed her keys. "Let's just say I would've gotten more work done on base."

"Well, that was fascinating," Petra said, holding open the door and switching off the light. "Let's go. I'm starving."

The dining facilities on base, or DFAC for short, were as crowded as Parker knew they would be. Food services did a great job of rotating favorites from most of the countries represented on base, but fried chicken nights were always crowded. Military personnel from every country seemed to love it despite the questionable country music some of the American soldiers managed to play in the background. As they opened the double doors and headed for the serving line, the steamy scent of mashed potatoes and gravy washed over Parker, relaxing her instantly as she grabbed a tray and ducked out of Petra's path. Petra was on a mission to get her favorites and loaded up her tray with a golden tower of thighs and wings that threatened to topple over as she tried to balance it with the sweet tea she'd filled to the rim in the other hand.

"I love this stuff. Is this really just cold tea with sugar in it?"

Petra glanced over at Parker as she filled her own glass and looked back. "No, good sweet tea is a mystery I'm not sure you can handle the details of. But it's most certainly not 'just cold tea with sugar in it.' And I'm going to pretend I didn't hear that."

They found a spot at a long table in the back of the room and set their trays down, shrugging off their coats and draping them over the backs of the chairs. Petra settled in and squeezed a scarlet lake of ketchup onto the corner of her tray.

"So what's in it?"

"Tea," Parker said with a wink in her direction. "And sugar."

Petra balled up her napkin and tossed it in Parker's direction as Maeve Waterbury walked up to the table and set down her tray across from Parker. The napkin landed squarely in the pool of gravy next to her chicken. Maeve paused, then picked it up with a dainty thumb and forefinger and looked up at Parker.

"I'm assuming you have room for an adult at the table?"

Maeve was British, and the rumor was she'd joined the British Armed Forces just to piss off her wealthy parents. She'd gone to the best London schools and spoke all the Romance languages fluently, so regardless of her motivations, she'd risen quickly in the ranks and been assigned to NATO as a translator and interpreter, a coveted position.

"Tell me, Maeve." Petra put down her fork and looked sweetly over the table at her. "Do you ever unclench your ass? Or is that even possible after all these years?"

Maeve glared at her and dropped the gravy-soaked napkin into Petra's lap.

"Oops. I was aiming for that pile of bones on your tray." She smiled back and folded her own napkin in a perfect square beside her tray. "You can see how I'd confuse that with your lap."

Parker put her hand on Petra's arm to keep her on her side of the table. "Jesus. Can you two go even a minute without acting like toddlers?"

Petra stifled a growl and went back to her chicken.

Parker looked at Maeve and took a stab at changing the subject. "Have you heard anything else about the conference in Greece?"

Maeve shook her head. "No. I don't know anything except that I'm locked into it and we have a briefing tomorrow morning at oh-six-hundred hours before we leave." She carefully peeled the breading off her chicken breast and dropped it on the side of her tray with a look of disgust, inspecting the meat beneath for any other trace of excess fat she could eliminate. "It's about domestic violence, right?"

"It is, which is why I'm on the list to go."

"God, I'm jealous," Petra said, reaching for Parker's glass of tea after she'd noisily reached the bottom of her own. "I'd love to go to Santorini again. It's literally pure blue ocean and whitewashed villages everywhere."

Parker tried not to laugh as she watched Petra consider returning the tea and decide against it.

"From what I understand, it's definitely different for the women who live there," Parker said. "In the poorer villages that surround places like Santorini, women are sometimes trapped in abusive situations because there are no resources for them."

"And in a lot of households, they're too valuable to lose, literally." Maeve looked around to see who was at the next table. "Most of them work in the tourist trade and bring in most of the household income, yet rape and domestic violence are huge issues in Greece and Italy."

"How do you know that?" Petra put Parker's tea back on the table and picked up a chicken wing.

"Oh, I don't know," Maeve said. "Basic education?"

Petra swallowed, then sucked the flavor off the end of the chicken bone before she tossed it over onto Maeve's tray. "Well, my English is better than yours, so it must have been basic."

Maeve closed her eyes and took a dramatic breath before she turned to Parker.

"Anyway, I was wondering if you wanted to get together and do some outside research if we have time? I'd really like to get out to some of the smaller villages at least for an afternoon and get a better perspective than what they hand us in the conference."

"So what does all this have to do with NATO?" Petra asked.

Parker ran her hand through her hair and glanced at Maeve. "For the most part it has to do with the changing nature of warfare. Female civilians are being increasingly targeted, but we can't ignore that they're also often a target of violence in their own communities. NATO is all about peace, so it's our job to reach those victims and help them become leaders."

Maeve nodded and continued. "And more leaders mean quicker progress when it comes to gender equality, and then that promotes peace and security in their home countries."

Parker picked up a chicken thigh and thought back to what she'd seen a few days before. She'd just finished working out at the gym on base. Parker was one of the only women there on a regular basis, so the small cedar sauna reserved for female soldiers was usually deserted, but that night when she'd walked in, Maeve was lying on one of the lower wood slabs. She was naked, her blond hair pooled like molten gold on the bench. Parker had paused, unsure of whether to go or stay, until Maeve opened one eye and looked her up and down.

"What?" she said. "Don't have the nerve?"

Parker climbed onto the slab above her and shed her towel, balling it under her head and closing her eyes as the warmth melted her naked body into the wood. After a few moments, Maeve stood and wrapped her towel around her body, which looked surprisingly delicate when Parker glanced in her direction—lean, but rounded by soft, full breasts. She left without a word, but as she did Parker saw the tattoo that spanned her back from shoulder to shoulder.

Your silence will not protect you.

CHAPTER THREE

The next afternoon, Parker shrugged off her uniform jacket and fell back onto the bed in her hotel room, arms outstretched. She'd always hated to fly, and the civilian plane she'd taken to Santorini was roughly the size of an Alabama farm truck and not nearly as safe. The fact that it had landed at all seemed like a miracle.

The door opened suddenly, and Maeve wedged through the narrow opening, tossing her pack onto the small table by the door before she glanced toward the bed. She stopped cold when she saw Parker there, watching her with an arm folded behind her head.

"What," she said, looking her up and down, "the hell are you doing in my room?"

"Nice to see you, too, Sergeant Waterbury." She sat up and pulled her shirt over her head, leaving only her sports bra and tank. She dropped the shirt on the bed beside her.

Maeve looked like she was ready to back out of the room and sleep in the hall. "I specifically requested a single room for this conference ages ago."

Parker walked over to the window and pulled open the curtains. The ocean below was a brilliant expanse of the palest turquoise surrounded by the whitewashed village. The horizon was just starting to warm with the setting sun, and seagulls swooped over the surface of the water, calling to each other over the waves below.

"And that's surprising? Clearly you're clearly new to military travel."

"But..." Parker followed Maeve's horrified glance to the one small bed in the room. "You've got to be kidding me."

"Feel free to ask if there's another room," Parker said. "But when I came in they were completely booked for the conference, which is probably why they put us together."

She tried not to smile as Maeve started unpacking her things with a clear air of displeasure. There was more to Maeve than met the eye, but whatever it was, she kept it well hidden.

"So what do we have to do this evening?" Maeve asked.

Parker picked up the schedule and followed the list with her finger. "There was an official welcome and introductions, but that was hours ago. We both got here after it started."

"When is dinner?"

Parker looked at her watch. "Petra should be here in about five minutes with a greasy bag of fried chicken."

Maeve stared over her shoulder with narrowed eyes. "You'd better not be serious."

"Relax, Sergeant." Parker smiled. "I'm just kidding. But we did miss dinner downstairs by about an hour."

"Great," Maeve said, hanging up the last of her uniforms and zipping her pack closed. "It's going to be dark in like five minutes and I'm starving."

"I know." Parker pulled on a fresh shirt and smoothed her hair back in a bun. "And no one serves food after dark."

Maeve's head whipped around.

"Kidding." Parker smiled again, looking out the window at the buildings that lined the shoreline. "We can just walk down from the hotel. There have to be a dozen little cafés and restaurants down there."

Maeve walked over and looked down, watching the streetlights flicker on and the glowing café lights strung between them sway in the breeze that swept across the sand. Parker saw her face soften slightly as her eyes followed a dolphin and its calf as they crested the waves and dove back under, then rose again in a smooth arc, their bodies the color of moonlight. Finally, Maeve turned back around and walked to the door. She opened it, looking back at Parker.

"It's been years since I've been here, but I know a couple of places. Are you coming?"

Parker grabbed her jacket and followed her out the door,

picking up the key Maeve had walked right past and slipping it into her pocket.

It only took about ten minutes to find a café that Maeve deemed acceptable, which Parker knew had only happened because she'd remained convinced she'd starve to death in Greece. They were seated on the front patio, where above each table an open wood frame was draped with bleached muslin, stiff with salt and rustling in the ocean breeze. The air smelled like baked seawater, and they were close enough to the water to see the foam rush onto the sand then slip silently back into the darkened sea. Fairy lights rimmed the edges of the patio area, and the sound of acoustic guitar washed in from somewhere down the beach.

The waiter filled their water glasses and handed them handwritten menus on clipboards. The name of the restaurant was penciled carefully at the top, almost as an afterthought.

"This is romantic," Parker said. "Is this all some big plan to get me into bed, Waterbury?"

"Ah...no," she said, not taking her eyes from the menu. "The plan is definitely to get you out of my bed."

Parker realized when she looked down at the menu that what she'd assumed was bad handwriting was actually Greek. "Do you think they have this in English?" She looked around for the waiter, who had quickly disappeared.

Maeve looked up from behind her menu. "What do you like when it comes to Greek food?"

"Wow," Parker said. "The South is just chock full of authentic Greek cuisine, so I can't really choose a favorite."

"Fine, then." Maeve rolled her eyes, which seemed to signal the waiter, who appeared suddenly out of nowhere. "You get what you get."

Maeve ordered in fluent Greek, and the waiter soon reappeared with a chipped, handprinted saucer of olives and two small glasses of a milky white liquid.

"Is that a shot?"

"Jesus." Maeve took a small sip of hers and set it back down on the table, stifling what had almost looked like a smile. "No. It's ouzo, you cretin."

Parker took a sip and set it firmly back down on the table. It tasted like liquid licorice and finished like powdered fire.

"Wow. That's…" Parker shook her head and searched for the words. "Wow."

Maeve smiled and chose an olive from the dish, staring into the waves that broke in a sudden white flash on the dark stretch of beach beyond the table. The waiter brought another dish, this time baby octopus in an inky sauce.

Parker raised an eyebrow. "Seriously?"

"What?" Maeve said, octopus dangling from her lofted fork. "Can't handle it?"

Parker speared a tentacle and put it in her mouth, trying not to think about the tiny suction cups on the underside. The texture was delicate, not at all what she'd been dreading, with a flavor like fresh mushrooms soaked in seawater.

"You like it, don't you?"

"Actually," Parker said, "I love it. It's nutty, almost buttery, with an umami note I didn't expect."

"What were you expecting?"

"Salty rubber."

Maeve laughed, the wind pulling a lock of her hair out of her bun and brushing it against her cheek. "That's pretty accurate if it's not prepared correctly, so you weren't far off."

The waiter brought a bottle of chilled pale gold wine to the table and filled their glasses, then returned with bread and a long platter of fish for the table.

"So what's this?" Parker said, trying not to look the fish in the eye. "I'm trusting you here, since that's my only option."

Maeve tucked another stray lock of hair behind her ear and cut into the fish with a delicate horizontal slice and put it on a plate for Parker. "It's sea bream, a local fish that they grill over open flame with fresh thyme and lemon. Take a sip of wine before you taste it. It's meant to be eaten with a dry white."

Parker took a bite. It was beautiful, simple, like fresh air and sun-warmed saltwater. The char from the fire fell from the skin to her tongue, as well as the olive oil and coarse salt rub, which gave the crispy skin a briny crunch.

"What do you think?"

"I think I may have to stay in Greece." Parker finally looked up and shook her head. "This is literally the best thing I've ever eaten."

Maeve laughed, her blue eyes sparkling in the candlelight. She tore a hunk of bread from the loaf on their table and sat back in her chair, taking the pins out of her hair and breathing in the night air. Her hair was the lightest cool blond and floated around her shoulders, reflecting the moonlight.

"I like you better after a shot, just for the record," Parker said as she refilled the wineglasses that held the reflection of the ocean.

Maeve smiled. "It's not a shot, Alabama boi."

"Ah, I see you've done your research." Parker squeezed a fresh lemon wedge over more of the fish and looked up as she put a big bite into her mouth. "So what made you go into languages?"

Maeve hesitated for a second before she answered.

"I'm good at it."

Parker smiled as she took a sip of wine. "That's not hard to imagine."

Maeve finished the last of her fish and sat back in her chair, watching the waves break on the shore for a few moments before she spoke.

"What made you want to work with women?" she asked finally.

Parker looked up and smiled. "I'm good at it."

"Yeah, I've heard." Maeve rolled her eyes, tossing an olive pit in her direction. "Specifically, what prompted you to go into gender issues in the military?"

"I'm kidding," Parker said. "I'm actually with the military police in the States, but I got orders to deploy to NATO when the officer assigned to Gender Perspectives was reassigned at the last minute. I felt like I was playing catch-up for the first few months, but I loved it."

"Do you work mostly with civilians?"

"I do. Unless there's an issue like sexual misconduct or gender-based inequality that comes up with our soldiers."

Maeve tucked a lock of hair behind her ear and glanced out at the sea. "And how often does that happen?"

"More often than you'd think," Parker said. "But fortunately not on my watch yet. Knock on wood."

Maeve looked toward the sea, then pulled a stack of euros out of her jacket pocket and laid them on the table.

"Will you excuse me for a moment?" she said, her words following her as she walked.

Parker finished her wine as she watched Maeve walk down the beach, pausing to remove her jacket and boots and leave them in a pile on the sand. She stood motionless at the edge of the water, her hair blowing around her face like a windswept silk scarf. Parker turned to pay the bill, then looked back at Maeve to find she was waist-deep in the water.

Seriously? Parker thought as she grabbed her jacket and walked down the beach toward her. *Maeve, the famously uptight Brit, is suddenly just wading out into the ocean in her uniform?*

Then she saw it: a dolphin breaking the surface of the water and gliding toward Maeve. It dove back under the surface, only to reappear a few seconds later and slip under her outstretched hand. Waves breaking on the shore were the only sound, and Parker slowed, sensing their need for space. She watched as Maeve lowered her body slowly into the water and touched her face to the dolphin's cheek, whispering, then ran her hand gently over its moonlit back once more before it turned and swam back into the black expanse of ocean, fin gliding like a crescent moon on the water until it, too, disappeared under the waves.

Maeve stood there, watching, then turned and walked back to shore, where Parker was waiting with her jacket. She pulled it on and laced up her boots, then they turned and walked back toward the amber glow of the streetlights.

Later, when she was almost asleep, Parker heard Maeve whisper into the darkness.

"Thank you for not asking."

❖

The next day was a whirlwind of seminars and information, and by the end of the day Parker was exhausted and hungry. She caught Maeve coming out of the last lecture and asked if she wanted to grab dinner.

"God, I wish," she said, glancing over her shoulder. "But I'm stuck eating here with my boss. He has a meeting with a French official and I have to interpret."

"Any suggestions?"

"Um, yeah," she said, looking at her watch. "Stay away from anything that looks familiar or fried."

"Seriously?" Parker wondered if anyone else could hear her stomach rumble.

Maeve glanced again over her shoulder and turned back to Parker.

"Go back to where we were last night and walk the shore until you smell night-blooming jasmine. You have that in the States, right?" Parker looked at her blankly, distracted by the thought of the beautiful grilled fish from the night before, until Maeve waved her hand in front of her. "Do you know what that smells like?"

"Yeah," Parker said. "Nothing like dinner."

"Well, that's when you know you're past the tourist stops and into some of the good local restaurants. Look for a place called Le Vélo Rouge."

Someone a few yards away signaled for Maeve, and she joined her colleagues as Parker went upstairs to change into civilian clothes. She chose a pair of khakis worn low on her hips, a sky-blue T-shirt, and white Chuck Taylors, and grabbed a black jean jacket as an afterthought. She warmed a bit of hair product in her hands and ran her fingers through her hair, pushing it off her face and into a low ponytail, then left the hotel and headed for the restaurants lining the beach. The sun was setting when she'd been out the night before, but today it was still fiercely gold, warming the expanse of homes stacked like dazzling white blocks up the side of the mountain. Doors and shutters painted brilliant turquoise, red, or bright yellow dotted the backdrop of buildings, and ancient vines of deep purple wisteria and delicate green ivy wound themselves around the edges of walls and corners, making them seem as if they were dripping color onto the winding staircases that seemed to all lead to the deep blue expanse of sea below.

A seagull swooped down to inspect an abandoned sandwich wrapper on the sidewalk, and Parker remembered suddenly that she was supposed to be looking for La Vélo Rouge. She drew in a deep breath, trying to remember the scent of jasmine. When she was a kid in south Alabama she'd spent many of her summer days outside, mostly in a treehouse at the back of her family's property. It was in an old live oak tree covered in hanging Spanish moss, which made it almost invisible if you didn't know it was there. She had Archie and Veronica comic books stacked in a milk crate, an old camping cot, and whatever mystery she was reading at the time, which was all she really needed. Her favorites were books from the Hardy Boys series, which her seventh-grade teacher had let her borrow from her classroom a few years ago since her middle school didn't have a library. After a while, Mrs. Rae started bringing her other books, two and three at a time, and they always had library cards in the back. Parker signed them and slid them carefully back in the envelope glued to the back cover before she gave them back to Mrs. Rae, just in case she was supposed to.

She'd always been a tomboy. Until high school she'd hung out with the boys on her street, but once they all started ninth grade she'd suddenly ceased to exist. Well, not literally, but she might as well have. After her eighth-grade summer, every girl she knew started wearing makeup and hanging around staring at boys, so it wasn't surprising they didn't know she was alive, but the neighborhood guys she'd grown up with looked right past her in the halls, too. Sometimes she went a whole day without anyone saying a word to her, which she learned pretty quickly wasn't the worst thing in the world.

Her freshman year, a new girl transferred to Red Cove High from some fancy school in LA, which she told everyone the second she met them. Her name was Tasha Banks and she looked like California—blond with blue eyes, and breasts you could see the shape of through her shirt. She caught Parker looking at her twice, and both times her eyes had narrowed and she'd turned around to whisper to her friends before the group of them inevitably turned their heads like a flock of birds to look at her. They never said one word to her face, but Parker had a feeling they said plenty behind her back.

Parker was in algebra one day about a month after Tasha arrived, and the guy next to her passed her a note from Tasha. It was folded into perfect triangles and written in red ink that smelled like strawberries.

I need to ask you something. Meet me in the boys locker room after class.

Parker stuck the note in her pocket. When the bell finally rang, she put her Trapper Keeper in her backpack, slung it over her shoulder, and waited until the halls were empty. The door to the boys' locker room was heavy and silent under her hands as she pushed it open and saw Tasha leaning against the lockers. Parker walked over to her and saw that she'd unbuttoned the front of her shirt halfway to her waist and wore a sheer yellow bra that showed the tawny half-moon of her nipples.

Then she saw them out of the corner of her eye, the other four girls in Tasha's group, as they came around the corner from the lockers. Parker looked through them to the door.

Tasha smiled and leaned closer. Parker felt the slick weight of her blond hair fall against her cheek. "You don't want to go just yet, do you?"

Tasha's voice was syrupy sweet, and she was so close Parker could smell her Dr Pepper lip gloss. She trailed a finger down the front of Parker's T-shirt.

"We need to ask you a question," she said, her hand moving under the fabric and across Parker's chest. "We were just wondering if you're a boy or a girl."

Parker had always been lean and athletic, with a chest that looked more like muscle than curves. She tensed and looked at the ceiling while Tasha ran her hand slowly across Parker's chest and slipped it under her sports bra. She felt her nipples harden under Tasha's fingertips. She wanted to cry but kept her eyes on the ceiling.

"Hmm..." Tasha glanced back at the circle of girls. "She might be a girl, but it's hard to tell."

"Stop," Parker said through clenched teeth. Her jaw tensed, and she tried to move past them toward the door.

That only made the other girls move closer, and one of the girls shoved her shoulders against the lockers so hard it made all the locker doors clatter. The cold metal pressed sharply against her shoulder blades, and Parker closed her eyes. She could see the door and she wanted to run, but she felt weak, frozen.

"I don't know, girls," Tasha said, looking over her shoulder, then back at Parker. "We might just need to find out for ourselves."

Suddenly there were scissors, the blades nicking her ribs as they sliced open her shirt from hem to neck. Tasha cut away her sports bra next while the other girls pulled at the pieces until she was naked to the waist. Parker looked down and watched the shards of who she used to be as they fell limply around her feet.

"Oh, look at that," Tasha said, picking up the clothes and tossing them into her bag. "She is a girl. At least I think she is." She stared at Parker's bare breasts, her head tipped to the side. "Guess I lost that bet."

Their laughter ricocheted off the cinder block walls until Tasha nodded at one of the girls, who started to dig around in her bag.

"You idiot," Tasha said to the girl, her eyes locked on Parker, running her fingers across Parker's nipples again before she stopped to leisurely squeeze one between her fingers. "Don't tell me you fucking forgot them."

The girl hesitated and looked up, her eyes following the tear that slipped down Parker's cheek. Tasha put her hand on her hip and waited, one eyebrow raised.

"No, here they are," the girl said softly, pulling handcuffs from her bag. "I just couldn't find them."

"Be sure and thank your brother for these." Tasha giggled, pulling on Parker's shoulders to find the wrists pressed between her back and the locker doors.

One of the metal hinges was digging into her left wrist, but she still felt frozen, like she was watching it happen to someone else. Parker's fists were clenched behind her, but Tasha still managed to bring them forward and click the handcuffs around them, then lean down to get a rope from her bag. Parker felt herself start to throw up as she watched her tie the handcuffs to one of the padlocks on the locker door, using the ends to loop it over again and tie it in a double knot.

She squeezed her eyes shut against the tears that slipped through, falling hot against her cheeks as she looked at the ceiling, barely holding back the vomit still stuck in her throat. The girls gathered at the mirrors and touched up their lips before they left, like she wasn't even there. They'd finally turned to leave, giggling, when Tasha paused and turned back. She walked back up to Parker and scrawled something in red lipstick across her torso. Parker didn't look at her, just kept her eyes on the ceiling.

It wasn't long before Parker finally leaned over and heaved onto the chipped tile of the locker room. Her legs gave way afterward, and she slumped down against the locker doors, arms still hanging from the locker above her head. She heard the bell ring for the next period at the same time a group of football players jostled through the locker room doors, shoving each other and laughing. They stopped suddenly when they saw her, eyes moving together across her body, their mouths slack and silent.

"Dudes." Jack Hearndon, the senior quarterback for the football team, looked back at the group. "Just get the fuck out."

They stood there, staring, until one of them opened his mouth to speak. Jack didn't give him the chance, shoving them all out the door and shutting it hard behind them. Parker shut her eyes again as she heard him say something to them about not letting anyone in. As he turned back to her, Parker looked up and dropped her head back against the lockers.

"Hey," he said slowly as he walked toward her. "I'm coming over there to get you untied, okay?"

Jack waited until she nodded, then fumbled with the knots for a few seconds before he gave up and rummaged through his bag for a pocketknife.

"Who did this to you?"

Parker didn't answer and Jack had the sense not to ask again, but sliced through the rope and put the knife back in his pocket as he pulled his own shirt over his head and laid it across Parker's chest, looking away until she lowered her arms as much as she could, just enough to hold it against her body.

"Hey, Jack." One of the guys popped his head through the door.

Jack stepped in front of Parker and yelled back before he had a chance to go on. "Get the fuck out of here, Cooper, and don't let anyone in here until I say."

"Well, you'd better get a move on, because Coach Hardwick is out here in the hall talking to the principal. He looks like he's heading here next."

The door closed again and Jack looked at Parker.

"We've gotta get those cuffs off you so you can put that shirt on."

He reached for her wrists and turned them over, examining the bracelets. Parker felt herself start to panic. She just wanted to pretend this never happened, but if Hardwick walked through that door, that was no longer an option.

"Well." Jack looked up and they locked eyes for the first time. "We're in luck because these are a piece of shit. They're plastic."

Parker tried to jerk them apart, but it was clearly going to take more than that. She stared at the door, biting her lip until she felt blood flow warm into her mouth.

"Don't worry, okay?" Jack met her eyes again and dropped his voice to almost a whisper. "We're going to get this handled."

He motioned for her to follow him around the corner to the showers, then turned her shoulders until she was facing the cinder block wall.

"I know this sucks, but you've got to let the shirt go for a second and raise your wrists above your head so we can get these things off you."

Parker raised her arms and the shirt dropped. Jack took her wrists in his hands and paused.

"You trust me? 'Cause if you move the wrong way, you're gonna get hurt. Just let me do it."

Parker nodded. Jack stood behind her and slammed the cuffs onto the wall again and again until they broke into pieces and dropped to the ground. Jack leaned down, grabbed his shirt, and handed it to Parker. She put it on and started to say something, but they heard the main locker room door slam open and hit the wall. Coach walked in, mumbling something about finding his keys. He couldn't see them from around the corner, but he was directly between Parker and the only other exit. Jack pointed silently to another steel door just beyond the main open area. It was the door into the gymnasium, and they both knew if she could get in there, she'd be able to walk out the front doors of the gym like nothing had ever happened.

Jack took the knife out of his pocket again, opened it, and slashed a long, shallow gash into the heel of his left hand. Parker gasped, and they both froze as they heard Coach's footsteps stop.

Jack locked eyes with Parker and pointed again at the door. She nodded, then watched as he walked around the corner and smacked deliberately into Coach, who was looking for his keys again.

"Damn, Hearndon," she heard him say. "What's wrong with you?"

"You gotta help me get this bandaged," Jack said, panic in his voice. "It won't stop bleeding."

"Here," Coach said. "You're bleeding all over the place. Let's get it over to the sinks and let's take a look. How the hell did this happen?"

Parker leaned out just enough to see them walking toward the row of sinks, their backs to her. She ran quietly across the room behind them and out the door. She stopped short once she was in the gym, assessing the surroundings, but thankfully the gym was mostly deserted, only a janitor pushing through the rear doors with his cart.

Then, in one endless minute, it was over. She was outside, filling her lungs with air so cold it burned. She wanted it to burn, wanted the pain to cauterize her memory. Eventually she started running and ran until she got home, but she didn't go inside. She didn't want to see her mother on the couch with the curtains drawn, or the medicine bottles overturned and empty on the coffee table. She didn't want to see her not look up when she came in. So she walked past the front yard and back to the treehouse. It wasn't until the next morning that she saw the word Tasha had scrawled across her body in lipstick, looking even more sinister in its backward reflection in the mirror.

Princess.

Parker shook her head to clear the memory of the smeared red letters she'd scrubbed at until her skin bled. It wasn't the word itself that bothered her, it was the tattooed memory of how it felt to be frozen.

A horn blared suddenly across the road and startled her out of the memory. A taxi was parked haphazardly against the curb, and the driver was staring at two women, one holding the hand of a child, standing outside the open door. Parker watched him tap his thumb on the steering wheel and look at his watch for emphasis. The women glanced at him hurriedly and embraced, then one of them pulled off her jacket, stooped down for a moment, and held it while the boy put it on. She stood up and brushed a tear from the mother's face, pausing to hold her close and whisper in her ear. Finally, she pulled sunglasses from her pocket and handed them to her, then stepped back onto the sidewalk as they disappeared into the taxi and it sped off into traffic, horn blaring.

The woman watched the car until it rounded the corner, pulled out her phone, and spoke into it as a sudden wind whipped her hair around her face. She hesitated at the edge of the road, then found a break in the traffic and crossed to the boardwalk. Parker watched as she dropped her phone back into the pocket of her jeans and wrapped her arms around herself, shielding herself from the evening wind sweeping across the beach from the water. Parker followed her as she started to walk. By the time she caught up with her, she smelled jasmine in the air.

Either that, or it was Alessia's perfume.

CHAPTER FOUR

Parker handed Alessia her own jacket as she fell into step with her as Alessia, for once, looked too shocked to say anything at all.

The wind seemed to pick up on cue and the sea crashed onto the rocks beside them, then swirled back onto the beach, edges lined in white foam. As they rounded the next corner, a restaurant stood out to the right, made of bleached wood with a turquoise tile roof. A white ceramic fountain splashed water into a small, sky-blue pool, but there was no sign, just an antique red bicycle leaning against a clapboard wall dripping with bright yellow jasmine vines. Parker slowed, breathing in the sweetwater scent that reminded her of humid Alabama evenings.

She stopped and nodded slightly in the direction of the door. Alessia hesitated, looking back in the direction they'd come from. Her hair was as wild as her eyes, cheeks pink from the cool wind still sweeping up from the beach.

"No offense," Parker said, one eyebrow raised. "But I'm starving, and you look like you could use a drink."

Alessia hesitated, then took one more look down the boardwalk before she walked through the door that Parker held open for her. Warmth enveloped them as they looked around, almost as if they'd walked into someone's kitchen, complete with crumbling brick walls crowded with hundreds of family portraits. Raw wood planks suspended from the ceiling held ivory candles lining the length of them. There were open fireplaces at both ends of the restaurant, sounds of laughter and clinking glasses from every direction, and the air was fragrant with crushed herbs and roasting garlic.

A waitress waved them over to a small curved booth tucked into a corner, and Alessia pulled Parker's jacket off as she slid in first, handing it back to her. She wore faded Levi's and a black shirt unbuttoned just enough to show the delicate line of her collarbone and soft curve of her breasts. Her face was bare and windswept, and there were two delicate emerald rings on her right hand.

A huge brick pizza oven sat in the center back wall, with the bustling, open kitchen swirling around it in a semicircle, separated from the dining area by glass. The same waitress, with a gunshot voice and sparkling eyes, fired off orders in Italian to the guys tossing dough into the air and spinning it on their fists. Eventually she stopped at their table, swiping at a red stain on her apron as she took out a small notepad. Alessia glanced at Parker before she ordered for them both in Italian.

"I can't believe I managed to walk into an Italian place in Greece," Parker said. "What did you order?"

"I ordered a bottle of Spanish tempranillo for me," Alessia said. "And an Italian tutor for you."

"Cute." Parker locked her eyes onto Alessia's and paused. "Now tell me why you have a Glock on your hip."

Alessia smoothed the hem of her shirt back down over the black leather holster. She didn't answer, but Parker didn't let her look away.

"Fine," Alessia said, sweeping her hair into a glossy bun at the nape of her neck. "I'll cancel the tutor and get you a wine you can handle, but we're not talking about that."

Parker sensed the edge to her words. Clearly she'd have to approach that subject later.

"What do you mean, 'a wine I can handle'?"

"Well," Alessia said, "this one tastes like tar and charred wood until you get into it, so I'm assuming it will be too much for you."

The waitress set down two large glasses and a dark bottle with a black-and-gold label, then turned to head back into the kitchen, stopping for an impromptu dance with one of the cooks as she passed.

"All right, wine girl," Parker said, nodding in the direction of her glass. "Hit me."

Alessia smiled, then poured a taste into each of their glasses, spinning one for a few seconds and handing it to Parker before she picked up her own.

"So what am I supposed to be tasting here?"

"No way." Alessia picked up her glass. "You almost impressed me once, which I'm positive was some kind of accident. Let's see if you can do it again."

Parker raised the glass, but Alessia caught her eye and lowered her own nose into the glass she was holding. She inhaled deeply and Parker followed her lead, closing her eyes against the intensity of the aroma before the wine even touched her lips. When she opened them, Alessia was watching her.

"What do you taste?"

"It's intense," Parker said. "Dark and dry like you'd expect at the start." Parker hesitated. "But then it...softens."

"What do you mean?"

Parker ran her hand through her hair, trying to wrap words around the layers of scent. "It becomes soft but almost acrid, almost like raw vanilla pods were dried over a fire and crushed into the wine."

The waitress appeared again suddenly, and they made room on their table for the antipasto platter she had balanced on three fingers. She put it in the center of the table with a small dish of olive oil, tucked a stray lock of dark hair behind her ear, and disappeared again.

Alessia picked up a brined green olive and glanced at Parker.

"Tempranillo grapes are aged in French oak. Some winemakers hand-flame the insides of the barrels to char them, so that's the smoke element you noticed." She met Parker's eyes and held them. "Most people don't pick up on that, or if they do, they call it something else."

Parker picked up a slice of baguette and dipped the crust in the oil, then layered it with a thin slice of dark, peppered meat and pickled red pepper before she handed it to Alessia.

"So, what are you doing in Greece?"

"Trying to bring you up to speed on the international wine scene, clearly," Alessia said with one eyebrow raised, taking a bite of the bread and handing it back to Parker. "What are you doing here?"

"I'm with Gender Perspectives at NATO, so I'm here at a conference about domestic violence."

"I thought you were an MP."

Alessia finished pouring them each a glass of wine, catching a single ruby drop on the side of the bottle with her thumb as she put it back on the table. The glossy slick of polish on her nails perfectly matched the wine.

"I am an MP in the States," Parker said. "But here I'm a Gender Perspectives officer. Officially I deal with wartime violence as it relates to women, but we also try to make a difference in surrounding communities when we can, and violence is a real issue here."

Alessia nodded, spreading baked garlic onto a toasted baguette slice. "Italian culture can be centered around men, but I think it's even worse in Greece."

Parker started to say something, then paused.

"What?"

Parker glanced at Alessia's shoulder and she brushed off what she thought was a string, realizing too late what it was as it fell through her fingers.

"So," Alessia said, taking a sip of wine and glancing back at her shoulder. "You just untied my bra strap in a restaurant. Is that standard training in the American military, or is that a Parker move?"

Parker's eyes followed Alessia's to her bare shoulder and noted that the delicate ribbon tied at the top was now gone.

Alessia raised an eyebrow. "You planning on tying that back together?"

Parker held her eyes and lowered her voice. "Unless you're going to take your shirt off for me, those straps might be hard to find."

"Well, I can't walk out of here with my bra undone." Alessia turned slightly in the booth to face Parker, holding the challenge between them. "So good luck with that."

Parker held her eyes as she unbuttoned two buttons of Alessia's shirt. She slid her fingertips over her skin, slowly tracing the warm curve of her breast until she felt the loose ribbon under her fingers. Parker brought it up and leaned closer to tie the two ends back together at her shoulder.

When she was done, she sat back and handed Alessia her

wineglass. "Maybe that should be an army move," she said. "Because you haven't taken a breath since I started."

❖

Later, as they walked out of the restaurant, Alessia turned to Parker.

"I want to show you something."

Parker stopped, smiling. "I tried to get you to do that in the restaurant, but you made me tie it back together."

Alessia shook her head, lifting Parker's jacket off her arm and slipping it on as she walked. "Actually, I think you'll find this more interesting."

She turned sideways to avoid a wide group of American tourists walking with maps in front of their faces, which wasn't entirely successful, and turned off the boardwalk away from the beach.

"So, are you ever going to tell me what you're doing in Santorini?" Parker asked as Alessia led her through a maze of back alleys and crumbling brick streets. Night was starting to fall, and the streetlights clicked on as they walked past a café filled with people and gold light that spilled onto the sidewalk, alive with the clink of glasses and laughter.

"No."

Alessia turned and started up a wide, whitewashed staircase.

"No, what?" Parker said, confused. "No, you're not going to tell me?"

"No, I am not going to tell you what is not your business." Alessia looked back from a few stairs above, her hands on her hips. "Do you need me to wait for you?"

Parker closed the gap between them and stopped on the step above her.

"Yeah, I can barely keep up," she said with a wink.

She turned and took the stairs two at a time to the next landing near the top of the city, surrounded by an expansive view of the deep golden sun setting just beyond the white-capped blue water.

"God, this is beautiful," Parker said, a railing the only barrier between her and the sea below that sparkled with the last of the evening sunlight. The waves had picked up closer to the shoreline, the only sound their crash against the seawall below. Birds circled overhead, and Parker caught sight of the pale outline of the waning moon on the dark side of the horizon.

Alessia caught up and paused for a moment at the railing, the wind blowing her hair around her face as she looked toward the next doorway, framed by a white archway. The door was a slick, juicy orange color, and she pulled a key from behind a potted lemon tree beside it. As they entered, a red tile hallway curved into a family room with a terra-cotta fireplace to the side and cozy sofas with linen slipcovers. The walls were old plaster, the current warm amber color accented by older hues beneath where the plaster had cracked and fallen away over the years, like turned-down pages in a book. Plank floors painted a shiny black reflected the light as Alessia turned on a lamp and slipped Parker's jacket off her shoulders and folded it neatly over the back of a worn red velvet chair.

"You have a house in Santorini? Or are we about to get arrested?"

Parker smiled as she looked through the French doors to a brick patio below.

"Very funny. I don't, but my aunt Lucia did until she died. My father kept it for my sister and me, although I'm the only one who comes here."

"That's Lexie, right?" Parker said, thinking back to what Giada had said about Alessia's sister in the café. "Is she older or younger than you?"

"Yes, Alexa, actually. She's older, but not by much." Alessia pulled a bottle of mineral water out of the fridge and reached up to an open shelf. "Not that anyone would guess that. We used to be close, but I've been waiting for her to grow up my entire life."

Alessia balanced on her tiptoes and reached for the cobalt blue glasses just out of her reach. Parker walked up behind her until she felt the warmth of Alessia's body relax against hers, then took two off the shelf and handed them to her.

"What's outside?" Parker asked.

Alessia glanced up as she was filling the glasses and flipped a switch on the kitchen wall.

"Go look."

Parker walked through the French doors and onto the first level of the red brick patio. A long wooden table sat at the edge, surrounded by forged iron chairs and handmade candlesticks of varying heights down the center of the table, and just above, light shimmered from a crystal chandelier hung from a branch of an old fig tree. Dense moss had grown between the aging bricks to form a maze underfoot as she followed the limestone steps to the curved lower level and a wooden arbor heavy with ancient wisteria vines. The dense clusters of flowers dropped down from the arbor frame in shades of violet and lavender like vivid pools of paint swirled together and dripping onto the floor. Lanterns hung from the four corners, illuminating the black night sky as Alessia came through the doors toward Parker, carrying the bottle and glasses. She set them on a small table under the arbor between two chairs.

"This is amazing," Parker said, running her hand over one of the wisteria vines wound around the corner post of the arbor. "Did your aunt do this?"

"I think my dad actually built the arbor." Alessia handed her the glasses. "My aunt loved it out here, so my dad kept expanding the patio over the years even after my grandparents died. She was a bit odd and never married, but she and my dad were always close."

"What did she do?"

"Well, at first glance," Alessia said, taking off her shoes and leaving them under the arbor, "not much."

"But that's not the whole story?"

Alessia looked over at Parker, eyes reflecting the steady light of the lanterns. "You could say that."

Parker sank down into one of the chairs as the breeze swept down and brushed a lock of hair loose from the low ponytail at the back of her neck. She slid the elastic out and wrapped it around her wrist, running her hand through her hair that fell just above her shoulders.

Alessia closed her eyes and drew in a long breath.

"Cedar. I love that scent."

"What, me?" Parker asked. "Is it my shampoo?"

Alessia nodded. "And your skin. Both."

Parker looked at Alessia, her eyes still closed, arms wrapped around her knees in the chair. The small, dark mole just to the right of her lips made her look like a silent movie star. "What else do you smell?"

"Just the night," Alessia said. "Some scents are always in the air here, like salt, stones in the sun, lavender leaves…they all deepen into something different at night."

"Is it different in Italy?"

Alessia nodded, opening her eyes. "I smell the sea in everything here. In Italy it's the earth, like turning over a handful of raw, dark soil before dawn."

She pulled a metal tin of lip balm out of her pocket and smoothed it on with her finger, setting it on the table between them, then tucking her dark, wavy hair behind her ear. The wind took it back and brushed it lightly against her cheek.

"No one ever asks me about scents," Alessia said. "They think wine is about flavor, but it's not, at least not for me. It's always been about the scent."

"How did you get started with wine?" Parker rolled up her sleeves as she spoke. "Did you go to school for it?"

"I did," Alessia said. "Which was challenging, but I'd been traveling with my dad and memorizing scents since I was a kid, so I think I approached it a different way. It took people a while to get used to it."

She picked up her water glass before she noticed it was empty, then glanced back at the house before she spoke. When she did, her voice was draped in memory.

"When I was six, my parents and Aunt Lucia took us to Grasse, in the south of France. Most of the flowers used in perfumes worldwide are grown there, so there are endless fields of roses and lavender, and even some of the rarer plants like narcissus and neroli."

"You must have loved that," Parker said, switching Alessia's empty glass with her full one and setting them back on the table. "Did they do it just for you?"

Alessia shook her head. "They had no idea about my nose at the time, no one did. Ma and Lucia just wanted to go to see the flowers. They'd just always thought it looked like a beautiful place."

"So what happened?"

"What do you mean?" Alessia picked up her glass and paused, the start of a smile on her lips.

"Something happened."

"Well," Alessia said. "You're not wrong. The first night we were there, my mom woke up and came in to check on us. Lexie was there, but I was gone and she was hysterical."

"I bet. Where did you go?"

"There was a window in the bedroom of the cottage we were renting, and I was restless. I couldn't sleep that night. There was a scent in the air that I'd never smelled before, and I just kept breathing it in. I knew it was a flower, but it had a strange, woody, resiny undertone." Her voice fell, slowed by the memory. "I loved it, and just wanted to be closer to it."

"So you crawled out the window?"

Alessia laughed. "Yes, sir, I did."

How Alessia had just referred to her wasn't lost on Parker. People frequently called her "sir" by mistake, especially when she was in uniform, but there was something intensely sexy about it when chosen on purpose.

"Let me guess," Parker said, smiling. "It took about two minutes for your mom to wake up the entire village to find you."

"That's pretty accurate. It was a full moon, so at least they had a little bit of light. When they finally found me, I was sitting in the field where I'd found that flower, and I'd stacked it and other flowers I'd collected into little piles, with tree leaves, crushed bark, and even a few handfuls of dirt I found in different fields."

"You had your own little perfume factory going on?"

"Yes, and I'd been working on it for hours, but my mother was not impressed. She scooped me up in her arms, but I started crying right away because she'd mixed up all my flowers."

"Did you go back in the morning?"

"No. I didn't have to. My aunt said she'd stay there with me until I was ready to go, and she just sat there watching me, at the edge of the field, even though it was almost dawn when I finally got everything back to the way I'd had it."

Alessia looked toward the house and Parker pretended not to notice the dark shimmer of tears. She looked almost fragile tonight, with her bare face and wild hair. Her jeans were faded to the color of air, with a rip at the knee that matched her bare face and feet.

Finally, she stood and picked up the glasses.

"Follow me."

Alessia led her through the open doors into the kitchen, where she opened a tall wooden door that led to a narrow hall. The walls and ceiling were lined in knotty red cypress, and the floor was raw stone that looked slicked with moisture in places, as if it had just rained. The hall extended about thirty feet before it disappeared around a corner.

Parker listened for a moment and turned toward the end of the hall.

"I hear something."

Alessia smiled and flipped a switch on the wall. "After you."

"I'm almost positive this isn't smart."

Alessia smiled. "Good instincts, soldier."

Parker walked slowly down the hall until it curved around the corner and opened into a stone room with a blue-and-white tiled pool at the center, lit with soft blue underwater lights. Just beyond the pool, the stone wall had been carved into a natural rock waterfall. Backlit water rushed over the rocks to the pool, where a sheer mist of silver steam rose silently off the surface. Hidden lights glowed from behind the rocks in the walls surrounding the pool. Two teak benches stood beside the water, stacked with fluffy white towels.

"How is this here?" Parker said, looking up at the ceiling. "We can't be underground."

Alessia laughed and opened a small wood-framed refrigerator by the door. She pulled out a bottle of white wine and gave it to Parker with an opener.

"It's not underground. This house is built into the mountain on the north side, which has natural hot springs running through it."

Parker cut the foil on the bottle of sauvignon blanc and eased out the cork, then handed it back to Alessia.

"I'm afraid there's only one glass," she said as she poured, then handed it to Parker. "So you'll have to share with me."

They sat at the edge of the pool, feet in the water, listening to the water tumble down the rock.

"Did your father build this?"

"He did," Alessia said, watching the light scatter across the surface of the wine. "My aunt had severe arthritis, and the hot springs were always the only thing that made her feel better. As she got older, Da didn't want her to have to climb up and down the staircases into town to go to the community pool, so he had someone tap into the hot springs behind the house and built this pool for her."

Parker handed the wine to Alessia. "They must have been close."

"They were." Alessia hesitated. "They had a rough start, so it's always been just the two of them against the earth."

Parker smiled. "Do you mean 'against the world'?"

Alessia raised an eyebrow. "The world is not the earth?"

"Fair point," Parker said, trying not to smile. "I stand corrected."

"Anyway," Alessia said, taking a sip of the wine and handing it back to Parker, watching the water move in swirling blue waves over her feet. "Their mother died when my dad was sixteen and my aunt Lucia was fourteen. So from then on, they only had each other."

"Was it sudden?"

Alessia looked into the water for a long moment before she answered. "You could say that."

Parker looked over at her and had the good sense not to throw words at the silence.

"One day they came home from school and found their mom beaten to death in the kitchen. The wall beside her was covered in blood to the ceiling, and the fire poker was still embedded in her skull when they found her."

"Jesus Christ." Parker shook her head and asked the only question there was left to ask. "Did they know who did it?"

"No one had to ask." Alessia leaned down to touch her fingertips to the water. "My grandfather was gone by the time they came home from school. They never saw him again."

Parker looked down at the water, searching for words. But there were none, and they both knew it. Alessia pulled herself up from the edge of the pool and brought back the wine bottle, refilling the glass in Parker's hand before she sat back down.

"So what about you?" she asked. "Are you close to your family?"

Parker shook her head, sifting through the possible answers to that question.

"I'm close to my brother, Wes, who runs the coffee shop in our hometown."

Alessia nodded. "What about your mom and dad?"

Parker balanced the wineglass on the stone edge between them. She watched a drop of condensation roll down the side as she spoke.

"Dad left us when I was eight."

"Left? What do you mean?" Alessia looked over at Parker, her dark eyes reflecting the blue shimmer of the lights in the water. "Did he die?"

"Maybe. I don't know."

Parker ran her hand through her hair, glancing back at the door as if she were looking for an escape route from the memory. But she'd lived with it long enough to know that the best way out was through, so she started talking.

"We were getting ready for bed one night, and Dad told my mom he was going out for cigarettes. I just went to bed like usual, but I got up in the middle of the night and went to the kitchen. I didn't know she was even there until I saw the tip of her cigarette burn red in the dark. She was just sitting there. In his chair at the table."

Alessia handed her the wineglass. "What did she say?"

"Nothing. She just sat there until the sun rose. She told me to go back to bed, but I fell asleep in the hall, waiting."

"And he never came home?"

"No," Parker said. "And she never really did, either. I mean, she was there." She paused, not sure how to phrase it. "But it was like she gave up or something. She was never the same."

Alessia's eyes shimmered in the flicker of the lights under the water, and she ran her hand through her hair. She lifted herself out of the pool and unbuttoned her shirt, then stepped out of her jeans and dropped them by the side of the pool, topped by the gun and holster. Parker forgot to breathe. Her eyes swept the length of Alessia's body as she sank into the water, then settled onto the underwater bench. Her black satin bra was soaked and clinging to her skin. Water streamed down the curves of her breasts in rivulets, disappearing into the center of her bra.

When Parker finally looked into her eyes, Alessia raised

a single eyebrow until Parker laughed, then pulled her own shirt and sports bra over her head. She stepped out of her chinos next, leaving only her black boy shorts. She lowered herself into the water beside Alessia, breathing in the salt steam hovering above the water, closing her eyes against the urge to pull Alessia close.

"I'm impressed," Alessia said, her eyes moving over the strong lines of Parker's shoulders. "Most Americans are shy about the naked."

"About being naked?" Parker smiled, trying to keep her eyes above Alessia's breasts. "Well, I guess I'm not most Americans." She leaned her head back against the pool edge. "You'll figure that out at some point."

The water tumbled down the waterfall rocks and into the pool, shapeshifting into a cloud of steam. Alessia ran her hands through her hair, letting it fall around her shoulders before she sank beneath the water and swam to the center of the pool. Parker watched as she stood and the water streamed down her body, her hair dark and slicked against her shoulders. When she swam back to the edge, her bra strap fell down her arm as she pulled herself onto the bench. Parker smiled.

"What?" Alessia said. "Deciding which one to untie this time?"

Parker ran a finger between the ribbon and Alessia's skin, watching it fall, taking Alessia's bra with it. It slowed and clung to her wet skin, hesitating just before it slipped off her nipples. Alessia put it on the side of the pool and sank back down into the water.

"So who was it?" Parker watched the pale blue reflection of the water in Alessia's dark eyes.

Her eyes fell to Parker's mouth, and when she spoke, her voice was soft. "What do you mean?"

"There must have been a girl?" Parker ran both hands through her hair. "Someone must have been responsible for making you appreciate American soldiers like you do."

Alessia smiled and shook her head. "You noticed."

"Hard not to," Parker said, settling back against the stone. "She must have been a piece of work."

Alessia shook her head, looking down into the water. She was silent for a long moment before she spoke.

"She was, but it wasn't her that broke my heart."

Parker hesitated, then pulled Alessia across her lap to face her, hands circling her waist.

"Who was it, then?"

Alessia didn't answer, just brushed her lips across Parker's so lightly that Parker wondered if it had been her breath. Parker slid one hand slowly up the curve of her back and into her hair. Alessia closed her eyes as Parker ran her tongue up the side of Alessia's neck, barely touching her skin, then across her earlobe, scraping it lightly with her teeth as she let it go. Then she froze, her body stiffening.

"Wait." Parker put her hand in the center of Alessia's chest and held her there, attention hard and focused, listening.

Alessia glanced at the door, her body stone-still.

"Someone's here," Parker whispered. "I just heard a door shut."

"Which door?" Alessia asked as they lifted themselves out of the water. She took the towel Parker handed her from the stack on the teak bench, drying herself quickly and pulling on her clothes.

"I think it was the front door," Parker said, glancing back at her as she looked down the hall that led to the kitchen. "Stay here."

Parker finished dressing, then walked to the door that led to the kitchen, opening it slowly and scanning the room as she stepped back into the house. Everything looked exactly as it had when they'd come in, but she still went upstairs to be sure the house was clear. The house was silent, eerily neat, and the boards on the stairs creaked under her feet as she walked back down to the front door. It was still locked from the inside.

"Did you find anything?" Alessia said quietly, peering out from the kitchen onto the back patio, where the wind swayed the chandelier from its fig tree branch. A lock of wet hair was clinging to her cheek, and her gun was strapped to her side.

"No. Everything appears to be locked from the inside." Parker walked to the patio door and tried the handle, which clicked solidly against its lock. "But I know I heard that front door close."

Parker glanced back at Alessia, who was now standing by the antique chair in the living room, Parker's jacket still looped over the back. Her hand shook as she pulled at the knife holding a photo to the arm of the chair, the red velvet behind it like a faded pool of blood. She handed the picture to Parker and sank into the chair, her eyes wide and motionless, fixed on the empty fireplace.

The photo was of Parker and Alessia under the arbor earlier that evening, taken from inside the house. The jagged slit where the knife had pierced the paper was all that was left of Alessia's face.

CHAPTER FIVE

"Ma, I didn't come in to eat. I'm here to drop yesterday's deposit at the bank for you."

Alessia held out her hand for the bank bag.

Giada slid the bag out of her grasp, put a cookie in her hand, and gestured toward the tables.

"Sit. You have time for the breakfast. I bring to you."

Alessia knew better than to argue, so she slipped behind the counter to make an espresso before she took a seat at a small table by the brick wall. She'd just bitten the edge off the lemon sugar cookie when she saw Father Declan Flaherty come through the door and greet her mother with a kiss.

Four years ago, the archdiocese had sent him from Belfast when Salerno's village priest had died suddenly from a heart attack. He'd charmed most everyone within weeks with his fondness for whiskey and irresistible smile, but her mother had declared there was no replacement for the village priest she'd grown up with. Declan was also much younger than their previous priest had been—the same age as Alessia—which was another initial strike against him for Giada. He persisted, though, and within a few weeks she was inviting Father Flaherty around for dinner. Even Alessia had grown fond of him; he'd ignored her habit of keeping most people at arm's length, and they'd grown close over the last few years.

He kissed Giada on the cheek as she handed him a long baguette wrapped in white paper, and on his way out the door raised an eyebrow at Alessia. She sighed as she threw her jacket back on.

"Ma, I'll be right back," she said in the direction of the counter where her mother was sliding a platter of rosewater cookies into the glass case. "I promise."

She squinted in the sudden bright sunshine as she opened the door and wove herself into the foot traffic until she rounded the corner of the building. She knew exactly where he'd be: at the edge of the wide river that flowed behind the café and into the center of town.

Indeed, Declan was there, sitting on a stone ledge watching the wind scatter petals from the flowering trees onto the pewter surface of the water. He lit a cigarette as she sat down beside him and handed it to her without a word. Alessia drew the smoke into her lungs, closing her eyes before she spoke.

"So," she said. "How is she?"

Declan lit his own cigarette and exhaled slowly, watching the smoke drift toward the river, an undulating reflection of the water.

"She came to confession yesterday."

"Fabulous," Alessia said, tapping her cigarette and watching the velvety ash disappear into a gust of wind. "Tell me everything."

Declan glanced at her with a half smile. "You know that's not how this works."

"Fine. I just need to know if she's okay. Ma's getting more worried every day."

"I saw you with your mother at sunrise mass twice last week." He glanced over at her with a wink. "If I didn't know better, I'd think you wanted to be there."

"Don't count on it."

He laughed and ran a hand through his hair, but the same dark wave always escaped and brushed across his left cheek, making him look even younger than he was.

"She's fine," he said, holding her eyes. "Well, as fine as she ever is. But she misses you."

"Declan." Alessia looked down and willed the sting of tears behind her lashes to disappear. "You know I can't forgive her. Not even for you."

"I know." His voice was suddenly gentle, and he leaned his shoulder against Alessia's. "And, saints preserve us," he said with a quick glance skyward, "I can't say I blame you." He squeezed her hand, and Alessia felt him choose every word before he said it. "But I've never seen anyone so in need of forgiveness, either."

They sat in silence for a few moments, until Declan reached over for the last of the cigarette Alessia had forgotten was in her hand, crushing it under the polished tip of his shoe.

"I'll see if I can get her to pop round the café and at least let your mum know she's safe."

Alessia smiled as she stood and buttoned her jacket against the breeze coming off the water. She pulled Declan to his feet and took the arm he offered as they started back toward the street.

"That might be the best plan. Otherwise," she said, tucking a wild wave of hair behind her ear, "I'll have to keep coming to mass, and we both know no good can come of that."

Once she was back in the café, Alessia gathered her things and promised to eat the toasted sandwich her mother had wrapped up and slipped into her bag. She kissed Giada's cheek and stepped out into the bright sunshine, only to stop one shop down and push open the heavy glass door of her father's jewelry shop.

Salvatore was behind the counter examining a ring he turned slowly in the light, looking at it through a jeweler's loupe. His silver shock of hair, which always seemed to be at the same urgent stage of requiring a haircut, fell forward and jockeyed for position with his every movement. When the door clattered shut behind Alessia, he glanced up and pushed the hair out of his eyes.

"Alessia," he said in a rush, as if he'd just solved the mystery of cold fusion, his head dipping once again to the ring. "You must see this."

She wedged herself and her bag into the narrow area behind the counter and leaned over to look.

"It's beautiful," she said, winding her hair into a quick bun before she took the jeweler's loupe from her father and peered though it for a closer look. It was a square-cut emerald set simply in pale yellow gold, deep green and shimmering on a thin gold band of medieval filigree. The stone reminded her of a lake at nightfall. Still, dark, and endless.

Sal turned up the light on the loupe.

"It reminds me of you. It would be a perfect engagement ring."

He was smiling, but worried lines framed his deep brown eyes. Alessia had noticed lately there seemed to be more of them than usual. He sighed as she handed him back the ring.

"I just want to see you settled and happy," he said, holding her eyes. "Maybe even making beautiful grandchildren."

"I am happy, Da."

Alessia looked up at him as Sal covered her hand with his, fingers smudged with black jeweler's grease. She'd loved the smell of it since she was little, along with the smooth, cool scent of gold that had always clung to his hands. She leaned in to kiss his cheek as a taxi passed the window with two wheels on the sidewalk, horn blaring as it sped off down the street.

"Da, you know I want to do that eventually, but I've got work to do first."

Alessia winked as she swiped a chocolate truffle from his stash under the counter, then closed her eyes as she savored the fresh raspberry and vanilla filling melting onto her tongue.

"Besides," she said, opening her eyes and licking a smudge of raspberry coulis from her bottom lip, "we both know how that turned out last time."

Sal smiled as he shook his head and dropped another truffle into her jacket pocket, this one wrapped in crinkly silver paper.

"You know, you remind me more of your grandmother every day."

He glanced back at a small black-and-white photo of his mother mounted on the wall behind the counter. Alessia had accidentally knocked it off the wall when she was little, and she still remembered the bright square of wallpaper she'd found under the photo, the edges aged and yellowed where the frame had been. In the picture, her grandmother had toddlers Sal and Lucia on her lap, holding them close and laughing, dark waves of glossy hair tossed around her face by the wind.

Sal touched the photo and smiled, making the sign of the cross as he turned to his daughter. "She'll send the right one for you when she's ready. She's still all around us."

He put away the ring and flipped the sign on the glass door to Closed as he locked the row of five deadbolts on the door.

"Maybe she shouldn't even bother," Alessia said, pulling her bag back onto her shoulder. "I'm starting to think I'm cursed or something."

Sal shot her the look she'd expected, then led her through the door behind the counter and pulled it shut behind them.

The back room of the jewelry store served as Sal's office. It had a scarred mahogany desk on one side, bathed in the soft green glow of a library lamp, and two worn leather couches that faced each other by the opposite wall. The coffee table Alessia had made for him, a split wine barrel with a hammered copper top, sat between them, topped by two short chipped glasses and a bottle of grappa. The office was one of those rooms that never really seemed to have enough light in it, as if the stone walls had slowly absorbed it, refusing to illuminate the dark corners or lighten the cold scent of damp limestone.

They sank into the couches and Sal dug in his shirt pocket for a cigar. She handed him the cigar cutter and matches from the coffee table and sat back, eyeing the glasses.

"Da, why do you always have glasses with chips in them?" Alessia picked one up and turned it around in her hand. "This one actually has three of them."

"So your mother doesn't steal them for the café," he said, examining the roll of the cigar for a long moment before deeming it acceptable and clipping the end. "Otherwise, the second she gets low next door, she swipes them and I never see them again."

He poured them each a small glass of grappa and recorked the bottle. Grappa was closer to jet fuel than liquor, which she suspected was why her father loved it. She clinked her glass to his and took a sip, closing her eyes against the sudden cloud of burning vapors at the back of her throat.

"Delicious," Sal said as his glass clattered back onto the slab of hammered copper. "Life without grappa is not worth living."

Alessia smiled, filling his cup up again before she sat back into the sofa. Sal's eyes met hers, and he glanced down at the bag sitting beside her on the sofa.

"So," he said, words slowly unfolding into the silence. "How did it go?"

Alessia pulled a folder from her bag and handed it to her father. "It went fine. I don't think anyone saw us."

Sal thumbed through the papers inside and pulled out a glossy eight-by-ten photo. He looked at it for a long time, then slid it back into the folder and laid it on the coffee table between them. The photo had a handwritten address on the back.

"So that's where they are now?"

"They will be." Alessia glanced down at her watch. "Olivia and her son should land at the Salerno airport this evening, and I'll have a car there waiting for them. By tomorrow, she'll be on a plane to France."

Sal held the lighter to the end of his cigar to relight it, drawing in air and watching the end glow and spread. "Who referred this one to us?"

Alessia picked up her glass and took another sip, smaller this time, and pointed at the paper she'd handed her father.

"Lina, she's a nurse at the hospital the woman was taken to after it happened."

Sal blew smoke toward the ceiling and watched as it disappeared. "How bad was it?"

"Bad." Alessia instinctively touched the gun at her hip, hidden by her jacket. "She's pregnant again and almost lost the baby."

Sal shook his head. It was a moment before he spoke. "Do you think she's ready to stay gone?"

"I think she is." Alessia leaned back into the couch and closed her eyes before she went on. "But her husband told her that if she didn't come home when they released her, he'd find them and kill her son in front of her. He also said he'd find me next, which seems to be a trend lately."

"Christ." Sal topped up his glass and settled back in his seat. "How dangerous do you think he is?"

"One a scale of one to ten, if the average dickhead we deal with is about a three…" She hesitated and glanced down at the folder on the table between them. "He's a nine."

CHAPTER SIX

After waiting nearly an hour for the car that was supposed to take her from the airport back to base, Parker finally got back to her room. She swung her bag onto her bed and sank down beside it. It was hard to miss the look Petra pinned her with from across their room.

"So," Petra said, raising an eyebrow. "How was the conference?" Her voice held an almost giddy note of anticipation.

"It was fine." Parker eyed her as she pulled off her boots and set them neatly at the foot of her bed. "Why?"

"Oh, no reason," Petra said, peering under random stacks of papers on her desk until she found the lid to the open jar of peanut butter in her hand. "I just overhead Maeve saying she got stuck in a room with you. One with a single bed."

"Oh, good Lord." Parker rolled her eyes. "Nothing happened."

"Sure," Petra said, smiling. "Whatever you say."

She continued to dig around in the piles of scattered papers on her desk that seemed even deeper than usual.

"Hey, don't get me wrong." Petra picked up a sticky note and discarded it in the vague direction of the trash can. "I think she's annoying as hell, but if she ever shuts up for a minute, it's hard not to notice that body. I'm straight, not blind."

She pulled a note out of the pile and attempted to smooth the wrinkles out on the surface of her desk, presenting it with a flourish and handing it to Parker.

"Colonel Williams wants you in his office tomorrow morning at oh-six-hundred hours. I think they tried to reach you on your phone, but you must have been still on the plane. His secretary dropped this off for you about an hour ago."

"Just an hour?" Parker said, holding the paper up by one corner and extending her arm. "That's all it took for you to make it look like you blew your nose on it?"

Petra studied it and tipped her head to the side. "I may or may not have put my banana on it. Loosen up, Captain Haven."

The next morning Parker dressed carefully and precisely. Being called to her commanding officer's office was rare, and as she walked to the administration buildings her mind sifted through the possible reasons for the meeting. Security at the door was noticeably heavy; as an officer, she was able to walk through fairly quickly, but she noted that there were MPs in place as well as the normal security officers. She arrived at her commanding officer's office with two minutes to spare.

Sergeant Allison Carver, who served as the administrative assistant for Colonel Williams, stood and saluted Parker as she approached, then handed Parker a gray folder with a stack of papers inside as she opened the office door and stepped in.

"Good morning, Captain Haven," she said, glancing at the clock. "He's ready for you."

She opened the office door just enough to see inside and spoke in a low voice. "Captain Haven is here, sir."

She held the door for Parker, then shut it quietly behind her as she left. Everyone in the room was of a higher rank than Parker, so she stood at attention at the desk until Colonel Williams invited her to sit.

"Have a seat, Captain Haven. We appreciate you coming in this morning." He took a sip of his coffee and set it to the side. "I assume you know Lieutenant Colonels Trobaugh and Hooper?"

Parker took a seat and noted they all held the same gray folder.

"I do," she said, with a nod in their direction. "Thank you, sir."

Trobaugh and Hooper were both from a Northern California Army base and had been deployed to NATO specifically because of their experience in international law. Parker knew enough about them to know they both started as detectives before transferring to law and had been assigned fairly recently to their posts in the military police. She also knew they were a couple.

Colonel Williams was one of the best commanding officers Parker had served under during her career. He was African American with a strong New York accent, just the beginnings of silver hair at his temples, and he was known for his deep, rumbling voice. His office was always immaculate, except for a signed NY Mets baseball on his desk and a gum wrapper beside it. She'd only been in his office a handful of times during her deployment, but the wrapper was always there, and it was always Juicy Fruit.

"Captain," Colonel Williams said, pulling the hem of his sleeve down as he spoke. "We are aware of the situation to this point, so let me get you up to speed."

Parker nodded and opened her folder. "Yes, sir."

"You might already have heard, but there was a murder just outside the airport yesterday afternoon, about two hours after your plane landed back in Italy. It's the first murder in Salerno since 1985."

Parker nodded.

"Ordinarily," Hooper said, glancing over at Williams, "this would be a civilian matter, but with this one, we're working alongside the local authorities."

Hooper was a tall woman, with pale skin, a strong build, and clear blue eyes. Her wife, Trobaugh, was the opposite, a petite blonde with an athletic body and more gold medals to her name than a treasure chest. They never commented on their personal lives, but it was obvious they were an item. Or at least it was to Parker.

Parker looked back at Williams. "That's a busy area, even at that time of day. Were there any witnesses?"

"The victim's name is John Haley. He was found dead at the wheel of a car in the pickup area of the Salerno Airport." He shuffled through a stack of papers on his desk and handed Parker a photocopied video still. "We've obtained the surveillance video. The victim pulls up to the curb in the waiting area, waits in the car for almost six minutes with his eyes locked on the exit doors of the airport, then slumps over dead across the steering wheel."

"How is that possible?" Parker said, looking carefully at the blown-up still from the security footage. "Even if no one saw the shooter, someone must have heard the gunshot."

"That's what we thought," Trobaugh said. "Local law

enforcement has been interviewing witnesses since it happened. No one heard anything."

Williams handed Parker a note with a last name and number at the top.

"I know this is a bit outside of the terms of your deployment, but as a senior MP and one of the only three detectives on base, you have the most investigative experience, so we're pulling you in as the lead on this investigation. You'll report back to me, of course, and you'll have Trobaugh and Hooper as well as the MPs on base to assist you." He glanced at the clock on the wall. "In fact, we have CSIs at the victim's hotel room right now collecting evidence."

He looked at his watch.

"You'll find the name of your point person for local law enforcement on that slip of paper, and you're expected at Hotel Saville in Salerno at ten for a briefing on the details. Don't forget to sign out your weapon. You'll want to keep it on you until we get this thing wrapped up."

"Yes, sir," Parker said, standing as Colonel Williams stood.

He walked around the desk and held out his hand to Parker, looking her in the eyes for a moment before he spoke.

"We've worked together for just under a year now, but it didn't take me long to figure out that if I need something done right, you're the person to put on it."

"I appreciate that, sir," Parker said, meeting his eyes. "I won't let you down."

As she turned to leave, she looked back at Hooper. "Ma'am, if you don't mind my asking, why *is* the military getting involved with this one? You mentioned that ordinarily it would be a civilian matter."

"The victim was an American citizen." Hooper removed her glasses and glanced at Colonel Williams, then back at Parker. "But he was also the only son of the governor of New York."

❖

Parker slid into a parking space in town and locked her military vehicle. Her holstered weapon felt heavy and unfamiliar at her side;

unless there was a direct threat present, she didn't usually carry a weapon on base, and she'd forgotten how heavy they were. She crossed the street, barely avoiding a rambling transit bus with no intention of stopping, realizing she didn't have any idea what this Italian detective looked like or if he even spoke English.

Pigeons swooped across the sidewalk in pursuit of a forgotten sandwich crust as she walked toward the hotel. The scent of baking bread and warm chocolate wafted through the open door of a nearby bakery, and small black bistro tables dotted the sidewalk outside, draped with wide ribbons of sunlight. Her stomach rumbled at the sight of the fresh apricot croissants being placed carefully in the display window. She hadn't eaten that morning, and it was pretty clear now she'd be busy through lunch and possibly dinner.

Parker finally reached the hotel and stepped through the wide double glass doors to the main lobby, which had an expansive white marble floor that instantly turned her footsteps into echoes in the empty room. An enormous ceramic vase of calla lilies stood silent in the center of the reception area as Parker circled it, scanning the lobby. Sunlight streamed through the skylight three stories above the floor, into a crystal chandelier that scattered it across the floor in pale gold pools. Parker stopped and examined the note again. It unnerved her that she seemed to be the only person in the room, if not the entire hotel.

"Captain Haven?"

Parker turned to see a woman at the entrance to the bar just past the reception area. She motioned to Parker to join her and took a seat at the bar. Parker watched her as she walked. She was petite, with dark hair pulled into a tight bun at the nape of her neck. She moved like spilled mercury, her fingers fluid and graceful as she poured water into a rocks glass as Parker took a seat.

"I'm Inspector Francesca Valle," she said, pushing the water toward Parker. She spoke perfect English with a strong Italian accent. As Parker pulled the case folder from her bag, she felt the woman's gaze on her before she heard her speak. "And I wasn't expecting a woman."

Parker met her eyes. She was startlingly beautiful, with soft brown eyes and a mouth that reminded Parker of the full, sensual curves of a naked woman. She wore a conservative pinstripe skirt that clung to her hips, with a white blouse and dark suit jacket.

"Well, I wasn't exactly expecting you, either." Parker smiled as she said it, and saw a flash of a smile in return. "So now that that's out of the way, why don't you fill me in on the details of the case?"

They talked for a few minutes as Francesca described the crime scene. The car was a rental, so it was nearly useless as far as forensic evidence. They'd identified the victim from his ID and found a key card in his wallet that led them to the hotel. Once the staff had opened his room, a passport in his luggage confirmed his identity.

"Well," Parker said, trying not to stare at her mouth as Francesca took a sip from her glass, "we know he was American, but any idea why he might have been in Salerno?"

"His passport stamps show he's been in Greece for three years, with only occasional visits back to the US." She tapped her nails on the slick mahogany surface of the bar and hesitated. "I hear his family has political connections in your country?"

"That's putting it lightly," Parker said, jotting down the information on the inside cover of the folder and putting her pen back into the pocket on the arm of her uniform jacket. "So obviously there's pressure to get this solved ASAP."

"A crime like this is extremely rare here in Salerno, so we're anxious to get it wrapped up as quickly as possible, too. Tourists bring in most of the city's income this time of year, and this story splashed across the news will bring that to a halt in a hurry."

Parker paused, her eyes skimming the curves of Francesca's breasts before she thought to stop herself.

"What was he doing in Greece for three years?" Parker asked, pulling out the video still Colonel Williams had given her. "That seems unusual."

"Partying, from the look of it so far," Francesca said. "His family has been contacted, and we've only spoken to them briefly, but they said he wasn't working. He had a trust fund in place, apparently."

"Anything unusual in his room?"

"The room is still being processed, but so far we've found about a gram of cocaine and a case and ammunition for a Smith and Wesson forty-caliber pistol. Everything else seems normal. No visible signs that a struggle occurred at any point."

"Would you mind if I take a look before I go?"

"I was expecting you'd want to; it's number three sixteen on the third floor. The hotel will be closed until my team is sure they've gotten everything and cleared it." Francesca looked at her watch. "I need to get back to the surveillance tapes at the station. So far we've only had a chance to look at the minutes just before and after the shooting, but not the rest of the footage. We might catch something new from a different angle."

"The thing that's been sticking in my mind is that no one heard the shot. It had to have been a sniper. This was too clean and silent to be anything else."

Francesca pulled a thin silver case engraved with her initials out of her bag and handed Parker her card.

"I agree. But there's a reason someone sent a sniper to take out a random American in a crowd of people." She slid the card case back into her bag. "And I want to know what it is."

Francesca made a quick call to her officers in the room to let them know Parker was headed upstairs and promised to email the footage to Parker that afternoon.

"You've got my card, so call me tomorrow morning after you've seen the tapes." Francesca put her bag on her shoulder and they walked out to the reception area, her heels clicking on the marble floor. "Or sooner, if you notice anything unusual. I'm going to try to see if they'll let me see the body by then so I can get a better idea of what direction that bullet came from."

She looked at her watch, then the door.

"It was nice to meet you, Captain Haven."

Francesca offered her hand and Parker shook it, meeting her eyes. "And please, call me Parker. I have a feeling we'll see each other again."

"Certainly. And please call me Francesca." Her eyes traced the lines of the muscles in Parker's arms as she excused herself and headed for the front doors, the sound of her heels reverberating in the deserted lobby.

Parker found the room and ducked under the crime scene tape

across the door, picking up a pair of latex gloves from the box on the counter and snapping them on as she looked around. The cocaine Francesca had mentioned was already bagged and tagged, as well as the weapon case, and the room was nearly full of crime scene investigators from both the military and Italian police. Maeve was standing by the window, looking down to the sidewalk.

"What the hell are you doing here?" Parker said as she crossed the room, trying to step out of the path of the CSI techs.

Maeve looked up at her, then went back to staring down at the sidewalk. "Knitting you a cardigan, obviously."

Parker raised an eyebrow in her direction.

Maeve sighed, pushing a wayward strand of blond hair out of her eyes. "What do you think I'm doing here?" Her soft British accent was a contrast to the sharp murmured Italian all around her. "They pulled me to go with the crime scene techs as an interpreter, but the Italian police all speak English, so they're doing just fine communicating on their own, as it turns out." She looked at her watch and went back to window-gazing.

"So what do you think?"

Maeve looked back at Parker. "What do you mean?"

"You've been here for a while, what do you think we're going to find in here?"

Parker held her gaze until Maeve realized she actually expected an answer.

"I think that what they've already found was lying in plain sight on the bed." Maeve sighed, glancing over at the evidence bags on the counter. "Beyond that, you're going to find fuck all."

Two CSI techs using tape to pull hairs off the carpet raised their heads and shot her identical looks.

"Don't hold back, Sergeant," Parker said, coughing to hide a laugh. "Good to see you making friends as usual."

Maeve turned back to the window.

"Look," Maeve said. "There hasn't been much to do for the last three hours, so I took a look at the key logs that show when the room is locked or unlocked when someone goes in or out."

She reached over to the counter for a sheet of paper and handed it to Parker. It had three lines of text on it.

"Your victim checked in yesterday afternoon and used his key card to open the door, stayed twelve minutes, then left and never came back."

"So you're saying it's unlikely that he left behind a truckload of hidden evidence in just over ten minutes." Parker nodded, stepping to the side and out of the way of one of the techs. "Fair point."

Parker took the log sheet from Maeve just as someone knocked on the open door of the room from the other side of the crime scene tape. Based on the uniform, he seemed to be a hotel employee, and a good twenty years past retirement age. His pants were belted around his ribs, and two tufts of gray hair, one over each ear, were the only contrast to his oily bald head. His floral shirt was slightly unbuttoned, highlighting his yellowed undershirt and wiry white chest hair. He started to step under the crime tape only to have everyone in the room look up and tell him to freeze, so Parker and Maeve joined him in the hall.

"Can you ask him what he's here for?" Parker said, looking at Maeve.

Maeve spoke to him for a moment in flowing Italian and was rewarded with a smile and long reply.

"What did he say?"

"He said someone asked for the video surveillance DVDs from the last three days, and they're in the security room. He brought the keys so we can go down and get them."

The old man was beaming. He looked Maeve up and down, then stepped forward to grasp her left hand and kiss it. Maeve gave him a perfunctory smile and stepped back, shooting a glance at Parker.

"What else?"

"He rattled off something about beautiful women, then offered to take us to the security room."

Parker and the old man said nothing, waiting for her to make a move. Parker smiled, then cleared her throat and looked at Maeve.

"Go ahead," Maeve said to Parker, nodding toward the elevator. "I'll wait."

The old man's gaze remained locked on Maeve, this time with one unruly white eyebrow raised.

"I hate to break it to you," Parker whispered, somehow managing to keep a straight face as she leaned closer to Maeve. "But I don't think it's me he's waiting for."

Maeve dropped her voice and plastered a neutral look on her face.

"Bloody hell," she said, her voice a hiss. "They really don't pay me enough for this shit."

Parker offered to go with her, but Maeve waved her off.

"He's all of ninety pounds," she said, brushing away the elbow he offered her. "I think I can take him if I need to."

Parker ducked back under the tape to finish looking over the room. Maeve was right; the CSIs from both the military police and Italian law enforcement were going through everything with a fine-tooth comb, but it looked like whoever had been there simply came in, loaded his weapon, and went back out. It didn't look like he'd even stepped foot in the bathroom, considering there was still a paper strip over the toilet put there by housekeeping.

Parker picked up the glass by the sink and held it up to the light to see if there was a lip print that might contain traces of viable DNA, but there was nothing.

"Captain Haven?"

Sergeant Carter, the MP's lead CSI tech, rounded the corner of the bathroom with a plastic tub of evidence bags, each of them labeled and stapled neatly at the top.

"We're done and heading out. Should I wait to release the room?"

"No, that's fine, Carter. I think we're done here."

"Yes, ma'am. I'll take the scene tape down on the way out."

Maeve stepped back into the room just as the CSIs left and handed Parker the DVDs.

Parker winked at her. "Have a good time?"

"Fucking hell." She unbuttoned the top button of her jacket and glared at Parker. "I need a drink."

Parker smiled as she took a final look around, and they stepped into the hall, locking the door behind them.

"I need to get these videos back to the base, but I'm going to starve before I get there if I don't eat," Parker said, glancing at Maeve as she pushed the button on the elevator. "You hungry?"

"Always." Maeve stepped into the elevator and carefully squared her shoulders in the mirror.

A few minutes later, Parker and Maeve rounded the corner of a brick alleyway and sidestepped the puddle in the center of the cobblestone walk.

"It's about to dump rain on us," Maeve said, looking up at the smudged charcoal cluster of clouds looming overhead. "Where the hell are you taking me?"

"Pipe down over there," Parker said with a wink. "Trust me, you're going to actually like this place."

Two streets and another alley later, Parker stopped at a brick pub with a Tudor-style white-plaster-and-timber-framed second story. The glossy black entrance door swung open and they stepped into a classic English pub, complete with Premier League coverage playing on the screen above the slick antique bar, snooker tables in the corner, and the scent of roast potatoes warming the air. Parker chose a small leather booth by the back window and slid in, taking her cap off and running her hand through her hair.

A lanky teenage boy with Justin Bieber hair and a Manchester United T-shirt ambled over and asked what they'd like to drink.

"A pint of Magners for me." Maeve looked up at the waiter. "And God knows what the American wants. Probably a diet Budweiser or something."

"Charming," Parker said. "But you're wrong. I'll have a regular Budweiser."

The boy flashed a smile at Maeve and returned to the bar, glancing back at their table on his way.

Parker picked up her menu. "I think you might have a fan there."

"How do you know?" Maeve said, swiftly lifting the menu out of Parker's hands and setting it back down on the edge of the table where it had been. "Maybe's he's gay and thinks you're cute boi candy."

Parker laughed out loud. "Cute boi candy? That's a first." She made another pass at the menu and was rebuffed. "Although come to think of it, I've been called worse."

"I bet you have." Maeve smiled at her with a raised eyebrow. "I've heard a few things around the barracks."

The boy reappeared with Maeve's pint and a bottle of Budweiser for Parker.

Maeve looked up at him. "Roast?"

He nodded toward a chalkboard at the end of the bar. "Aye," he said in a thick Scottish accent. "It's Sunday."

"Perfect," Maeve said, handing him back the menus. "We'll take two of those, and a bag of Walkers Prawn Cocktail crisps for me."

Maeve took a sip of her pint.

"What the hell just happened?" Parker asked, then paused, eyeing Maeve's glass. "And what are you drinking? It looks like apple juice."

"It's Magners, an Irish cider." Maeve pushed it toward Parker. "I'd say you might like it, but go easy. It's probably higher alcohol than you're used to."

"Jesus." Parker looked up and smiled. "What did you do with your time before you had me to throw darts at?" She took a sip of Maeve's pint, then switched it with hers. "And surprisingly, this isn't terrible. Just for that you're losing it."

"Cheeky bastard." Maeve flashed her a rare smile that lasted until she tasted the Budweiser. She swallowed with effort and pushed it to the edge of the table. "I'm not drinking this. It tastes like piss."

Their waiter dropped off the crisps and looked down at the bottle Maeve had pushed away.

"I don't want to talk about it," Maeve said in answer to his unspoken question. "But it seems the American has grown an actual pair of bollocks, so I'll be needing another pint of Magners."

The boy laughed, pushing his hair out of his eyes and shaking his head as he walked back to the bar.

Maeve opened the bag of crisps and put one in her mouth, closing her eyes and sinking back in the booth with a sigh.

"I hate to admit it, Haven," she said, finally opening her eyes and reaching for another. "But I'm in love with this place. How did you even know this was here?"

"I saw it once when I was looking for something else, and I remembered today it had a British flag over the door. I figured you'd like it."

"You did well." Maeve smiled as heavy rain started to pelt the window beside them. "I'm almost impressed."

Parker smiled back, then looked down at the foil bag in Maeve's hand. It was pink, with a picture of a sliced potato and a large shrimp dancing on the outside.

"I'd ask what the hell you're eating, but I'm not entirely sure I want to know."

"You don't. I think that may just be too much for you to handle."

Parker watched the rain come down in sheer silver sheets outside the window. It was good to think about something besides the case for a few minutes. The lack of evidence in the room hadn't been a great start to the investigation.

"So," Parker said, "did you meet Francesca?"

The waiter reappeared suddenly and pushed her empty bag of crisps to the side as he put down two steaming platters of roast beef and vegetables with brown gravy in front of them.

"Oh, my God," Parker said after a long pause, eyes locked on the plate in front of her. "This looks amazing."

Tender hunks of roast beef glossed with a rich brown gravy and vegetables sat on large, mismatched plates. Crispy, golden roast potatoes piled high on the side were accompanied by something that looked like a small collapsed soufflé. Parker lifted the edge of it gingerly with her fork.

"Except for this," she said, examining it closely. "What's this?"

"Just eat it," Maeve said, dipping hers in the gravy and popping half of it into her mouth. "It's heaven."

She was right. They were quiet for the next few minutes, the only sound the clink of cutlery on the chipped floral plates and the sound of the rain pelting the window outside. The roast reminded Parker of the Crock-Pot dinners her mom used to make when she was little, before her dad left. The rich, meaty scent of it filled the whole house, and she'd sneak into the kitchen and stand on a chair to lift the glass lid when her mom wasn't looking, breathing it in.

Maeve looked up at Parker, fork in hand.

"I did meet Francesca, by the way." She took a sip of her pint and looked over the glass at Parker. "She looks like your type." She glanced at her watch, suddenly puzzled. "It has been three hours… have you slept with her yet?"

"Very funny, Waterbury," Parker said, savoring the crispy skin on her last bite of roast potato. "How would you know what my type is, anyway?"

"Because I'm gayer than you, and your type is obvious, to say the least. You like classic, curvy femmes with big tits. I've seen you check out a few on base."

Parker put down her fork and stared. "You're gay?"

Maeve looked up at her with one raised eyebrow, glass in hand, and pushed her plate away, carefully crossing her fork and knife across it. "Didn't suss that one out, did you, Detective?"

"Wow." Parker smiled and shook her head. "That one went right past me, obviously. Although I don't know why it surprises me. You keep your cards pretty close to your vest."

The waiter came and collected their plates, which Parker gave up with some reluctance, despite being too full to even think about finishing the last few bites. As he left, he asked Maeve if she'd like another cider.

"We'll both take another," she said, nodding at Parker's empty pint. "Cheers."

Parker smiled, folding her cloth napkin onto the table and meeting Maeve's eyes. She smiled back, tucking her blond hair behind her ear.

"What?"

"So, what's your type, then?"

Maeve pulled the cuffs of her uniform jacket to her wrists in a perfect line. "Let's just say I wouldn't kick Francesca out of bed."

"Great." Parker rolled her eyes and glanced up at the sky through the window. A loud crack of thunder rattled the panes that were crisscrossed with iron detailing in small diamond shapes, which made the room look more like a Harry Potter set than a pub. "Now I have to try to get that image out of my head. Thanks."

Maeve laughed, then glanced at her phone. "That reminds me. My sister had her baby." She held up a photo of a newborn girl with strawberry-blond hair wrapped in a fluffy pink blanket. "She told me to tell you it's yours."

"What?" Parker said, shaking her head slowly. "I didn't even know you had a sister."

"Ski trip to Germany," Maeve said slowly, clearly enjoying her confusion. "Last Christmas? Gorgeous redhead who locked herself out of her cabin in the snow?"

Maeve watched the memory flash across Parker's face as the waiter put their drinks down on the table.

"Emma?"

Maeve nodded, one eyebrow raised, a smile spreading slowly across her face. "What? You didn't know you'd slept with my sister?"

The lanky teenage waiter didn't bother to hide his laugh as he shook his head and walked back to the bar.

CHAPTER SEVEN

Back on base, Parker watched the surveillance tapes until her vision blurred, but there was just nothing there beyond the obvious. The senator's son, John Haley, had checked in, entered his room, then walked out of the hotel a few minutes later. The hotel's surveillance equipment was outdated to say the least, but it was clearly Mr. Haley, so the identity of the victim was not in question. Why he'd been targeted in the first place was the question that seemed to have no answer.

The identity of the victim had not been released to the press yet, but because of his high-profile family connections, that information would be difficult to keep under wraps for much longer. Parker leaned back in her chair and ran both hands through her hair. She had a briefing with Colonel Williams first thing in the morning, and she needed to show a clear direction of where the case was headed. She pulled on her jacket and slid her case files into her bag. It had already been a long day, and Giada's espresso was the only thing that was going to clear the fog from her head.

Parker drove off base and into town, the sun gilding the windshield with slick molten gold. She turned off the air conditioning and lowered the window, breathing in the scent of the blossoming lime trees. It was delicate, more like honey than citrus. In a week's time, the blossoms would be gone, replaced by the earthy scent of rosemary and oregano fields, stretched out over the rolling Italian countryside like rumpled patchwork blankets. The rosemary was her favorite. The smell of it intensified in the evening sun, the scent warmed and strengthened by the fading rays, a contrast to the cool, dark scent of soil beneath that clung to it.

As she rounded a sharp curve, she remembered suddenly what Maeve had said about the ski trip. Of course Emma had been Maeve's sister. She had enough experience to know that the whole encounter had gone a bit too smoothly to not snap back and bite her in the ass.

Parker had been given leave the previous Christmas and she'd spent a few days at Garmisch, a ski resort reserved for military members and their families in Germany. She'd gone with Petra and a few of their friends, and they'd all rented a cabin at the base of the mountain between Christmas and New Year's Eve. On their last night there, after a few rounds at the bar in the lodge, Parker had decided to head back to the cabin and pack for the flight back to Italy the next morning. The trail to the log cabins was up the hill from the lodge and carefully groomed, with deep banks of glittering snow to either side. The air was brittle but somewhat warmed by the scent of burning evergreen from the cabin fireplaces, smoke curling up from every brick chimney on the same path toward the stars.

Parker pulled her jacket tighter around her and zipped it up to her chin, digging her wool beanie out of the pocket and pulling it over her hair, which seemed to resist, wild with static from the cold. She tucked her hair behind her ears and trudged up the path, lit on both sides with streetlights, casting a frozen glow onto the icy bricks. Her cabin was still a good fifteen-minute walk from where she was.

"Shit!"

The word shot out of the silence and startled Parker, who stopped in her tracks. She cautiously rounded the corner to see a petite younger woman in thermal underwear and a wool cardigan standing outside one of the cabin doors. She was turning the door handle, one way and then the other, barefoot in the snow, wild waves of copper hair falling across her shoulders and down her back.

"Ma'am?"

Parker said the word softly, trying not to startle her. It was pitch dark unless you were directly under one of the lights, and Parker knew it might seem to the woman that she'd jumped out of the woods like a big bad wolf with an Alabama accent. But the woman hadn't even seen her yet, just hopping from foot to foot and turning the door handle with all her strength, cursing not quite under her breath.

"Ma'am," Parker said, stepping off the path and walking over to her. "Can I help you?"

The woman whipped her head around and took an unsteady step back, falling into the snowbank beside the cabin. Parker stepped over to her and held out her hand. She didn't take it.

"Who the hell are you?"

She had a soft British accent and deep blue eyes, framed by the fiery copper waves of hair that made her look like an unfortunate mermaid stuck in a frozen ocean wave.

"I'm Captain Parker Haven," Parker said, her arm still outstretched. "I'm staying in one of the cabins just up the hill."

She looked Parker up and down, then took her hand. As she stood, Parker noticed her bare feet were soaking wet and bright red from the cold.

"Here," she said, shrugging off her jacket and laying it on the ground. "Stand on this while we figure out how to get that door unlocked."

The woman reluctantly stepped onto the jacket, her eyes moving across Parker's shoulders and down her arms. Parker smiled, then met her eyes.

"What's your name?"

She looked at Parker for a moment before she spoke. "Emma."

"Just stand there for a minute, Emma, okay?"

Parker knelt in front of the door until her eyes were level with the lock, then unclipped the Leatherman from her belt.

"There's no way to get it open without the key. I've already tried," Emma said, her voice choking up with frustration, words tumbling over each other in a rush. "My sister left me a key because her flight got delayed in Paris and she won't be here until morning and it's the only one but I left it inside and it's way too late for the office to be open to let me in, so—"

Parker clicked the lock free and swung the door open. She held her hand out to Emma, who now looked reluctant to step off the jacket she hadn't wanted to step onto in the first place. Parker watched her put her toe back in the snow for a single second, then place it firmly back onto the down jacket. Parker shook her head, smiling.

"You don't make things easy, do you?"

She turned and stood in front of Emma while Emma hopped onto her back. She walked her into the cabin and put her down on the hearth in front of the fire, then went back and retrieved her jacket and shook it out in the doorway.

"It's soaked," Emma said, peering at it from the hearth. "You can't walk back up the hill like that, you'll freeze." She looked at the open front door. "But it will dry in like five minutes by the fire."

Parker hesitated, but Emma got up, took the jacket from her, and draped it over the back of the chair closest to the fire, then padded into the small kitchen. Parker looked around the small cabin that was much like her own, cozy couches with fringed cashmere throws facing the enormous stone hearth, the night pitch black and silent against the windows. The snow had started falling again and the flakes shimmered as they floated past the panes.

Emma walked back into the main room and handed Parker a glass.

"What's this?"

"Don't get excited," she said, wrinkling up her nose and winding handfuls of unruly waves into a quick bun at the base of her neck, securing them with an elastic she pulled off her wrist. "It's just American bourbon. It's absolute swill, but it's my sister's favorite, so I brought her a bottle."

"And why am I the only one drinking the swill?" Parker said, one eyebrow raised. "Despite your charming disposition, you could be trying to poison me for all I know."

"Well," Emma said, smoothing her hand over her belly, "I'd join you, but I think the baby might not appreciate it."

Parker's eyes dropped to Emma's tummy, where she saw just the beginning of a baby bump. "Congrats. How far along are you?"

"Four months," she said. "But it already feels like twelve."

Emma plopped down on the couch and pulled the throw over her legs. Her eyes were the deepest blue, almost violet, and as Parker sat at the other end of the couch, she had to suppress a sudden ridiculous urge to kiss her.

"Are you excited?" Parker said, glancing quickly at Emma's

mouth and pulling her eyes away. She wore no makeup but her full lips were the palest shade of pink, outlined at the edges by faint freckles the color of honey.

"Certainly not." Emma laughed, her hand around her belly. "But she's kind of growing on me, so you never know, I may be before it's over."

"What does the father think?"

Parker realized as she said it that it was none of her business, but Emma just shrugged.

"He doesn't know."

Parker met her eyes, phrasing her next question carefully. "And do you want it to stay that way?"

"I guess, although I wouldn't even know how to track him down at this point, so it doesn't matter."

She picked at a loose thread at the end of her sleeve and wound it around her thumb. Parker watched Emma's thoughts flash across her face as the wood crackled in the fireplace, shapeshifting into coals that glowed red and dense in the bed of velvet gray ash.

"It sounds stupid, but I was too old to be a virgin, and I guess I just got sick of waiting. So I slept with some French backpacker I met at the pub one night. I just wanted to see what all the fuss was about."

She looked up and smiled, her eyes dropping to Parker's mouth. "I have no idea why I'm telling you all this, by the way."

They both turned to look at the window as the wind picked up suddenly and scraped itself across the panes hard enough to make them rattle.

Parker smiled, picking up her glass. "I tend to have that effect on women."

Emma glanced down at Parker's glass and pulled herself up from the sofa before Parker could protest, returning with the bottle of Evan Williams Reserve. She poured a bit into Parker's glass and set it on the coffee table in front of them.

"What did you think after it finally happened?" Parker's eyes dropped to the curves of Emma's breasts before she caught herself. She was bare underneath her soft yellow cardigan with a deep V-neck. Parker's eyes traced the soft swell of her nipples, and she made herself look away.

Clearly the girl is straight, she reminded herself as she took a sip of the bourbon and glanced over at the fire. *Get a grip.*

"What did I think about what?" Emma said, raising an eyebrow. "The sex?"

Parker held her eyes and smiled until Emma laughed.

"I think I still don't know what all the fuss is about," she said. "I'm not even sure I want to do it again."

"Well, if that's the case," Parker said, then paused, looking into her glass as she spoke, "then he wasn't doing it right."

"That's almost certainly true," Emma said, pulling the elastic out of her hair and letting it spill over her shoulders. "But I didn't know what I was doing, either. I've never even been on an actual date."

Emma looked at the fire as a burning log split suddenly and fell through the grate, the center cracked open to show a fiery orange middle with blue flames licking at the edges. It was a long moment before she spoke again.

"After what happened, my parents brought in tutors to teach us at home. They literally didn't let us out of their sight until we went to university."

The second the words were out, she slapped her hand over her mouth.

"Sorry," she said, shaking her head. "I'm talking too much, and I'm not even the one drinking."

"Lightweight," Parker teased. She paused, catching Emma's eye. "Or maybe it's something you need to say."

The fire had finally managed to chase the chill from the air, so Parker pulled her navy wool sweater over her head, leaving just her white T-shirt and sports bra. Emma's eyes dropped from Parker's shoulders to her abs before she looked away.

"Besides," Parker continued, "that snow just turned to ice, so you might as well spill it. It doesn't look like I'm going anywhere soon."

Just then a hailstone hit the window and Emma jumped, covering her heart with her hand until her breathing finally slowed. She smiled but was quiet for a while, staring into the fire. Parker waited in silence, swirling the ice in her glass. The bourbon was warming her from the inside out, and the situation was starting to get interesting. There was something mysterious about Emma, something simmering just below the surface.

Emma started to say something, then stopped and looked back to the fire. Her eyes were still there a few moments later, watching sparks chase each other up the chimney, when she spoke again.

"It was my fault," she said, her voice different than it had been before, a melded swirl of half voice, half memory. "I was supposed to walk home from school with her that day, but I skipped my last class and just went off with my friends. I was the reason she had to walk home alone."

Parker got up and tossed another log on the fire, then sank back down on her end of the sofa, facing Emma.

Parker leaned up and laid her hand over Emma's when she saw her blink back sudden tears. "What happened?"

"She just never came home." Emma bit her lip, pausing twice before she allowed the words to fill the space between them. "It happened when I was nine and she was eleven. We didn't see her again for nine months."

"God," Parker said finally, her voice low and dense in the silence. "I'm so sorry."

Parker reached out and caught the tear on Emma's cheek. She didn't turn her head, just closed her eyes as another tear dropped from her lashes.

Parker's voice was soft. "How did the police finally find her?"

Emma rubbed her eyes slowly with her fingers, then took a deep breath, as if trying to clear the memory from her mind.

"They didn't," she said, finally. "She found them."

She wiped her eyes with the heel of her hand and smiled for the first time, making a half-hearted play for the bourbon before Parker lifted it swiftly out of her reach. She laughed, a sound like tinkling bells that Parker instantly wanted to hear again.

"So, what happened?"

"The man who'd kidnapped her stopped to get petrol one day but the card reader on the pump was broken, so he left her in the back of his car while he went inside to pay. She was looking out the window and watched a guy in a military uniform get out of another car and walk into the store behind him. It was an older one, with no power locks. There was no one else around, so she ran to his car, climbed into his trunk, and shut herself in."

"Holy shit," Parker said slowly. "That took some guts. She sounds like a badass."

"Yeah." Emma laughed, then picked the bottle up and topped up Parker's glass. "You have no idea."

"What happened after that?"

"The poor guy had some explaining to do, because when he went back to base and stopped at the gate checkpoint, she started raising hell in the trunk, screaming and kicking the trunk lid. Long story short, he was arrested and held until they figured out why he had some random girl in his trunk. She told me years later that she'd seen his military uniform and knew she'd be safe with him."

"Good God." Parker sat back on the sofa and watched the reflection of the firelight in her glass for a moment before she spoke. "What was it like when she got home?"

"She didn't speak for over a year," Emma said softly. "Not one word."

They sat in silence, listening to the sharp crack of green sap in a chunk of firewood. It sizzled down the side of the log, filling the air with the scent of charred evergreen. Thick pine branches, heavy with snow, cast charcoal shadows on the wall beside the hearth.

"The next summer, our parents took us on holiday to the beach in Cornwall. It was our last afternoon there and I was just wading around in the shallows, looking for shells." Emma glanced up as a branch grazed the window, scraping the frost into an intricate pattern on the glass. "Mum and Dad were on chairs farther up the beach, but for once they weren't really paying attention to us."

"What was your sister doing?"

"She was going way too deep into the water. I called out her name, but she didn't turn around. She walked until she was into the water up to her shoulders."

"Did you tell your parents?"

"No, they'd told us not to wade in past our knees, so I knew she'd get into trouble." Emma bit her lip, as if she was watching the scene in her mind before she spoke again. "The water was really calm, and the sun was just starting to set. I remember the way it glittered on the dark surface of the waves." She paused and smiled, as if awash in the memory. "And then I saw them."

Parker realized she was holding her breath and let it out slowly. "Who?"

"The dolphins." Emma's voice was soft, almost a whisper, as if the words were a secret. "There were three of them, just swimming around her. It was surreal to watch. Even now I still just have flashes of that memory—I think I just couldn't take it all in at the time."

Emma brought her knees to her chest and wrapped her arms around them.

"I remember how she slid her hand over their backs, and how gentle they were with her. I don't know how to describe it, they seemed…protective, almost." She shook her head. "I know it sounds strange, but it's like they were talking to her, only with no sound."

Emma sat with the memory for a moment, staring into the fire. Parker tangled her fingers into Emma's, and they watched the flames turn to embers until she was ready to go on.

"It seemed like they were out there forever, but it was only a few minutes. I remember one of them holding its face to hers for a long time, and then they were gone. She stood there until she couldn't see them anymore and then just walked back to the shore and sat down beside me."

Parker glanced over at Emma. "What happened then?"

"She stood up after a few minutes and held out her hand, and said, 'Let's go.' It was the first time she'd spoken in over a year."

Parker shook her head, then got up and walked into the kitchen, filling the electric kettle and switching it on.

"What do you take in your tea?"

"How did you know I wanted tea?" Emma said from the living room, peering over the back of the sofa at her.

"Because you're British." Parker flashed her a smile as she retrieved a pint of milk out of the refrigerator. "And I've been here for almost an hour and I have yet to see a teacup in your hand, so you're overdue."

"I'm impressed. You must know someone from home," Emma said with a laugh. "Milk and two sugars, please."

Parker brought the tea into the living room and set it on the coffee table in front of them.

"Are you not having any tea?" Emma asked. "Although I'd be having a real drink, too, if I could." She looked longingly at the rocks glass. "I'd even drink whatever that is."

"Not on my watch," Parker said as she picked up her bourbon, glancing at Emma as she did. Her pale skin had just a touch of an apricot undertone, awash with freckles across the tops of her breasts where the cardigan dipped between them.

Emma smiled. "You don't have to pretend not to look at my breasts, by the way. They're spectacular right now, trust me. I just wish they'd stay this way forever."

Parker laughed, nodding as she glanced at Emma again with one raised eyebrow. "Well, you're not wrong there."

She settled back into the couch and took a sip of her bourbon.

"So, before I get myself in trouble, tell me what happened after you came back from Cornwall with your sister."

"My parents were over the moon that she was talking again, but the morning after we'd come back, she was sitting at the kitchen table at the break of dawn, fully clothed, before my parents had even gotten up to make tea. She'd never spoken about who'd taken her, so I think everyone assumed they'd never catch the guy, but she suddenly wanted to go to the police station before the sun was even up. Mum was worried, she thought she was acting weird, having some sort of a breakdown, but Dad said he'd do whatever she needed him to do. So he took her to the station."

"Did she tell them what happened?"

"She told them every detail, apparently, although she was adamant she did not want Dad in the room, even though he was supposed to be there because she was underage. Somehow they got around it."

"God, she must have been so scared. She didn't even know those people."

"She had so many details, of where she'd been held and exactly what had happened to her, that the detective thought she was creating a story in her head to help make sense of it in her own mind. He said it would have been understandable. But she never wavered on even one detail, then refused to leave the station until they drove her to where she'd been kept. It was only about five kilometers from our home, in a run-down council house."

"Did she let your parents go with her?"

"She had to. Mum had gotten to the station by then, but my sister flatly refused to tell the police anything else unless both of them were in a different car. The detective told my parents later he'd never seen anything like it, that she was like steel. After they pulled up, she just sat in the car and stared at the house from across the street."

Emma tucked her feet under Parker's legs and put her cup back on the coffee table.

"In the end, they got a search warrant and went inside, then pulled up the disgusting carpet in the room where he'd kept her locked up. She'd told them she'd made a mark for every day she'd been there with a pencil on the plywood underneath the carpet, which she had, and a drawing." She hesitated, trying to find the words. "Like a map of the scars he'd left on her body, like cuts and cigarette burns."

"Jesus Christ." Parker shook her head and squeezed Emma's hand. "So obviously they arrested the guy?"

"They found him that day and charged him. Her body held every scar she'd marked on the map, precisely where she'd drawn it, so it didn't take much more for him to go down."

"Did she have to testify?"

"Yes, but the judge let her do it privately. She's told me some of what happened to her over the years, but Mum and Dad don't know much at all. She didn't want them to have to live with it."

Emma took a deep breath. "And then it was over. He got life in prison."

"And what about her?" Parker asked, getting up and putting another log on the fire, blowing on it gently until it flamed to life. "How was she after all that?"

"She's different than she was before it happened, but I don't know how anyone wouldn't be. The detective was right, she is like steel." Emma hesitated. "But fragile steel." She turned to Parker. "I know that doesn't make any sense, but that's the only way to describe it."

"It makes perfect sense," Parker said, sinking back down on the couch and swirling the bourbon in her glass.

Emma stretched her legs out over Parker's, her hair slipping through her fingers as she pushed it back from her face and let it fall over her shoulders. Firelight hovered like desert heat in the room. Parker had turned out the light in the kitchen, so except for an amber glass floor lamp glowing in the corner, the fire was the only light in the room.

Emma winced and slid her hand over the slight swell of her belly. "I think she's moving."

"She must be feisty." Parker let her eyes move over Emma's body, finally looking up with a smile. "Strange. I wonder where she'd get that from?"

Emma picked up Parker's hand and laid it across her belly, covering it with her own as the flames painted slow light across her face. Parker let out a ragged breath and closed her eyes.

"This is dangerous ground, Emma," she said, looking up at her, then dropping her eyes to Emma's mouth.

"I know."

When Parker spoke again, it was a whisper. "What do you want?"

Emma shook her head. "I don't know."

Parker moved her hand up to cover Emma's heart. Emma's cheeks were flushed, her blue eyes darkening slowly like a steel-blue storm. Parker relaxed her hand against Emma's heartbeat.

"Do you want me to show you?"

Emma nodded slowly as the first button of her cardigan slipped through Parker's fingers like water.

❖

Alessia pushed through the door to the jewelry store, her bag slipping off her shoulder as it closed behind her. There were two customers in the shop. Her dad was helping one of them while the other waited, so she slipped behind the counter and showed the sapphire rings to the second customer. Her dad glanced up at her as she put them away and headed back to his office a few minutes later, and Alessia gave him a look that let him know to turn the Open sign over on the door when he was done.

Alessia had the grappa poured and on the coffee table before her father came through the door, her shoulders set, mouth tense.

"I'm afraid to ask," he said with a sigh, sinking down in the leather chair and folding his glasses into his shirt pocket. "I know that look."

Alessia nodded, twisting the thin silver ring on her thumb. "We have a situation."

"Is it about yesterday at the airport?"

"You heard?"

Sal nodded. "Is Olivia all right?"

"She called me yesterday from the airport, and she's in France now." Her father was patting down his pockets with a distracted look until she handed him a lighter from her bag. "Do you remember Mirelle Savi? She's our connection in Paris that's hosting Olivia and her son while they set up her new identity."

"Have we used her before?"

"Yes, about a year ago. She texted me late last night to say they'd arrived safely."

Sal exhaled loudly, leaning forward and holding up his glass for a toast.

"Don't get excited, Da," Alessia said, pulling off her black leather jacket and laying it on the couch beside her. "That wasn't our problem."

Sal downed the shot of grappa and leaned back in his chair. "All right," he said. "Let's hear it."

"There was a reason Olivia called me from the airport. Did you hear about the shooting there?"

Sal nodded, leaning forward to listen.

"When she walked out of the terminal, she was looking for the car I'd said would be there, but the incident had just happened, and police were taping off the area. She saw the dead man in the driver's seat of the taxi, though, as his body hadn't been removed yet."

"I must be getting too old for this," Sal said, shaking his head slowly. "What does all this have to do with her?"

"The dead man was an American. John Haley." Alessia picked up her shot of grappa and threw it back without as much as a wince. "The boyfriend who threatened to kill Olivia if she left him."

CHAPTER EIGHT

Parker wedged her bag and stacks of folders onto a small corner table in the far corner of the café by the brick wall. There wasn't much surveillance footage, just under seven minutes, and even fewer angles, but she needed to go through the rest of the airport surveillance frame by frame. The kitchen doors swung open and hit the wall behind as Giada appeared with an armful of warm baguettes dusted with flour. Parker reached the counter just as they started to slip, and took them from her while she placed them in the bakery case one at a time.

"Parker," Giada said when she'd finished, looking her up and down. "The army does not feed you? You look skinny."

"Trust me," Parker said, "I'm eating plenty. It's just not nearly as good as your food."

Giada beamed, dusting the flour off her hands and starting Parker an espresso. "I bring you some lobster linguine from the back. I made this morning."

She finished off the espresso and put the cup on a tiny white saucer, handing it to Parker with a nod. "Sit. I bring to you."

Parker smiled as she walked back to her table. It had been a few days since she'd been at the café, and as much as she didn't want to admit it, she'd missed Giada fussing over her. She slid into the seat and looked up just in time to see Alessia burst through the door, hair flying and cell phone in hand.

"Ma," she said as she turned sideways to avoid a customer on the way out. "Do you still have my cell phone charger behind the counter?"

Giada dug underneath the register and produced a tangled white cord.

"Great," Alessia said. "Because my phone just died, and last week I somehow lost the charger that's supposed to be in my car."

Another customer stepped up to the counter, and Giada shot her daughter a look over her shoulder as she turned to help him.

"You're on your phone too much, Alessia. Maybe if you don't have it, you learn to live without it."

"Ma," Alessia said, looking suddenly tired and rubbing her temples. "Just trust me. I need the phone."

Giada passed the order slip to her daughter, who suppressed a sigh and dropped her bag by the espresso machine as she poured milk into the pitcher and started steaming it.

"Ma, seriously? I'll make this one for you, but I'm not here to work," she said over her shoulder on her way back to the espresso machine. "I just need my phone to charge for a few minutes so it works until I get home."

Giada leaned back to look her daughter. "You are home by nighttime?"

Alessia shook her head, dipping the steel thermometer into the pitcher to check the temperature of the milk. "I don't know, why?"

Giada shook her head and winked at the elderly Italian man at the counter as she handed him his change. "Those phones have everything, but now the young people know nothing about their own city?" They smiled together as he took his bag and headed for the door.

Alessia poured the espresso and milk into the takeaway cup and used a spoon to top it with a dense, velvety foam.

"What are you talking about?" she asked. "The American who got shot at the airport?"

Giada nodded as Alessia clicked the lid into place and handed it to her mother. She finished with her customer and turned back to her daughter, who was busy pilfering a lemon lavender cookie from the pastry case.

"Ma," Alessia said as she stood and dropped the cookie into a small paper bag. Her voice was tense. "You worry too much. I can take care of myself."

She checked her phone and disconnected it, wrapping the cord around itself and handing it back to her mother with a kiss on her cheek.

Parker caught Alessia's eye as she was on her way out the door and motioned for Alessia to join her. She hesitated, but Parker held her gaze until she reluctantly sat down at her table with a pointed glance at her watch.

"No offense, Parker," she said. "But I have to go."

Giada appeared suddenly carrying a wide, steaming bowl of linguine in cream sauce with a wedge of fresh lemon on the edge. She gave Parker's shoulder a squeeze as she set it down in front of her and hurried back to the counter.

"She has linguine back there?" Alessia said, glancing back at the kitchen door. "She didn't tell me that."

"Maybe that's because she likes me better," Parker said, turning back the cuffs of her uniform jacket and twirling the creamy pasta around her fork.

Alessia rolled her eyes as she picked up the lemon and squeezed it over Parker's dish.

"That's possible, but only because she didn't just see you try to get that pasta into your mouth without half of it sliding off your fork. If I had more time, I'd teach you how to eat it properly."

Alessia looked pointedly at the door as Parker went in for another bite and then sighed, leaning back in her chair. Parker finally put her fork down as if she'd remembered something she'd forgotten.

"I look forward to that," she said. "But before you go, I just need to know one thing."

She pulled a folder from the stack on the table and handed Alessia a glossy eight-by-ten of John Haley, slumped over the wheel of the taxi, the side of his head slicked with blood.

Parker picked her fork up and speared a tender chunk of lobster.

"How exactly did you know the victim was an American? That info hasn't been released to the public yet."

She twirled the pasta against the side of the bowl, watching the color drain from Alessia's face as she laid the picture face down on the table.

"It was on the news."

"Nope," Parker said, folding the pasta into her mouth. "Try again."

"Parker." Alessia closed her eyes as she rubbed the tension from her forehead with her fingers. "With all due respect, this really doesn't concern you."

Parker nodded to the stack of folders and surveillance tapes beside her. She waited, one blond eyebrow cocked like a hammer, until Alessia made the connection and sighed again, looking at the photo again before she handed it back to Parker.

"I have to do a consultation with a vintner this afternoon." She stood, running her hand through her hair. "Come by the house afterward, about seven, and we'll talk."

Parker nodded, holding her fork aloft. "Want me to bring you some leftovers?"

Alessia headed for the door, pulling on her jacket as she walked, muttering *asshole* not quite under her breath.

❖

Parker pulled up to Alessia's house just after seven and parked, her eyes locked on the side of Alessia's yellow Citroën. The driver's side window was shattered and the entire side of the car looked like it had been dragged across a concrete wall. The side mirror dangled by a thin wire, the breeze rocking it gently back and forth against the door.

As Parker walked up to the door, she noticed it was ajar. She knocked lightly and paused, listening to the sound fall flat in the empty room. There's a kind of quiet that only happens when something's out of place, and this was one of those times. She stepped inside, moving instinctively to pull her weapon from the holster. A bottle of white wine sat on the counter—she guessed by the condensation it had been there for less than five minutes—with two crystal glasses sitting to the side of it. Parker scanned the living area, but nothing seemed different, and a recent fire crackled in the fireplace.

"Didn't anyone teach you it's bad manners to wander into people's houses when they're not there?"

Parker swung around to see Alessia leaning against the doorframe, a blood-streaked plate in her left hand. She wore white jeans with a navy linen shirt tied at her waist, and leather sandals. Pieces of her hair had fallen out of her bun, and the wind had brushed them across her cheek as she stood in the doorway, the last of the afternoon sun falling over her in a sheer wash.

Parker lowered her weapon but continued to clear the house until she was satisfied they were alone. She reholstered her gun and took off her cap, finally letting out a slow breath.

"Hasn't anyone ever told you it's bad manners to disappear and leave your door open like you've been abducted?"

Alessia shot her a flash of a smile as she closed the door, then clicked three locks and a deadbolt into place. Parker watched as she walked into the kitchen and dropped the plate into the dishwasher, then tucked a wisp of hair behind her ear and handed Parker a glass of the wine.

Alessia clinked her glass to Parker's. "Cheers."

"Cheers," Parker said, nodding toward the front door. "Now what the hell happened to your car?"

"It's somewhat charming, this concern for my well-being, but I assure you I can take care of myself."

"I have no doubt about that. But just for fun, let's at least clear up why you were carrying a bloody plate into the house just now."

She shrugged off her uniform jacket and folded it over the stool beside her. Alessia paused, studying the tense lines in her face, then looked at her watch.

"That," she said, nodding toward the west wall of the house, made of wide timbers supporting floor-to-ceiling windows, "you can actually see for yourself."

Alessia crossed the room and sat at the base of the windows, leaning against one of the wide hardwood beams, arms wrapped tight around her knees. The setting sun was a slow copper blaze, streaked with thin, steel-blue clouds, but her gaze was fixed on the ragged edge of the canyon just beyond the windows. Gnarled olive trees held on to a few scraps of earth at the edge with arthritic roots, but the world seemed to drop away beyond that, leaving only a steep slope into the rocky canyon that seemed to have no end.

Parker sat beside her, and her gaze followed the beam up to the soaring thirty-foot oak ceiling, where mahogany beams and black ironwork gave the space an artsy but distinctly industrial feel. In the northwest corner, tucked up almost to the ceiling, was what looked like a floating wood platform constructed of the same honeyed oak as the ceiling above it and framed in mahogany, suspended at all four corners by thick, forged iron chains. If you didn't know it was there, it would be easy to miss altogether.

"I'm almost afraid to ask," Parker said hesitantly as she nodded toward the ceiling. "But what is that?"

Alessia glanced up, then back down at the ground outside the windows. "Nothing," she said distractedly, still peering at the edge of the canyon. "Just my bed."

Just then, the scraggly bushes at the edge of the canyon path rustled, and Alessia put her finger to her lips. Parker sat motionless, following her gaze to the ground where a slender gray wolf wound her way through the bushes to the base of an olive tree. She lifted her head to stare at the windows, then sniffed at the chunks of raw meat laid out on a large flat rock beside the olive tree. Her coat was every shade of moonlight, uneven but dense and glossy, and muscles rippled in her shoulders as she devoured the meat. When she was finished, she swung her head up to meet Alessia's eyes. She paused for a moment, then loped back down into the darkening canyon, disappearing into the blackness.

"Friend of yours?" Parker smiled as she stood and offered Alessia her hand to help her up. She took it.

"I heard her howling one morning in the canyon and hiked down close enough to see that she'd gotten one of her feet pinned between two boulders. I knew right away she wouldn't be able to get out of it by herself."

"And she let you help her?"

"She didn't want to let me near her, but I think we both knew that was her only chance of getting free. I spent half the day just trying to get close enough to see how bad her injuries were." Alessia opened the fridge and pulled out several wedges of cheese wrapped in white paper and tied with twine. They were labelled in small, careful handwriting, and she unwrapped them as she spoke, placing them on a large slab of wine-stained barrel wood, bound at the ends with hammered copper and rivets.

"So what happened?"

"With Luna?"

"You named the wolf Luna?"

Alessia glanced at the window. "It just seemed to fit her, and by the time we finally got her foot unstuck, there was only moonlight." She crumbled a bit of cheese from one of the slices and tasted it, then placed it on the board. "I had a bottle of water in my bag, so I tried to get her to drink out of my hands, but that took almost an hour, and I'm lucky I still have all my fingers."

She paused while she cut into the rest of the cheeses. A dense, creamy cheese coated in black pepper was first, then a hard cheese that looked stained with wine, as if it had been soaked into the rind. It flaked a bit as it was cut, falling apart like chiseled slate. The third cheese was flecked with cranberries, and as Alessia sliced it, the edges crumbled onto the board. She smiled when she saw Parker staring and handed her a piece of it.

"What kind of cheese is this?" Parker said, taking it and letting it melt onto her tongue. Tiny crystals crackled in her mouth as she finished, but the flavor was dense and seductive. "That was intense," Parker said. "Like burnt caramel. But what are the crackly bits in it?"

Alessia smiled and handed her another piece. "It's a cave-aged Oud gouda. The crystals form in the aging process and give it some crunch."

Alessia poured some deep red wine into a new glass from another bottle on the counter and pushed it toward Parker.

"It should be eaten with an inky red with some body to it, like a petite sirah. This one is from Toscano Winery over the hill. Save the white for the softer cheese I cut into first."

"You distracted me with this cheese," Parker said, popping another slice into her mouth. "What happened next with Luna?"

"After she drank, I stayed close and she relaxed enough to let me look at her leg, but if I moved too quickly she growled, so I had to be careful to move slowly."

Alessia ran a handful of fresh raspberries under cold water and scattered them onto the wood slab beside the cheese, then sliced a peach beside it and topped that with an airy pile of fresh mint.

"I was finally able to shove one of the boulders out just enough to loosen the gap, and she pulled it out. She put pressure on it fairly quickly, so I don't think it was broken. It looked like she'd just stepped in the wrong place and gotten stuck." She paused, glancing out the windows. "And I guess we've had a bond ever since."

Alessia pulled a baguette out of the basket on the counter and sliced it, then seared each slice in a cast-iron skillet with a sprinkle of olive oil and salt. Parker watched her from the other side of the counter, trying not to stare at the satiny slice of skin between her jeans and the shirt tied at her waist, which proved to be impossible. It was slender and mouthwateringly taut, accented even more by the lush curves of her ass.

"Okay," Alessia said finally, turning to place the cheese board between them on the bar. "The meats in the middle are sliced prosciutto, and then there's peppered calabrese next to that. And the cheese…" She hesitated. "You won't know the cheeses besides the gouda you just ate, but trust me, they're beautiful."

The basket of toasted baguette slices sat to the side of the cheeseboard, along with two small pottery plates dripping with a bright aqua glaze.

"So," Parker said as she topped a slice of baguette with the softer, herb-laden cheese. "Is this when you tell me what the hell happened to your car?"

Alessia looked up, balancing a slice of peach on her fork, then back down with a soft sigh.

"You don't want to know."

"Alessia." Parker's voice was soft, and she tipped Alessia's chin up gently with her finger until she met her eyes. "You're going to have to start talking to me. You seem to have inside information about my case, and your safety has been threatened enough for you to have been carrying a Glock on your hip when I ran into you in Greece. I need to know why."

Alessia put down her fork.

"I don't know what to tell you." She paused, and they both looked suddenly toward the windows, where a hawk screeched as it sailed past the glass and soared over the darkening canyon. "Or maybe it's more truthful to say that I don't know what is safe to tell you."

"Okay," Parker said, then paused, sensing she needed to change tack. "Let me ask you some questions to start with, and you just answer as well as you can. Do you think you can do that?"

Alessia nodded and bit her lip. Parker realized that for the first time since she'd known her, Alessia actually looked nervous, and she had to stop herself from reaching out and pulling her into her arms. Alessia pushed her plate away and took a long sip of the inky wine.

"Are you protecting someone?"

Alessia paused, then nodded.

Parker chose her next words carefully.

"Do you have any connection to the murder here in Salerno?"

"I had knowledge of it," she said. "Probably before you did."

Parker looked up in surprise. "And why is that?"

Alessia shook her head slightly and said nothing, the gold flecks in her eyes catching the light and shimmering against the velvet brown.

"Okay, you can't tell me that," Parker said, mostly to herself, then paused, clicking the tip of her pen against the polished wood bar. "Let's go back to that knife through your picture in Greece and today's damage to your car. I think it's safe to assume those two things are connected, but why would someone do that?"

Alessia shook her head and smiled as she picked up the knife she'd used to cut the peach and put it into the sink. "You'd be surprised. There are a few reasons."

"Whoever this was was close enough to kill you in Greece," Parker said slowly. "But he didn't. And he didn't make sure you were fatally injured today. He's toying with you."

Alessia spun the wine in her glass, watching it move like languid liquid sunlight. There were fine lines around her eyes and her jaw was set, tense. Parker watched her for a moment, then took the glass gently out of her hand and set it back on the bar.

"Do you think all of this is connected to the murder yesterday?"

"Maybe," Alessia said. "But I've been thinking all day, and I don't see it."

Parker rubbed the back of her neck with her hand and leaned back on the stool. "Tell me what happened today."

"I was driving home from the café and someone followed me. When I got past town, he pulled up directly behind me and hit the back of my car with his."

"Did you recognize the driver?"

"No, not really. It was a man, wearing a hat pulled down to his eyes. I didn't recognize him, but I couldn't really see him that well."

"What happened after that?"

Alessia let out a slow breath and pulled the pins out of her hair. She shook it, loosening the thick, glossy waves with her fingers, then rubbed her temples with the pads of her fingers, eyes shut tight.

"Not much," she said, slowly opening her eyes. "He pulled up beside me and tried to run me off the road."

"What did you do?"

"The only thing I could do—I let him do it. I took a chance that he'd leave me alone if he thought he'd hurt me, so I let my car run off the road and into a tree." She stopped herself. "Well, the side of it, anyway."

"And he kept going?"

"Yes. He slowed down at first but then he took off. I waited until I was sure I wasn't being followed again before I came home."

Alessia folded a wafer-thin slice of calabrese onto a baguette slice with a smear of soft cheese, then handed it to Parker. There was a bit of cheese on her thumb, and Parker watched as she put it in her mouth and swirled her tongue around it. She felt a sharp jolt of arousal and made herself look away, but it was getting harder not to think about pinning her against the kitchen wall, holding her wrists above her head, and ripping every button off that shirt.

"Okay," Parker said. "Let's go back to the murder victim."

Alessia took a breath and rolled back the cuffs of her shirt.

"I can tell you he was involved with a woman in Greece and it was an abusive relationship. He almost killed her the last time it happened, and she's four months pregnant." She paused. "He made it clear that if she left him again, he'd kill her."

"How do you know all this?" Parker took a pen out of the loop on her uniform sleeve. "I need her name."

Alessia shook her head again. The strain was showing on her face, and her hand shook slightly when she raised it, which Parker pretended not to notice. Alessia set her glass on the bar and sank down onto the stool beside Parker, who put her pen away and turned, holding one of Alessia's cold hands in both of hers.

"It's been a long day for you, hasn't it?"

Alessia nodded, eyes closed tight. Her lashes were suddenly dark and wet, and a tear slipped down her cheek. Parker slid her hand around the back of Alessia's neck and pulled her closer until she felt Alessia's forehead rest against her shoulder. The small, dark mole near her mouth, reminiscent of golden era actresses, was soft under her fingertips as she stroked Alessia's cheek.

"Let's take a break, okay?" Parker's voice was low and gentle. "Why don't you show me that trapeze bed? I might die of curiosity if you don't, and then that would be all your fault. I don't know if you want that on your conscience."

Alessia sat up after a moment, turning her head to wipe away the tears on her cheeks with the tips of her fingers, but she smiled as she reached for two clean glasses and a new bottle of wine, and motioned for Parker to follow her to the stairs.

Wide slabs of polished cypress with beautiful organic edges were anchored into the wall by small iron bars underneath each step, so they appeared to float with no visible means of support. The stairs wound their way up the wall in a curve, each step slightly wider than the last as they neared the top of the three-story wall, like an unfurled spiral staircase with no frame. A handrail made of thick, twisted grapevine and anchored by cables to the ceiling was the only barrier between the floating stairs and the floor thirty feet below.

"You've got to be kidding me." Parker's eyes followed the stairs up to the platform. "That's the only way to get up there?"

"Too high for you, soldier?" A smile flashed across Alessia's face like sudden sunlight.

"I didn't say that," Parker said. "But why in the world do you have your bed up there?"

She looked into Parker's eyes for a moment and Parker saw her pause, then decide to tell the truth.

"Because if someone gets into the house, I can shoot him before he even thinks to look up."

CHAPTER NINE

When Parker and Alessia finally reached the top of the stairs, they stepped onto a small wooden landing, and Parker saw that the bed platform was suspended from the ceiling on chains just beyond that. She took it in for a moment, then ran a hand through her hair and unwisely decided to look down.

"Who designed this? This has to be against some kind of building code." She paused, examining the forged iron chains at four corners of the bed platform that allowed it to hang freely from the ceiling. "Make that every building code. Everywhere."

"It took some patience, but the architect finally got it passed. It's a converted winery, and officially a historic building, so there were some loopholes there." She smiled. "And apparently I had to stop talking about sleeping up here."

There was an antique pine box just to the side of the bed that served as a nightstand, and Alessia clicked on the stained glass lamp that sat on it, scattering warm amber light across the bed and illuminating the wine. Only a few inches separated the bed platform from the landing where they stood, and there were two nautical hooks on short chains with iron loops on the other side that anchored them together.

"I hesitate to ask," Parker said tentatively, stealing a glance at the floor through the gap between the bed and the landing. "But why not just build a single platform here with your bed on it?"

Alessia lifted the hooks out of the loops, then gave the end of the landing a push with her foot. The bed swung gently toward the windows, giving an unobstructed view of the stars over the canyon.

"Because platforms don't swing. Do you like it?"

"I think it's amazing," Parker said, stopping the swing and stepping onto the platform to sit carefully on the bed beside her. "And scary as fuck. In that order."

Alessia lay back against the pillows and looked out at the black night sprinkled with a glittering haze of stars. Her face was bare, and the lamp beside the bed lit up the amber freckles across her cheeks. Parker unlaced her boots and left them on the landing, then lay back on the bed with Alessia, watching the stars start to disappear behind a slow-moving cloud the same color as the pewter moon.

"Do you feel safe up here?"

Alessia turned toward Parker, propping herself up on her elbow. She bit her bottom lip, thinking before she spoke. "I never feel safe. But sometimes you make the choice to trade safety for something more important." She ran her fingers lightly over the embroidered initials *LC* on the raw edge of her linen pillowcase. "I know someone's trying to kill me. I've known it for a while. I just have to stay a step ahead of him."

Parker tucked a stray wave of dark hair behind her ear, then left her hand lightly at the back of Alessia's neck, stroking it with her thumb.

"I can't tell you anything else about this," Alessia said, her eyes dropping to Parker's mouth. "At least not yet."

"Tell me one more thing," Parker said, turning toward her. One delicate button on Alessia's shirt had come undone, and Parker's fingertips brushed the warmth of her skin as she buttoned it back up. "Why would anyone want to kill you?"

Alessia smiled. "I'll have to narrow that down and get back to you."

"What did you do?"

She just shook her head as Parker traced the outline of Alessia's lower lip with her thumb. The scent of her skin, like lavender soap and salt air, shimmered between them like desert heat. Alessia held Parker's eyes as she reached up for her hand, her breath warm and soft on Parker's palm before she drew the tip of her finger into the warmth of her mouth, stroking it slowly with her tongue.

"Fuck." Parker closed her eyes and let out the breath she didn't know she was holding. She knew she was on dangerous ground, her toes at the knife edge of a sheer cliff, and any touch would start her fall. Parker took back her hand with a low growl and raked it through her hair.

"Alessia," she said, her voice low and controlled. "That's more than I can take without touching you."

"What if I want you to touch me?" Alessia whispered the words into her ear, her breath warm against Parker's neck.

"I can't." Parker turned to look into her eyes, her voice dropping to a whisper. "I shouldn't even be here."

She reached out and slowly pulled every inch of Alessia's body into hers, spooning her, their heads resting on the same pillow. Alessia melted back against the warmth of Parker's body as Parker traced the curve of her hip with her palm.

"I turned you around because I don't trust myself not to kiss you," Parker said, her mouth close enough for her lips to brush the delicate skin of Alessia's neck.

Alessia took Parker's hand and laid it in the center of her chest, covering it with her own. Parker held her breath again for a few seconds, then slowly relaxed.

"Have you ever been in love?"

Alessia whispered the words, as if she knew the answer was a secret. She waited, and Parker counted her breaths before answering.

"I haven't. That's not really my style."

"Why not?"

Parker shut her eyes against the silent movie on fast forward in her mind. The images were quick, edges blurred together but still sharp enough to cut as they flashed through her memory. Her mother, sitting on the couch with empty eyes, overturned pill bottles littering the floor. The cold steel locker against her naked back as she hung from the handcuffs in the boys' locker room. The whispers that followed her like a thin trail of smoke in her tiny Alabama town. *Dyke*.

Parker pulled her closer, the words soft and low against Alessia's neck. "The same reason your bed is dangling three stories above the ground."

Alessia nodded, tangling her fingers into Parker's as she held it to her heart. "Because it's safer that way." It was a statement, not a question.

"What about you?"

Parker felt Alessia's heart beat faster under her hand, as if the memory were an intruder, armed and untraceable in the dark.

"I was in love once. We were engaged." Her words were flat, like she was reading a story from a newspaper. "But it ended about a year ago."

"What happened?"

It was a long time before Alessia answered. "We broke up the night before the wedding."

"Wow." Parker squeezed her hand. "Why?"

Alessia shook her head. Parker gave her enough silence to decide to speak.

"In Italy, the practicing dinner the night before the ceremony is almost as important as the wedding."

Parker smiled behind her. This was not the time to correct her choice of words.

"And we had ours on the patio of the restaurant where Liz had proposed, looking out over the sea. My sister Lexie hadn't shown up yet, but she's late to everything, and I still remember feeling so happy." She paused, as if reluctant to leave that moment. "Everyone I loved was crowded around one long table, and the sun was setting. My father had just stood up to speak when the one of the waiters came over to the table with something that had been dropped off at the door for us. So I opened it."

Parker held her a little closer. "Why do I not like the sound of that?"

"It was a voice recorder."

"What was on it?"

"It was Lexie and Liz. They were fighting over whether Liz was going to tell me before the wedding that they'd been sleeping together behind my back for a year."

"Holy shit." Parker felt Alessia stiffen slightly in her arms, tensing against the memory. "What did you do?"

"It suddenly made sense why my sister wasn't there, and explained why Liz ran out the door the second the recording started. Everyone kept trying to turn it off, but I made them leave it on. I wanted to hear all of it."

"Did you have any idea something was going on before that?"

Alessia shook her head and Parker squeezed her cold hand, warming it with her own.

"Evidently, Liz had been playing both of us the whole time. Lexie thought Liz was in love with her, and when Liz refused to tell me what was going on before the wedding, I guess Lexie figured out she had no intention of leaving me for her. So she recorded their conversation and had it delivered to the dinner to punish her."

"And you were just collateral damage?"

Alessia glanced back at Parker. "What does that mean?"

Parker hesitated, trying to wrap words around that concept. "It means that you did nothing wrong and still got hurt."

"I don't think she meant it to hurt me. I don't think she even thought about me before she did it." Parker heard the torn edges of Alessia's heart in her voice. "And I haven't seen her since."

Parker rolled Alessia toward her, her words as light as air on her cheek. "You deserve so much better."

Alessia's hands slipped under Parker's shirt and up the strong lines of her back as Parker moved over onto her body and hesitated only a moment before she kissed her, her hand resting at the base of Alessia's neck, their breath mingling, hot, intense as flash fire. Arousal shot through Parker like lightning, stealing her breath when she slipped her leg between Alessia's thighs and felt her arch underneath her, her hands tangled in Parker's shirt, pulling her closer.

"I need your skin." Alessia's words were a whispered rush as she pulled Parker's shirt over her head and dropped it on the floor beside them.

The buttons on Alessia's shirt fell through Parker's fingers, revealing a sheer silver bra that clung to her skin like mercury. Parker dipped her mouth to hover over one tense, taut nipple, touching it only with the heat of her breath for a few long seconds. She waited until she felt Alessia's nails on her back before she started circling it with her tongue through the gossamer fabric, teasing it almost into the wet heat of her mouth.

She paused long enough to slip her hand underneath Alessia's back and flick open her bra, then dropped it on the bed beside them as her eyes swept her body. Her breasts were full and firm with a dusting of freckles between them, rising and falling with her breath. Parker drank her in for a moment, then pulled off her own sports bra and lowered her body slowly down onto Alessia's.

"You're so beautiful," Alessia whispered quietly, her eyes moving across Parker's lean, athletic frame. She followed the lines of her arms and shoulders with her the tips of her fingers, tracing the sharp edge of every muscle. "The strong kind of beautiful."

"Beautiful." Parker smiled. "No one's ever called me that before."

She dipped her head and let her mouth hover over Alessia's nipple, brushing it with her lips. Alessia's fingertips were at the back of her neck, her breath still until Parker drew her nipple hard and slick into her mouth, all at once, stroking it with her tongue. She scraped it with her teeth, lightly at first, but then with more pressure when she heard Alessia's breath catch and felt her hand grip the back of her neck, pulling her closer. She lifted her head, meeting Alessia's eyes as she held her breast with both hands and pulled her nipple back into her mouth, swirling her tongue around it achingly slowly, then harder when she felt Alessia's hips buck underneath her.

She parted Alessia's thighs wider with one of hers and lifted her hands above her head, holding her wrists against the pillow. Parker held her eyes as she sank into her and rocked until she felt the slow melt of Alessia's body against hers and watched her skin start to flush a deep pink, like a stroke of rosewater across the lush curves of her naked breasts.

Alessia pressed her wrists against Parker's hand, smiling when Parker raised an eyebrow.

"I'm…" Alessia's voice trailed off to nothing, but her eyes stayed locked onto Parker's.

Parker let her wrists go, touching her thumb to Alessia's lower lip, her hand soft and warm at the base of her neck. "Tell me what you want."

"I don't know," Alessia said softly, her fingertips tracing Parker's arms. She was silent for a moment, and Parker watched her thoughts gather behind her eyes like a twilight storm. "I've been only with one person…"

Parker held the silence, letting her have the space to find her own words.

"And it was not like this." Alessia met her eyes before she let her gaze drop to Parker's mouth. "This is…"

Her soft Italian accent had become more noticeable, which Parker knew meant she was nervous. She paused for a moment, then offered a word. "Intense?"

"Yes." Alessia nodded. "Intense."

Parker lay down beside her and pulled her into her arms, breathing in the scent of her skin. "Tell me what you're worried about."

Alessia trailed her fingertips over Parker's abs as Parker bit her lip to distract herself from the jolt of electricity it sent straight to her clit.

"You've been with a lot of women, right?"

Parker laughed, catching Alessia's hand in hers and holding it to her chest. "What would make you think that?"

Alessia raised up on her elbow and held Parker's gaze, one eyebrow raised, until Parker relented and brought Alessia's hand up to her mouth, kissing the tips of her fingers. "Okay," she said. "I'm not sure why I'm admitting this, but yes, I've been with a few."

"This feels so different," Alessia said. "What if I'm not…what you're used to?"

"You're already not what I'm used to." Parker pulled her back into her arms. "But I like it."

Parker sifted her fingers through the delicate layers of Alessia's hair, trying to think about anything but the gorgeous breasts that were pressed against her body. Maybe it was her military mindset, maybe she was just a decent human being, but clear consent was important to Parker, and Alessia wasn't there yet. Which wasn't ideal considering the most beautiful woman she'd ever seen was lying nearly naked against her chest.

"So," Parker said. "This is none of my business, but was the sex good with Liz, even if it wasn't…intense?"

Alessia was silent so long Parker started to wish she'd kept her mouth shut, but then Alessia started talking, the words falling out in a rush.

"I wish I had someone to compare it to. I was so busy trying to break into the wine business and helping my father with...some family business, I just never even noticed anyone around me. And then when I got involved with Liz, I didn't have anything to compare her to." She hesitated. "But I know Liz liked girls that were more *boy* than me. Girls that looked like you."

"She liked tomboys?"

"Yes. Tomboys," Alessia said thoughtfully. Parker felt Alessia's fingers tense and covered them with her own. "But I think it was more important to her to be with someone that everyone else would think was beautiful. Even if she didn't."

"Trust me," Parker said, choosing her words carefully, "she thought you were beautiful. She'd have to be blind not to see that. But chemistry is unpredictable. You're attracted to people or you're not, and a lot of people tend to have certain types we're drawn to."

"And what do you like?"

"You." Parker let her gaze sweep her body, her words low and soft. "Just you."

❖

Parker left Alessia's house just before sunrise and somehow managed to get back on base, shower, and make it to her meeting with Colonel Williams four minutes early. They'd talked most of the night, then Alessia had fallen asleep in her arms. It had been hard to leave her at dawn, and even harder to go down that damn staircase in the dark.

When she was shown in by Allison, the colonel's assistant, Trobaugh and Hooper were already there, coffee in hand. Colonel Williams stood and handed her the remaining cup of coffee on the edge of his desk.

"No need to stand at attention, Captain Haven. I think we can dispense with that at this point. I had Allison call and speak to your roommate this morning, and she said you take your coffee black?"

"I appreciate that, sir, and yes, black is perfect."

Parker took the coffee and sat down, pulling the case file from her bag.

"Detectives, let's start with you." Williams nodded at Trobaugh and Hooper as they sifted through the papers in their files.

"We knew Captain Haven was headed to the victim's hotel yesterday," Trobaugh said, looking around and patting down her pockets until Hooper pulled a pen from the loop on the sleeve of her uniform and handed it to her. "So we showed up at the medical examiner's office to see what he could tell us about ammunition used or trajectory of the bullet itself."

"And what did you find out?"

"Haven was right—the round did come from a sniper rifle, and the bullet was McMillan Precision ammunition, which is high end and designed for close- to mid-range hunting."

"If I had to guess, I'd say the rifle was a McMillian TAC-50," Hooper interjected. "If you're familiar with that grade of specialized ammunition, it follows that you'd have a rifle at that level as well."

Trobaugh pushed her wire glasses up on her nose, pulled a sheet of paper with photocopied images out of her file, and handed it to Colonel Williams.

"We inspected it, and the spiral lands and grooves are consistent with the TAC-50, but that's not much to go on, and unless we recover a firearm that ballistics can test with a comparison microscope, it won't us get very far."

"What about the direction it came from?" Williams said, handing the paper back to Trobaugh. "Did the ME give you any clue on where the bullet could have come from?"

"The parking garage."

Hooper and Trobaugh answered at the same time, and after a quick glance at her partner, Hooper continued.

"Based on the angle and trajectory of the wound, the bullet could have only come from the parking garage just across the street from the airport."

"We measured and remeasured based on the specifics that medical examiner gave us last night, and went to the crime scene again to get accurate measurements of the parking structure," Trobaugh said, sketching a rough representation on the back of the paper and holding it up. "And based on that information, we think it's most likely the center portion of the third level."

Colonel Williams slowly unwrapped a stick of Juicy Fruit gum, crumpled the wrapper, and added it to the tiny pile on his desk.

"That's a solid start," he said after a moment. "The parking garage is still taped off as a crime scene, and I know you've already been out there to take measurements, but our evidence pool is nonexistent at this point. It can't hurt for you three to get out there this morning and look for anything the shooter may have left behind for us, which I'm guessing is zero."

Williams gave Parker a nod. "Haven, what did you dig up yesterday at the hotel?"

"Surprisingly little, unfortunately. We checked the surveillance video and use of his key card," Parker said. "But he was only in the room for a total of twelve minutes. We bagged and tagged about a gram of cocaine and the case for his weapon, but he didn't have time to leave much beyond that."

"And how did our team and the Italian CSIs mesh?"

"They actually seemed to work well together."

Parker took another sip of her coffee and willed the caffeine to kick in soon. Yawning in her boss's office wasn't going to happen, but on her way back to base she'd counted up the hours of sleep she'd gotten. It took two fingers.

"And it was a huge help to have Sergeant Waterbury on-site. I think it would have taken us a lot longer to get those surveillance tapes if she hadn't been there to translate. I'd like to keep her involved if I can."

"Absolutely. I'll make sure she's cleared for as long as you need her. And I've had Allison call down and authorize a vehicle for as long as you need it."

The colonel made a quick note on his desk pad and looked back at Parker.

"I was also able to dig up some further information on the suspect from a private citizen that may be helpful."

"All right," he said, leaning back in his chair. "Who is he?"

"She," Parker replied, ignoring the instant raised eyebrow from Trobaugh. "And I don't know how much help she'll be, but I'll keep you posted on any new information. As for what I know right now, Mr. Haley was in Greece for a significant amount of time before the murder and had a relationship with a woman there that was allegedly abusive, although I don't know her name. It might be worth running his name through Interpol and seeing what pops up."

"What about her, your informant?" Hooper asked, leaning forward on her elbows. "What do we know about her?"

"I have a personal connection to her, so I'm respecting her anonymity at this point," Parker said as slow, thick dread settled in her stomach. "But I realize later on that may not be possible."

Williams tapped his pen on the desk. He was silent for a moment, almost as if auditioning the words to phrase his next question.

Parker saw Trobaugh and Hooper look at each other from the corner of her eye.

"Putting your connection to our informant aside," he said, looking up at Parker, "do you trust her information?"

Parker nodded. "At this point, yes, I do."

Colonel Williams sat up and closed the folder on his desk. "That's good enough for me. Let me know about any potential evidence you find at the parking garage this morning." He paused, glancing over at Parker. "And Haven, see what else we can find out about John Haley. We need to know why the hell he was sitting in that cab at the airport, and who else knew he was here. This was anything but random."

"Yes, sir." Parker gathered her things and headed for the door with the other detectives.

❖

"You've got to be kidding me, right?"

Hooper looked horrified at Parker's suggestion. They'd been at the parking garage all morning and had come up with a big bag of nothing.

"You want me to roll around on the ground?"

"It's not the ground," Parker said, trying not to smile. "It's concrete. Think of it as urban flooring."

"Urban flooring my ass," Hooper muttered, sinking into a sitting position. "I might as well be wallowing around in the dump."

Hooper and Trobaugh were both look-twice attractive, but Hooper's dedication to a pristine uniform was well known, and she wore it well. She was a tall woman, with a strong build and dark hair, a striking contrast to her ice-blue eyes. Her wife was her exact opposite, a California blonde with a quick smile and a lean, muscular build that hinted at her past as an Olympic athlete.

"Yeah," Trobaugh said, rolling onto her back. "It took her hours to pick out that outfit she's got on. And by 'outfit,' I mean the same uniform we wear every freakin' day."

Hooper playfully flipped her off and Parker placed herself on the ground so that they were all about fifteen feet from each other and positioned to roll in different directions.

"The object of this is to look at an old scene with fresh eyes. The entire garage is shut down, which means we don't have to worry about any vehicles, so keep your eyes open as you roll. It's worth it to potentially see something we've overlooked from a standing position."

Hooper rolled her eyes, scooting away from a wad of gum flattened on the concrete like it was on fire.

"We'll see how 'worth it' it is when I catch some flesh-eating bacteria and I'm clinging to life by the time breakfast rolls around."

After about ten minutes, Hooper was right in the middle of a rant about the oil stain she'd just rolled into when she stopped abruptly, the sudden silence echoing through the empty garage.

Trobaugh and Parker stopped rolling and peered over at her. She was crouched over a drain, snapping on a pair of latex gloves.

"I realize I'm going to catch shit about this forever," she said. "But it seems your filthy little tactic worked, Haven."

They joined her at the drain just in time to see her pick up a brass shell casing that had fallen between two of the parallel bars of the drain, slightly too wide to fit through them but just below the surface level and out of sight.

"Well, hot damn," Trobaugh said as Hooper picked up the casing and dropped it into a paper evidence bag. "Maybe you should get on your hands and knees more often."

Two hours later, Parker felt comfortable that they'd collected the only evidence the killer had left behind.

"Thank Christ," Trobaugh said, wiping down her jacket with a baby wipe, which had the same effect as swiping it across an Alabama dirt road. "I need to eat or I'm going to kill somebody myself."

Hooper peeled off her jacket and shook it, holding it at arm's length with her thumb and forefinger. "No need. I'm sure the flesh-eating bacteria is already taking care of that."

They drove back into the center of old downtown and parked like the locals with two wheels on the sidewalk, wedged into the last parking space available. Trobaugh looked horrified and insisted that it must be illegal until Parker had her look at the rest of the vehicles surrounding them. All were haphazardly parked an inch from each other, and most occupied some portion of the pedestrian walkway, so she just shook her head and snapped her attention back to the search for food.

They finally found a tiny—and slightly tilted—brick pizzeria in a back alley and chose a secluded booth in the corner. The air was rich with the scent of charred peppers, mozzarella, and fresh oregano, and because Italians tended to linger for hours over a meal, the clink of glasses and laughter still hovered in the air despite the midafternoon hour. The waitress came to their table to take their order, and as she left Parker saw Trobaugh glance back to watch her walk away while Hooper was digging in her bag.

"Eyes front, soldier," Parker said under her breath just as Hooper finally emerged with her favorite pen. Trobaugh whipped her head around just in time, gave Parker a wink, and pulled out her iPad.

"What's this?" Parker asked as Trobaugh set the tablet up on the table.

"This is footage from the camera located at the only entrance to that parking garage. I had the footage from that day sent over but didn't get it until late last night. I'm not going to tell you what I saw until you watch it. I want to see if either of you notice it."

"Tell me you also have the tapes from the third level of the garage," Parker said, twisting the top off the bottle of sparkling mineral water the waitress dropped off at the table.

"No such luck; they only have one camera. It sits over the entrance to the structure and tapes over itself every three days. I asked for it just in time and had it sent to the base. Only three vehicles entered within the time frame of the shooting, and only one of those had no passengers and left less than a minute after the incident."

Parker and Hooper watched carefully until Trobaugh pointed to the screen as a black SUV entered the parking lot nine minutes before the shooting. The quality of the tape was surprisingly good, and she ran the tape in a loop until Parker suddenly leaned closer and hit pause just as the suspect reached for the parking ticket from the machine at the entrance.

"Can you zoom in there?"

"Zoom in to what?" Hooper squinted at the screen. "I don't see anything."

Trobaugh took her glasses off and handed them to her across the table, then zoomed in on the machine just as the suspect was taking the ticket. The tinted glass obscured everything above the suspect's elbow, but the hand was visible for just a second as he ripped off the ticket and drove past.

"What am I supposed to be seeing?" Hooper leaned across the table, chin in hand.

Parker pointed to the ticket and looked over at Trobaugh.

"Look closer." Parker smiled. "Study that hand."

The waitress appeared just then with a breadboard topped with a fresh loaf and a small dish of oil and crushed herbs. She was beautiful in a soft, accidental way, with her hair falling forward from a loose bun at the nape of her neck and sparkling warm hazel eyes. She was also wearing a white button-down shirt that all but fell open when she put the board on the table. Before she left, she asked Parker if she needed anything else, and her eye contact lingered long enough to make it clear she wasn't talking about mineral water.

"What the hell?" Trobaugh shook her head as the waitress walked away. "How do you get women you don't even know to throw themselves at you on a daily basis?"

"Women throw themselves at me?" Parker sliced a piece of warm bread off the loaf and dipped it into the spicy oil. "That has never been proven. Where exactly are you getting that information?"

"Um…" Hooper muttered, distracted and visibly torn between two thick slices of bread she'd cut from the small, still steaming loaf. She finally just piled both onto her plate and looked up at Parker. "Everyone on base knows that."

"I mean, I get it." Trobaugh mashed her bread into the oil until it sloshed over the side. "I guess you're not horrible to look at, if you're into that kind of thing. But no one so much as flirts within a hundred yards of me."

Hooper cleared her throat and pointed to the gold ring on her finger that exactly matched the one on her partner's hand. "And what exactly would you do if they did?"

Trobaugh broke into a smile and winked at her. "I would point them in Haven's direction, of course."

"That's better."

"Not to break up this tender moment," Parker said, pulling the iPad back to the center of the table, "but let's get back to the tape. What do you notice about the left hand, the one reaching for the ticket?"

Hooper looked at it for a moment, the forgotten bread she was holding aloft and dripping oil onto the table.

"Well, would you look at that?" she said, looking up after a moment to pop the bread into her mouth. "It seems our badass sniper likes to wear nail polish."

"When I noticed that, I pulled the most common driver's seat measurements for late-model SUVs to get a rough idea of the suspect's height, which is about five foot three." Trobaugh paused, one eyebrow raised. "We're looking for a woman."

"Are we positive it's not just a short dude with a thing for the latest trends in nail art?"

Parker and Trobaugh looked at her with blank expressions, fingers poised over the Play button.

"What?" Hooper said, mopping up the rest of the olive oil with the last crust of bread she'd plucked from the board. "He could be French." She paused, the bread an inch from her mouth. "Or from Portland?"

Trobaugh pushed Play again, and the woman pulled her hand back in the vehicle and turned back to the steering wheel. Parker hit Pause.

"Is there any way to have this footage digitally enhanced?" Parker asked, leaning in and squinting at the screen.

"This is enhanced," Trobaugh said as Hooper handed over the glasses she was wearing to Parker. "I had one of my buddies back home in digital forensics do it for me overnight, and he emailed it back this morning. This is as good as it gets."

Parker started the tape again just as the food arrived. A wide platter of lemon parmesan pasta to share clattered onto the table, topped with fresh pecorino shavings and toasted pine nuts, plus a side of marinara for Hooper.

"What is that? You ordered a side of random sauce just in case you decide to ruin the pasta we ordered?"

"Back it up, Haven," Hooper said, serving herself a large pile of fragrant pasta, then dousing it with a river of red sauce. "I know what I'm doing. And we both know you're just jealous you didn't think of it first."

Trobaugh shot her partner an affectionate look and started to serve her own pasta from the platter. "I take no responsibility for any of what's going on with that marinara."

"I like your glasses." The waitress they'd forgotten was still there looked at Parker and smiled. A wisp of hair fell across her face, and as she blew it gently away, all three women at the table suddenly dropped their eyes to her full, sensual mouth. "They suit you."

She walked away with another glance at Parker, and Trobaugh shook her head, pasta still dangling over the platter from the serving forks she was holding.

"Jesus Christ," she said. "I'm never going anywhere with you again. My ego can't take this shit."

"Watch yourself, Haven," Hooper said around a mouthful of pasta. "Someday your next first kiss is going to be your last."

Trobaugh and Parker looked up at her with the same expression of alarm.

"And you'll never see it coming."

It was early evening when they finally left the restaurant, and as they walked back to the car all three of their phones pinged at the same moment. It was a text from Allison, Colonel Williams's assistant.

Report to Col. Willliams office ASAP. Please reply with ETA.

"Damn, Hooper," Trobaugh said, rolling her eyes. "Word about your crimes against pasta shot to the top fast. Now we're all going down for it."

"Something must have happened," Parker said, wedging herself into the tiny European car she'd been assigned by Williams. "Have either of you ever been called to his office with no notice?"

"No, ma'am," Hooper said from the miniscule back seat that looked approximately the size of an almond with her six-foot frame folded up in it. "I have a feeling this case just got a lot more interesting."

It didn't take them long to get back to base. Allison greeted them when they arrived, then showed them into Colonel Williams's office and shut the door quietly behind her as she left.

They sank down into the same chairs they'd been in that morning as Williams sorted through a pile of papers on his desk, then leaned forward and pressed the button on his intercom.

"You're free to go, Allison," he said. "I appreciate you staying late and getting this info together for us."

He went back to the papers and sorted them into three piles and stapled them together.

"Thank you for coming in so quickly," he said, handing each of them an eight-by-ten glossy photo with two sheets of paper stapled behind it. "Take a look at this."

The photo showed a black car, in what looked to be a residential neighborhood, with one window rolled down. Slumped against the other window was the body of a man with one bullet to his temple, his face striped by wide rivulets of dried blood that ended in a dark, congealed pool around the base of his neck.

"Another one?" Hooper looked up and shook her head. "When?"

"The victim's name is Anton Perelli. He's Italian. And the MO is way too similar to our John Haley incident," Williams said, rubbing his forehead with the heel of his hand.

He looked tired. The tiny lines around his eyes that had always made him look kind were deeper, and two empty coffee cups sat at the edge of his desk. "This was about two weeks ago, in Paris. I just heard about it this morning. Someone based in Paris at Interpol saw the report about our airport murder and thought there might be a connection. I emailed you all of the details we know concerning the victim's identity."

"What was their report from ballistics?"

The colonel shook his head, tapping his pen on the surface of his desk.

"Like our murder, there wasn't anything to speak of in the way of physical evidence, so all they had to go on was an educated guess as far as ammunition." He ran a hand over his hair and squeezed the back of his neck. "Needless to say, it's not ideal that we may have an international serial killer on our hands and not one of us has a shred of evidence."

"Well," Parker said as she pulled the sealed evidence container out of her bag and laid it on his desk. "There's this."

"What's that?"

"It's a shell casing from the crime scene, specifically the section of the parking garage that Hooper and Trobaugh had narrowed down to be the shooter's location. Hooper found it."

Williams's face exploded into a smile and he slapped his desk with his palm. "Now that's what I'm talking about, Hooper."

"I'd love to take the credit, but Parker made us literally roll on the concrete until we came up with something. I found that in a drain that was just below ground level, and because of where it was, it would have been impossible to locate from a standing position."

The colonel raised an eyebrow and tried not to smile. "You did that in uniform, Hooper?"

Trobaugh made a weak attempt to hide her laughter with a cough. Hooper just shrugged, symbolically dusting off her sleeves. "We all have to make sacrifices."

"Tell us more about this murder," Trobaugh said, taking off her glasses and rubbing her temples. "What do we know about it?"

"Well, we know he was a Greek national, so that ties in with the connection to Greece that our current victim has. He was married, although in the midst of a divorce, and had some brushes with the law." He thumbed through some pages in the notebook on his desk. "Mostly domestic disturbances fueled by alcohol, by the looks of it."

Hooper got out her notebook and jotted down the details. "Why was he in Paris?"

"We don't know, and that's the problem." Williams leaned back in his chair and paused. "Someone's got to put all this together and find this bastard before he kills again."

"Speaking of that," Parker said, glancing at Trobaugh and Hooper, "you should know that either we've got a metrosexual sniper on our hands, or...the shooter is a woman."

A long moment passed while that information sank in.

"Are you kidding me with this?"

Parker took the iPad that Trobaugh handed her and set it up on his desk. "We'll show you exactly why we think he is a she, but we're fairly certain we're looking for a female."

Williams laughed, reaching for the jacket on the back of his desk chair and shrugging it on as he slid his laptop into his bag.

"Well, I'm going to listen to why you think the suspect is a female, but I'm familiar enough with your work to know that if all three of you think she's a woman, then chances are...she's a woman."

He looked up at them as he unplugged his phone and dropped it in his bag.

"After that I'm going to go home and have a large scotch, because at oh-five-hundred hours I have to be on a video conference call with Interpol to tell them they're looking in completely the wrong direction."

Parker pressed Play on the iPad.

"Which," Colonel Williams said, unwrapping a stick of gum and folding it into his mouth, "I can tell you now is going to go down like a screen door in a submarine."

CHAPTER TEN

L ate the next afternoon after the café was closed, Alessia let herself in, dropped her bag on the counter, and walked through the double doors into the kitchen. Her father was sitting at the prep table eating a large bowl of Giada's lasagna, complete with a glass of wine and a cloth napkin draped across his rounded belly.

"Da! You'd better not let Ma see you eat that before dinner."

"She left me to fend for myself," he said with a full mouth and his best pitiful expression. "She and her friends from her…"

"Book club?"

"Is that what they're calling it?" He paused to muster his most indignant look. "They all went out to eat and left their poor starving husbands at home."

"Well, you're clearly barely surviving," Alessia said, kissing him on the cheek and retrieving a wineglass from the rack overhead. "However will you cope?"

"I know." He winked at his daughter and pulled her in to kiss her cheek. "It could have gone either way there for a minute."

Sal loaded his fork with the steaming lasagna and lovingly pushed a bit of cheese and sauce onto it with his knife before he put it in his mouth, beaming contentedly.

"So what's up, Flower?" he asked after a moment as the silence grew heavy, using his childhood nickname for her.

Alessia sighed, turning the silver cuff bracelet on her wrist. "I think we have another problem," she said. "A bigger problem."

"Is it about the American?"

Alessia looked up, surprised. "Parker?"

"Sure." He winked at his daughter and waited for her to take the bait. "You can tell me all about that if you'd like."

"Da," Alessia said, suppressing a smile. "There's nothing to tell about Parker. But we do have another dead body. This time in France."

Sal put down his fork and the smile faded from his face. "Please tell me this is not connected to one of our clients."

"It is, but it goes deeper than that." She paused to smile at his untucked shirt and wild hair. "But it can wait until you finish. I'll go next door with you, and we can talk in your office when you're done."

Sal put his napkin on the table and leaned back on the stool— at least until he remembered it had no back and nearly toppled to the floor, catching himself just in time. Alessia shook her head and inspected his wine, quickly confiscating it and opening a new bottle from the rack. She replaced her father's glass with a clean one and filled it to just under half, swirling it until it opened up a bit, then handing it to her father.

"What was wrong with the other one? I found it open in the cooler."

"Where red wine should never be. At least not at that temperature. And you're drinking it from a champagne flute." Alessia smiled, picking up her own glass. "Clearly, you should not be drinking unsupervised."

Her father went back to devouring his lasagna while she tried to remember everything Parker had said when she'd called her that morning to ask her if she knew anything about the murder in France. It was obvious Parker wondered if she knew the victim's name, but she hadn't asked. At least, not yet.

Sal finished his pasta and Alessia put the bowl and their wineglasses in the sink, then they locked up the café and went next door to Sal's jewelry store.

"Da, it always smells like wet rock and old saddles back here." Alessia dropped her bag on the old leather couch in the back room while her father clicked on the stained glass lamps that instantly gave his office a cave-like ambiance. He settled himself on the chair across from her and started patting his pockets for a lighter.

"I can fix that for you, you know." Alessia raised an eyebrow in her father's direction. "I can come in and spritz everything down with some rosewater and lavender oil."

"Don't you dare." Sal winked at Alessia as he poured the grappa into two floral teacups with gold trim, one missing a handle, and handed one to his daughter.

"Salute," he said, lifting his glass and clinking it to hers.

"Salute."

They sipped the grappa in silence. Alessia felt herself tense under the weight of having not one but two dead bodies all but in the room with them. She knew her dad well enough to know what he was thinking: *One is a coincidence. Two is a plan.*

She sank back into the couch, rubbing away the start of a headache from her forehead and staring at the stone wall opposite. The light from the lamps was just enough to illuminate a spiderweb in the corner where condensation clung to the spun silver strands, shimmering as a fat black spider made her way across it.

"Da," Alessia said. "Do you remember that conversation we had in the café a few weeks ago?"

"I think I know what you're talking about," Sal said, pushing his glasses back up on his nose. "It was right after the Anton Perelli case. He showed up at the train station in Rome and threatened to kill you because you'd just put his wife on a train."

"That's right. So we sat down in the café that evening and wrote down all the details we had about Anton and that other guy who threatened to hunt me down earlier, Matteo Carvasio. Both of them knew I'd helped their wives escape, and threatened to kill them and then come after me."

She wound her hair into a quick bun and speared it with the pen she'd found in her pocket, only to have it promptly slide out and disappear into the sofa cushions. She sighed and started again.

"You wanted to see if you could find a connection between the two," Alessia said, finally getting the pen to stay in her hair.

"And I looked for weeks. I never found anything that connected them."

"Maybe there was nothing to find," Alessia said, twisting the lid off her lip balm and smoothing it across her lips with her ring finger.

She leaned back into the couch, closing her eyes and letting out a slow breath. "We both know it's my fault. I've been so distracted since the…since Liz."

She looked down to blink away the burn of unwelcome tears as she tucked her lip balm back in her pocket.

"We've been doing this together for how many years?" Alessia asked as she looked up at her father. "And in all that time, none of those men knew who I was or where to find me. Now three of them have threatened to kill me, and at least one seems intent on backing that threat up."

Sal shook his head and started to say something, but Alessia held up her hand.

"Da, it's okay. I know I've been sloppy, and with the Underground, that can get us killed. There's no excuse for it."

Sal looked at his daughter with warm eyes and leaned forward in his chair. "You talk like you are not human, Flower. Like you don't have a heart that was shattered into a thousand pieces." He reached out for her hand and squeezed it gently between both of his. "It takes time to find them all and put those back together again. To be able to focus on anything else."

He leaned back in his chair and pulled two cigars out of the box on the end of the coffee table. "You will smoke with me, no?" He waited for her to smile, then cut the ends, taking his time lighting one of them and handing it to his daughter, who shot a playful glance at the door.

"You know Ma will kill you herself for turning me to the dark side, right?"

"What?" Sal drew on his cigar and examined the end until he was satisfied with the burn. "The Underground? She always knew you'd step in when your aunt Lucia died. We just don't talk about it."

"No, Da," Alessia said, puffing out a perfect ring of velvety gray smoke that lingered above their heads like a ghost in the room. "Cigars. She knows about the Underground. I meant she'd kill you if she knew you ever taught me to smoke."

"Ah!" Sal nodded enthusiastically and dropped his lighter on the coffee table with a clatter. "Yes, that is a certainty."

They smoked in companionable silence until Alessia looked over at him, something just occurring to her.

"Maybe there's not a connection between the names on that list." She reached over and pulled the terra-cotta ashtray over into the center of the coffee table. "Anton saw us leaving the house and followed us to the train station, so that explains how he knew who I was. And who knows how Matteo found out? His ex-wife could have written down my name and he saw it, or someone at the hospital could have told him. It could have been anything."

"But what do we know about this dead body in France?" Sal asked. "Do you know who it is?"

"Maybe. Do you remember that woman in Sicily who escaped after being held in a basement for weeks by her ex-husband?"

"That one stood out," Sal said, finishing his grappa and setting the teacup down on the table. "She's the only one that has ever contacted us herself to ask for help. You handled most of that one, though, so I never knew much about it."

"We knew her as Mary at the time, but that was Marianna Perelli, Anton's wife."

Sal nodded slowly, putting the pieces together in his mind. "And how did she find out about us?"

"She wouldn't say." Alessia kicked off her sandals and pulled her legs underneath her on the couch. "But I think a connection in the hospital tipped her off. She was in there for days with an armed guard at her door after she escaped."

Sal paused, puzzled. "But we placed her in Finland, not France. How does she connect to this?"

"We did send her to Finland with a new passport and papers, but Anton showed up at her door there three weeks later. Fortunately, someone else was in the house and called the police, so no one got hurt."

"And where was I?" Sal asked, finally producing his lighter from his jacket pocket with a flourish. "I don't remember any of this."

"You were in Napa Valley with Ma when it happened." Alessia refilled her father's glass with a short pour of grappa. "Remember, that trip I got you for Christmas?"

"Ah…I do remember that. Excellent chardonnay." He locked his eyes onto Alessia's. "But what I don't remember is my daughter telling me anything about it."

"I didn't need to ruin your holiday, Da. I handled it. I got in touch with Mirelle, our French connection, and we placed Marianna in a new safehouse."

"Oh, no," Sal said, reaching for the bottle of grappa and holding it aloft as the thought formed in his head. "You said we have a body in France…"

"It wasn't Marianna. She's thriving and wants to be part of the Underground someday, apparently. I called Mirelle this morning to make sure she's still safe." She paused. "The body is Anton Perelli, but no names have been released yet. It looks like they're keeping this one pretty quiet."

"So how do you know this?" Sal rubbed his head, standing his wiry hair on end. "Did someone tell you it's Anton?"

Alessia ran her hand through her hair. "Parker told me about the murder."

Sal held Alessia's gaze, then tapped his cigar ash into the ashtray. "But not the identity of the victim?"

"She can't." Alessia pulled her legs underneath her on the couch. "I'm not sure if they know yet."

Sal paused, gaze fixed on his daughter, then took another sip of his grappa and went to his desk and shuffled through the top drawer.

"I'm still not sure what Anton and Matteo have in common besides the obvious. But there has to be something. And if I'm remembering right," he said, ducking to look toward the back of the drawer and yanking out a handful of stuck-together sticky notes, "there were three men on the list, and that's just two." He looked up, rumpled sticky notes fluttering down into a pile at his feet. "Who was the third?"

"John Haley, the one that got shot at the airport. I had you add him the first night Parker came for dinner out on the patio. Ma had me meet Parker at the café door downstairs, and I called you while I was waiting for her. You were still here at the jewelry store."

Sal nodded, still digging into the drawer with one hand while trying to fling a stubborn lime-green sticky note off his other palm.

"I hadn't gone to Greece yet, we were just starting to work the case, but I just had a bad feeling about him."

Sal stood up slowly, clutching a fistful of papers. "And now he's dead."

Alessia nodded, tossing her grappa back in one shot and setting her cup back down on the table.

"Yes," she said. "It seems he has that in common with Anton."

"Doesn't Mirelle's brother work with law enforcement there in Paris?"

"Yes, but all he could tell her is that the victim had the address of Marianna's new safehouse in his shirt pocket, and he was one block from it with a loaded gun in his lap when he was killed."

"So," Sal said, giving up and wedging the drawer shut with papers still hanging out of it, "three men on that list threatened to kill their partners, then come after you. And if that's Anton, two of them are now dead."

"So the question is," said Alessia, locking eyes with her father, "where is Matteo?"

CHAPTER ELEVEN

Parker pulled up to the entrance of Toscano Winery at sunset, shoving a small notebook in her uniform jacket and scanning the endless rows of trellises. Alessia had called her late in the afternoon and asked Parker to meet her at the vineyard but had hung up before Parker could ask where to find her when she got there. She walked toward the sun that hung low and heavy over the mountains, glazing the fruit with a copper shimmer. The air was still except for the warm wind that moved through the vines, shifting the leaves and picking up the scent of the lush coral roses planted at the end of every row.

As she locked the car, she caught a glimpse of Alessia halfway down a row of trellises. She was on her knees, her face dipped close to the ground. Parker started down the row, trailing her fingers across the green, luminous grapes dripping from the vines. They were still warm from the sun and glided like suede across her fingertips.

"Don't come any closer," Alessia said, still kneeling with her face to the ground. "Your scent will mix into the air and alter what I'm getting from the soil."

Parker stopped where she was, a smile forming against her will at the sight of Alessia on her hands and knees, ass in the air, her hair falling onto the ground around her face like a pool of brown silk. "Don't come any closer" was not typically what women said when they were in that position in front of her, but Alessia was far from typical.

She sat up after a few moments, twisting her hair at the nape of her neck, then dipped her hands into a zinc bucket of water under the low-hanging grapes. She dried them on the hem of her simple white linen dress, her brows knit together in thought.

"Permission to approach?"

Parker waited until Alessia looked up and smiled before she walked down the row. When she got to her, Parker slid her hand around the back of her neck, as soft as thought. Alessia closed her eyes and leaned slowly into Parker's chest.

Parker smiled and held her close. "If I didn't know you were a super-tough outlaw, I'd almost think you're happy to see me."

Alessia smiled up at Parker. "Don't get excited, I am a super-tough outlaw." She glanced down at Parker's hand. "And watch the thigh harness."

Parker assumed she was kidding until she ran her hand up the outside of Alessia's thigh and encountered the handgun, cold and heavy against her palm.

"Jesus," she said, shaking her head. "You're serious."

"I'm always serious." Alessia leaned down to pick up the zinc bucket and wine bottle waiting under the vines. Parker took them from her and emptied the water, tucking them both under her arm as they started walking back down the row.

"What were you doing back there?"

"I was studying the scent of the soil," Alessia said, stopping to pick a handful of grapes and hold them up to Parker. "Tell me what you smell."

Parker leaned in. "I don't want you to be intimidated by my skills here, but I smell…warm grapes?"

"That's good," Alessia said. "But is it a clean smell? Or do you smell something else, like mold or rot?"

"No, it actually smells great."

"Very good," Alessia said with a smile, starting to walk again. "But for the owner of the vineyard, Christian, that's confusing, since his estimated yield this year looks to be about half of what it was last year, and that doesn't happen for no reason. If we can identify the problem and fix it in the next three days or so, the grapes that are lagging behind will still have time to mature before harvest."

"Is that why he called you in?"

"Yes, but he called everyone else first. I was his last resort."

"And why was that?" Parker said, glancing over at Alessia,

who had paused to lay the picked grapes carefully at the base of the vines. "Word has it you're the best in the business. And by 'word,' I mean Google."

Alessia laughed, her warm brown eyes sparkling in the last of the sunlight. "You googled me?"

"Maybe. And it seems you are the wine industry's answer to just about everything. *Vintner Magazine* called you 'The Grape Whisperer.'"

"I don't know about that," Alessia said, taking a turn into another row. "I think I just smell things that other people might not. And from that, I usually know what they need to add to fortify their soil or how to fix an issue with the actual product, like I was doing today."

"So why would he not call you first?" Parker asked. "He must know your reputation."

"It's been a hard couple of years for Christian." Alessia leaned down and untangled a knot of new vine shoots at the base of the row. "He's more of an academic than a vintner. His brother was into actually crafting the wine hands-on, but Christian has been a judge with Court of Master Sommeliers for ten years—the organization that awards the title of Master Sommelier." They reached the end of a row and Alessia guided them into the next. "He was also the only person that voted against me when I took the exam in Austria."

The sun sank behind the mountain, turning the light into a soft violet haze, and the owls were just beginning to call within the trees surrounding the vineyard. The air suddenly felt cool. Parker shrugged off her uniform jacket and put it around Alessia's shoulders.

"Why would he do that?"

Alessia looked up and smiled, waiting until she saw the answer flash across Parker's mind.

"Seriously? Because you're a woman?"

Alessia nodded. "I had a nearly perfect score on all three sections of the test, and it was the first time I'd sat for it. Some people take years to pass even one of the sections, and the candidates are almost always men. He just instantly disliked me."

"But they awarded it to you anyway?"

"Right." Alessia smiled at the memory. "And that didn't go over well with him either. I knew when he called me for advice on this problem with his grapes that I had to be his last resort. Like, last-last." Alessia pulled her arms through the sleeves of Parker's jacket and held it around her as she walked. "His brother died unexpectedly and left him the vineyard last year, so he's had to learn on his feet. He's actually in Rome now at a training seminar, and asked me to stop in and see what I could find."

Parker stopped and squinted at what looked like a small building about a hundred yards ahead of them. "What's that?"

"That's a wine house." A breeze blew a dark wisp of hair into Alessia's eyes, and she tucked it behind her ear. "There's usually at least one in most European vineyards, and it's usually just more of one open room than a house. Before harvesting got as sophisticated as it is now, it served as a shelter for anyone who needed to spend the night in the vineyard to keep an eye on the grapes at harvest."

"So most are abandoned now?"

"Most aren't used for the original purpose now, but I've seen several set up like open-air bars in the summer, where the vintner's friends and family can sit and drink surrounded by the vines."

She took Parker's hand and led her through the rows until they came into the clearing for the wine house. It was made of grayed cedar shiplap boards, and the window openings had shutters that were held back by iron clasps, but there was no glass in the frames, allowing the wind to sweep lazily through the house, lofting the edges of the bleached muslin curtains. A simple wood deck spanned the front of the house, adorned only with a square yellow table and two white iron chairs.

"I love this," Parker said, trailing her fingers over the hammered copper hinges on the door, streaked with green and pale turquoise from the rain. "Do you think anyone ever comes in here?"

"Let's find out."

❖

Alessia turned the door handle and swung open the door, which protested with a loud creak. The inside was darker than the light still falling over the vineyards, but Parker could still see an old farm table with peeling sky-blue paint to one side of the single room, as well as the raw wood floors. Across from the table there were several square leather ottomans on rollers. They were pushed together to form an expansive square big enough for several people, topped by dozens of huge down pillows covered in in varying textures of linen and cotton, and all in shades of the ocean: sand, sky, and water.

"Whoever decorated this needs to come to the NATO base and take a shot at the barracks." Alessia smiled as Parker examined the burnished copper oil lamps mounted on the walls. "Is this the only light source?"

"Looks like it. Most of the wine houses don't have electricity." Her eyes scanned Parker. "Do you have a lighter in any of the ninety-two pockets on that uniform?"

"You're in luck." Parker reached into the inside pocket of the jacket that Alessia was still wearing and pulled out a slim bronze lighter. "I do happen to have a lighter, which is good since it's almost too dark to see in here already."

Parker walked around and lit the five copper lamps, turning the key on the side of each to adjust the flame. Warm light flooded the room, illuminating the glass rack on the wall made of old shipping crates, some still stained with wine.

"Is this why you brought the wine?"

Alessia laughed. "No, I actually thought I'd be done by the time you got here. But if you bring me a few of the grapes off the closest vines out there, I'll show you why I had it with me."

Parker brought in a small handful of grapes and watched as Alessia rubbed the sides of them gently over the dark glass of the bottle. She held up the bottle and turned it in the light.

"Do you see anything?"

Parker leaned closer but shook her head.

"Come with me."

Alessia took the bottle outside and found a darker spot between the trellises, just beyond the reach of the gold light streaming through the wide window frames. She held up the bottle to Parker and held it level, turning it just enough to reveal several swipes of what looked like silver dust.

"Where did that come from?" Parker asked, touching it gingerly with the tip of a finger.

"That's Fantasma Marcisce, or Ghost Rot in English," Alessia said. "It's rare in Italy, but it's actually a mold that's odorless and invisible to the naked eye." She stood so her back blocked the light of the rising moon. "But if it's disturbed, like what I just did by dragging the grapes against the black glass of the bottle, it luminesces in the dark."

"Can he reverse it in time for harvest?"

"The grapes should be misted twice a day with a mixture of neem oil and potassium and will need to be monitored, but they should bounce back in plenty of time. I've already called him; he's sending someone out tomorrow."

They returned to the wine house and took the bottle outside with the glasses and opener that were hanging on the wall. Parker opened the bottle gently, handing it to Alessia to pour.

"So," Alessia said, swirling the dark cherry-colored wine in her glass, then handing it back to Parker and picking up her own. "I know you're not here just to talk about grapes."

"I wish I was," Parker said, her eyes brazenly sweeping Alessia's body. "There's plenty of things I'd rather be doing."

Alessia took a sip of her wine and set it back on the square yellow table between them. "So there's another body? Do you think it's connected to John Haley's murder?"

"We're not positive, but the two victims were both shot in their cars, both appear to have been shot by a sniper, and both have had recent arrests for domestic violence." Parker smiled and swirled the wine in her glass. "At this point, we think it's a safe bet to assume the two might be connected."

Alessia said nothing, but she felt the color draining slowly from her face, and just for a moment, she thought she might be sick. She closed her eyes to refocus, then opened them again and asked the question she didn't want to hear the answer to.

"Are you sure it's a sniper?"

"Almost positive. We do have a casing from a bullet manufactured for professional-grade sniper rifles from one of the crime scenes, but even aside from that, it's the only thing that makes sense, especially in John Haley's case," Parker said, her eyes dropping to the tense set of Alessia's jaw. "There were dozens of potential witnesses at the airport, but not one of them saw the shooter, which pretty much eliminates anything close range. We've examined the CCTV footage a thousand times. One minute he's staring at the airport exit like he's waiting for someone, the next, he's slumped against the steering wheel with a bullet in his head. It had to be a sniper."

Alessia was quiet for a long moment before she looked back at Parker. "Do you know the name of the victim in Paris?"

"We ran his prints and they came back to an Anton Perelli."

Parker stopped for a moment and looked at Alessia, trying to read the thoughts swirling around her.

"Evidently he's had a string of arrests for domestic violence and was out on bail at the time of the murder, but other than that, we don't know much. There was an address in his pocket for a house fairly close to the murder scene, but it belongs to an older couple. They've been interviewed twice, but there's nothing that connects them to the victim so far."

Alessia picked up her glass and cupped it in her hands. Dense silence shimmered between them, and Alessia was thankful for the darkness. She was used to being in danger; that was a risk she took on when she started working cases with Aunt Lucia. She'd accepted a long time ago that, as part of the Underground, she was painting a target on her back. But compromising the anonymity of her clients—the only thing that kept them safe—was something she wasn't willing to do. The one other person that knew what she did was Declan. Her father told her once that the only thing that got him through some of the cases was talking about them in confession.

"You knew the victim was Anton Perelli, didn't you?" Parker looked over at her and leaned back in her chair as an owl screeched in the distance. Alessia let out a slow breath and nodded.

"How?" Parker said, frustration starting to creep into her voice. "Did you know about it before it happened, or after I told you he was dead?" She took a breath and slowed down. "Is there another target after Anton?"

Alessia looked over the crest of the mountains just visible in the distance. Suddenly, she wanted to be anywhere other than where she was.

"Alessia," Parker said, leaning back in her chair and rubbing her forehead with her fingers. "People are dying here." She paused, looking up at the rising pewter moon, then ran both hands through her hair and locked her eyes onto Alessia. "If you have information, I need to know."

Alessia bit her lip. She started to say something, then paused. "The couple in that house have nothing that will help you. Don't waste your time. They're not involved."

"Why was he killed?" Parker locked her eyes on Alessia. "The two victims both have recent arrests for domestic violence. There has to be a connection, but we can't seem to locate either of their partners."

Parker waited for Alessia to say something. She didn't.

"Do you know where we can find them?"

"They're both safe, and they couldn't tell you anything even if you found them, so leave them alone." Alessia's voice came out harsher than she'd intended. She closed her eyes and rubbed her temples. "Parker, you don't understand everything involved. Just trust me. I can't." She leaned forward, choosing her words carefully. "Even if I wanted to, I can't."

Everything inside her wanted to tell Parker what she needed to know, but that wasn't her choice to make. She rubbed her forehead next, trying to remember the last time she didn't have a headache. The wind moved over the trellises, sweeping down the hill like an invisible hand, ruffling the leaves to scatter the moonlight, then shifting direction and smoothing them again. The air suddenly had a chill to it, and Alessia pulled Parker's jacket around her and crossed her arms over her chest.

Parker glanced at her and pushed Alessia's wineglass toward her with one finger.

"Drink."

Alessia turned to her with a puzzled look.

"Did you just tell me to drink?"

Parker smiled, edging Alessia's glass even closer. "Yes, ma'am."

Alessia's sudden laughter swept away the tension from her face like a cool wind. "And what makes you think you can tell me what to do?"

"Nothing," Parker said. "I'm smarter than that. But something's going on behind those eyes, and wine might just smooth the edges."

"If I didn't know better, Captain Haven," Alessia said, picking up her glass, "I might think you're trying to get me drunk."

Parker didn't smile, just held out her hand until Alessia took it, then warmed it between both of hers. She held her gaze as she spoke.

"It's not that," Parker said softly. "I just can't stand to see you upset."

Alessia walked over and sat facing Parker on her lap, her hair falling around both of their faces as she kissed her.

❖

By the time they walked out of the vineyard, the full moon was high and provided just enough pale silver light for Parker to see Alessia tuck the edge of her skirt behind her holster, then leave her hand on the grip.

"Did you drive here?" Parker asked, looking for her car.

"No," Alessia said. "That *Dukes of Hazzard* moment the other day totaled it, so I'm driving my father's ancient Jeep right now until I buy another car. But my property line actually meets Christian's at the base of the hill, so I just left it at the house and walked over."

"How do you know about *Dukes of Hazzard?*"

Alessia smiled. "Let's just say Da is a big Daisy Duke fan."

"Well, we definitely have that in common," Parker said, scanning the parking area for any other cars. "Did you tell your dad what happened?"

"God no," Alessia said. "He doesn't need to worry about me any more than he already does."

Parker opened the door of the car for Alessia, and as they pulled out onto the road, both of them watched the rearview mirror for followers, but there was nothing behind them but the moon. The air was deeply cool, and night scents were beginning to rise. Alessia closed her eyes and breathed them in slowly.

"What do you smell?"

She opened her eyes to find Parker smiling at her from the driver's seat.

"Everything." She closed her eyes again and rolled down her window, the wind tossing her hair and sweeping the tension from her face for the moment. As they pulled up to Alessia's house, she unbuckled her seat belt quickly.

"I knew I was forgetting something," she said as she opened the car door. "I cut up meat for Luna before I left but forgot to put it out."

Parker put her hand on Alessia's shoulder. "Stay here. Let me clear the house."

Alessia handed over her keys and Parker stepped out of the car, hand on her weapon. Once she was inside and satisfied the house was safe, she returned to the front with Luna's plate in her hand and handed it to Alessia, who took it and walked around to the back, tipping the meat carefully onto the wood slab at the base of the tree. As she turned to leave, the bushes rustled and Luna stepped out. Their eyes met and Alessia reluctantly stepped away, rounding the corner with a smile. As she walked back into the house, Parker was choosing glasses from the overhead wineglass rack, peering at them like they were painted with foreign script.

Alessia smiled. "Are you pouring white or red?"

Parker paused, glancing down at the glasses in her hand. "Red?"

Alessia took the glasses and slid them back on the rack, replacing them with two Riedel cabernet glasses. She pulled a dark bottle of French syrah out of the wine rack and put it on the counter, then went to sit at the base of the windows, watching Luna devour the last of her dinner. Parker joined her, handing her a glass as she sat carefully beside her. Luna's head swung around, the muscles in her neck flexing slowly as she stared at Parker. After a few seconds, she went back to the last bits of meat, licking the juices off the slab before she lumbered back down into the canyon.

"She likes you."

"I don't know about that," Parker said as she took a sip of her wine. "It's either that or she'd like to eat me; I can't tell which. She trusts you, though. That's not hard to see."

"I don't know why, but she makes me feel safer out here." Alessia glanced over at Parker. "Before I met you, I think I'd forgotten how that felt," she said, her velvet brown eyes soft as she looked from Parker's eyes to her mouth. "But I'm starting to remember."

Parker kissed her slowly, then stood and held out her hand. "Let's go to bed."

Alessia smiled and left her shoes at the bottom of the stairs as she started to climb. "Don't look down," she said, tossing the words over her shoulder to Parker. "That's the secret."

"Right. That's what all the badass outlaws say," Parker said, sneaking a peek back down between the stairs at the rapidly disappearing floor. "The real secret involves a Xanax dispenser at the base of the staircase."

Alessia laughed as they reached the top, stepping onto the platform and dimming the lights below with the controls mounted on the wall. She let her hair fall out of the twist at the back of her neck and set their glasses on the wine box bedside table. The bed looked more like a puff of smoke than a bed, with endless pillows in cream and white, lofty dove-gray duvets, and slinky linen sheets that offered up wrinkles like a secret story.

"Jesus Christ, this is surreal," Parker said as she took off her jacket and looked down at Alessia as she sank back into the pillows. "Somehow, the most beautiful woman in the world is lying in bed waiting for me, with her dress around her hips and a Glock strapped to her thigh."

Alessia laughed as she flipped the buckle on the thigh harness and unholstered her weapon, clicking the safety on and laying it on the bedside table. Parker sank down beside her on the pillows and pulled Alessia over to sit across her. She ran her hands slowly up Alessia's thighs, edging the dress back up around her hips. Her panties were beyond delicate, just a sheer glaze of gold across her bare skin. Parker held her gaze until Alessia closed her eyes and leaned back slightly, her hands braced behind her on Parker's thighs.

Parker ran her thumb lightly across Alessia's clit, over the sheer fabric, touching her slowly until the slick heat of her soaked her fingertips. She circled her clit leisurely, then lightened her touch, teasing her until she felt Alessia's legs tense against her hips, the quiet swish of her hair brushing against Parker's uniform pants the only sound in the still air. Parker watched Alessia's nipples harden under her dress as her hips started to meet Parker's touch, her breath deepening when Parker slipped under her panties.

"Parker," Alessia said, eyes shut tight, her voice a rough whisper. "Please."

In one flash of motion, Parker unclipped her knife and sliced through Alessia's panties at the hip. Alessia's breath caught and Parker laid the warmth of her hand over Alessia's heart until it finally slowed against her palm. Parker returned to her clit with longer, deeper strokes. When she spoke, her voice was rough.

"Take your dress off."

Alessia lifted her dress over her shoulders and dropped it on the platform behind her, where it slid slowly off the edge and fluttered to the ground thirty feet below. Parker drank in the naked length of her, then pulled one of her nipples into her mouth, swirling it with her tongue, then letting it go with a soft scrape. She flipped Alessia quickly underneath her before she pulled off her own T-shirt and sports bra, leaving her naked to the waist.

"Are you..." Parker's words melted against the curve of Alessia's neck. "Sure you want this?" She traced the edge of Alessia's ear with her breath before she moved to her mouth, fingertips memorizing the outline of her lips. Alessia nodded and Parker covered her body with her own, lifting her thighs to wrap them around her hips. She moved against her, her hands everywhere, kissing her until she felt Alessia pull her harder against her body, her words urgent and breathless.

"Parker," Alessia whispered against her mouth. "I need..."

As her voice trailed off, she raised her eyes to Parker's, who bit Alessia's lower lip gently and stroked it with her tongue, letting it go only when she was sure Alessia knew it belonged to her.

"You need to not be in control?"

Alessia nodded, closing her eyes as Parker parted her thighs with her knee, sinking into every soft curve of her body. She placed a hand at the base of Alessia's neck and held her gently to the bed as she pulled Alessia's nipple into her mouth, massaging it with her tongue until it relaxed then claiming it again, hard enough to make Alessia weave her fingers into Parker's hair and hold on. Parker finally leaned up, tracing the other nipple with her thumb, then turned her until her shoulders faced the edge of the bed closest to the landing.

"Hands above your head," Parker whispered, holding her eyes until Alessia lifted her arms, crossing her wrists above her head.

Parker tugged the top bedsheet free and wound it around her wrists, then threaded both ends through the iron loop on the landing and knotted it twice. Alessia closed her eyes until she felt Parker's breath warm against her ear as she moved back over her body.

"I'll untie this the second you tell me to," Parker said, her fingertips moving up Alessia's side, tracing the curve of her breast. Parker leaned into her, her thigh pressed warm against Alessia's clit. She opened her eyes and Parker held her gaze in the dense silence shimmering between them. "But you won't."

As she said the last word Parker slid inside her, moving her fingers with the slow, deep rhythm of Alessia's breath. Her other hand moved from Alessia's neck down between her breasts, holding her strong against the bed as her mouth slid down her body. Parker tasted every inch of her, licking, sucking, and biting from her neck to the sensitive slope of her inner hip. She sank down deeper between her legs and pulled the delicate skin of her inner thighs into her mouth, hard enough to leave a painting of mottled color behind.

Parker moved toward her center achingly slowly, touching her only with the lightest brush of her lips. She drank in the sight of her as she slowly entered Alessia again, finding the tense spot inside her that pressed against her fingertips and begged her for more. She focused her touch there, watching Alessia's wrists strain against the sheet as Parker lowered her breath to Alessia's clit and stilled her fingers. The lamplight shimmered in translucent layers across Alessia's damp skin, rising and falling with her breath, as if it, too, was waiting.

Then, suddenly, Parker gave her what she wanted. She enveloped her clit with the slick heat of her tongue, swirling the tense bud in circles until Alessia's breath told her she was close. She stopped and drew it into her mouth, teasing just the sides of her clit with the tip of her tongue. Her fingers moved slow and sure inside her, until Alessia arched hard into Parker's mouth, her chest shimmering with a fine mist of sweat. Parker stopped just as suddenly as she'd started and held Alessia's eyes.

"Tell me what you want." She slid up Alessia's body and turned her hand so that three fingers were inside and the heel of her hand rested lightly against Alessia's tight clit. "I'll give it to you, but you have to ask me for it."

Alessia's eyes were heavy with desire. "Make me come for you."

Parker captured Alessia's mouth with her own and thrust deep inside her, her hips guiding the pace, the base of her hand slicking across Alessia's clit as she moved inside. Parker moved against her with the entire length of her body, stronger than she'd expected to because every inch of Alessia's body was begging for it. She felt Alessia bite her shoulder, then lose her breath as Parker leaned more heavily into her clit. Parker felt it then, building inside her, until Alessia's walls tightened around her fingers and the force of her orgasm shook her body until there was no breath left.

Parker slowed gradually, then laid her other hand flat and warm in the center of Alessia's chest until she relaxed, smoothing the damp strands of hair back from her forehead. Finally, Parker reached for the knots above her head and untied them, pulling Alessia deep into her arms, whispering for her to settle. Within a few minutes, Parker heard her breath relax into sleep, and she tangled Alessia's fingers into hers, trying to quell the growing realization that she was in love with the enemy.

CHAPTER TWELVE

I've got to stop doing this to myself," Parker muttered under her breath as she attempted to search her uniform jackets for the one she wanted without waking Petra, who was snoring on the other side of the room. She'd left Alessia in bed just after dawn and arrived back on base with barely enough time to shower and throw on a clean uniform before she was due in the MP offices to meet with Trobaugh and Hooper. As an officer and lead investigator on the case, she wasn't technically breaking any rules by spending the night off base, but she wasn't making her life any easier either.

She smiled as she lifted an empty Doritos bag off Petra's head and pulled the covers over her and the pile of crumbs beside her. She'd missed seeing her lately, but Petra knew her well. If they spent any time real together at this point, Petra would know something was wrong, and Parker didn't want to talk about it. She didn't want to think about it either, but she'd lain awake for hours last night in Alessia's bed learning that wasn't an option.

Parker ducked her head to look in the mirror attached to the closet door and warmed the hair product in her hands, raking it through her hair and pulling it back into a tight regulation bun. She was anxious to see what information Trobaugh and Hooper had come up with over the last day so the three of them could start building a profile of who they were looking for. The problem was Parker knew female snipers were rare, and almost nonexistent in the civilian world. And the chances of finding a female sniper with a motive to kill both their victims was even more remote. The only person that fit that profile was lying naked in her bed right now with a gun on the bedside table.

So, Parker thought as she reached for her cap on the way out the door, *I need another suspect. Any other suspect.*

After a quick stop at the DFAC for coffee, she wandered through the maze of MP offices in the main administration building until she found Trobaugh's office, but the door was half-open and the office was empty. She checked the time on her watch and looked around. It was too early for anyone else to be in the station, and definitely too early for the faint country music she heard coming from down the hall. As she rounded the corner toward the conference rooms, Parker peeked through one of the doors to see Trobaugh and Hooper doing a perfect two-step to a Gary Allan song coming from a phone on the conference table.

Parker stepped into the room, making a halfhearted attempt at a courtesy cough. " 'Nothing On but the Radio,' huh?"

"Shut up, Haven," Hooper said, straightening her jacket and switching off the music. "Haven't you heard of cardio?"

"Not this kind. Clearly, I'm missing out. What have I been doing with my life?"

"Not all of us look this good naturally," Hooper continued, dropping the phone into her pocket and looking Trobaugh and Parker up and down. "Well, okay, maybe you two do, but everyone knows you're freaks."

Trobaugh laughed and high-fived Parker on her way down the hall as Hooper expertly evaded Parker's attempt to get her to dance. As they reached Trobaugh's office and sat down, Parker scanned the wall across from her as she pulled the files out of her bag. It was covered in pictures of Trobaugh competing in martial arts and track events over the years, including a photo of her expansive collection of medals and trophies.

"Damn, Trobaugh," Parker said, looking closer at a photo of Trobaugh bending at the waist to receive a gold medal in what looked like a martial arts competition. "You're putting the rest of us to shame."

"Yeah, whatever, she's a badass," Hooper said with a sniff, picking a nonexistent piece of lint off her shoulder. "But I'm the boss."

Trobaugh coughed discreetly and winked at her wife. "Absolutely."

"Yeah, yeah, you guys are adorable." Parker rolled her eyes and snapped open her notebook. "Now tell me you've got a suspect."

"Well, obviously we've got several." Hooper dug a protein bar out of the top desk drawer and unwrapped it with a flourish before dropping the wrapper on Parker's lap. "Female snipers taking out random civilians are everywhere. The hard part has been narrowing them down to a shortlist."

"Actually," Trobaugh said, pulling up an image on her laptop and turning it toward Parker, "a civilian turned over some interesting footage to the local authorities yesterday, and they passed it on to us. Check this out."

A soft knock made all three of them look up, and Maeve stuck her head into the room.

"Am I late?" she asked, glancing at her watch as she sat down in the chair next to Hooper. Her ice-blond hair was pulled into a sleek bun, and the smudge of dark liner around her blue eyes made them look like framed sky. The memory of Maeve lying naked on the cedar slab in the sauna flashed through Parker's head, followed quickly by the tattoo she'd seen on her back as she'd walked out the door. Suddenly, Emma's story of Maeve's abduction and the words inked across her back clicked into place like the last tumbler in a lock.

Trobaugh introduced Maeve to Hooper and glanced over at Parker.

"I remembered that you asked Colonel Williams at our last meeting to keep Maeve on the case, so I called her and asked her to sit in on the meeting this morning. She's been briefed, so we all should be up to speed on what we know."

Maeve glanced at Parker with a raised eyebrow as Trobaugh pressed Play. Murky footage of several parked cars jerked to life. It had been shot from a much lower point than most surveillance footage, and the images seemed to be static until a dark figure flashed by, visible for a single second at best, then seemed to disappear into a dark SUV and pull out of the frame.

"What the hell was that?" Parker said, still squinting at the screen after the video had stopped. "Is that our shooter?"

"Possibly," Trobaugh said. "And it's blind luck we even have this. A resident of Salerno was parked in the airport garage the day of the murder. She was inside the terminal at the actual time of the incident, but apparently she has one of those expensive security systems in her vehicle that records the surrounding area while it's parked. When she saw the shooting on the news, she thought to check it and handed it over to local law enforcement yesterday afternoon."

"Where was she parked?"

"We went to the garage with her last night and had her show us," Hooper said. "Her vehicle was parked over that vent where I found the shell casing, directly beside our suspect's SUV. We do need to get a look at it in the daytime, though."

"Maeve and I can do that after this since you guys have already been out there," Parker said, looking back at the screen. "So is that our shooter's profile?"

"Well," Hooper said. "Approximately thirty-three percent of it, yes. Between the knit hat she has pulled down as far as possible and the collar of that shirt, we can see just that slice of her face from her cheekbone to her lower lip."

"Well, that's thirty-three percent more than we had yesterday," Parker said.

"And we were able to nail down her exact height using the dimensions of the informant's vehicle, give or take a bit for the footwear she has on." Trobaugh pulled up a photo of the informant's Lexus SUV. "We were close when we took a guess from the parking garage surveillance. It looks like she's between five three and five five."

"And she has long hair," Maeve said, rolling up the sleeves of her jacket and buttoning them neatly at the elbow.

"How do you know that?" Hooper tapped the keys on the laptop and brought the video up again, pausing it at the point the shooter passes the camera. "We can't see her neck because of that damn shirt collar, and everything else is under that beanie." She took off her glasses and rubbed her eyes. "Believe me, we spent all night looking at this footage, and there's not much of it. I don't think we missed anything, although we did send this to be enhanced today, so we might catch more after that."

"It's not that you missed anything, I just think you may have been looking in the wrong spot." Maeve scooted her chair closer to the desk that held the laptop. "Can you move it frame by frame, as slowly as possible, as she gets into the vehicle?"

Hooper started the footage while Trobaugh put her glasses back on and slowed it almost to a halt. All four of them leaned closer to see it.

"There," Maeve said. "Right as she climbs into the vehicle and puts her right hand on the steering wheel."

Hooper backed it up again and played that portion frame by frame. The suspect's hand was only visible for a second as she reached for the steering wheel; after that, the door shut and everything disappeared behind the tinted window.

"Okay," Maeve said. "Stop it at the exact moment her hand hits the steering wheel."

Hooper backed up the tape, her eyebrows pushed together in concentration.

"Do you see that dark line?"

"What dark line?" Trobaugh switched out her glasses for her wife's to take a second look. "There's nothing there."

"I'll show you a different way," Maeve said. "Pull up your internet browser and let me search for a minute."

Trobaugh handed her the laptop and turned to Parker.

"What did you find out yesterday about the second victim outside Paris? You said the private citizen you've been speaking to might have some info?"

"Actually," Parker said. "She did. When I talked to her yesterday she told me that the victim's ex-wife—"

"The same one involved in the domestic dispute charges?"

"That's her. Her name is Marianna. It looks like he was stalking her again. He was found with a gun in his possession. In his lap, actually."

"How do we know he was intending her to be the target?" Hooper asked, folding a piece of gum into her mouth.

"Because he was found less than a block from her safehouse and had her address in his pocket."

"Yep. That'll do it."

"Wait," Trobaugh said. "Didn't the first victim, John Haley, have some issues with domestic violence?"

"I've got it." Maeve handed Trobaugh back the laptop. The

screen was filled with random photos of young women, all with long hair past their shoulders.

"Tell me what these women have in common," Maeve said, pointing at the screen. "Look at their hands."

Hooper and Parker leaned in until their foreheads almost touched.

"Holy shit. You're right," Trobaugh said. "I've got it." She looked up and flashed a smile at Maeve. "It's been a while since I had long hair."

"Translation?" Hooper said. "Someone needs to give me and Haven the CliffsNotes or something."

"I think we can do a rough estimate of the age based on her profile, so it's clear we're not looking for an older woman here." Maeve switched back to the tab showing the paused footage and pointed to the suspect's wrist. "And just like most of the women with longer hair you just looked at, our suspect has what looks like a hair elastic around her wrist."

Hooper flipped back to the collection of pictures Maeve had shown them. "I see what you're saying. Every one of these women has one." She tilted her head and looked closer. "But how do you know it's not a bracelet or something?"

"By the angle of her wrist," Trobaugh said, pointing at the steering wheel. "She's reaching at a steep upward angle to the top of the steering wheel. If it was a bracelet, it would slide down. This one stays stationary on her wrist."

"And she's probably right-handed," Maeve said, leaning back in her chair and crossing her legs. "Most of us keep it on our dominant hand."

"Damn, Sergeant." Trobaugh closed her computer and leaned back in her chair. "You don't miss much, do you?"

"No," Maeve replied, without a hint of a smile. "Not usually."

They wrapped up the meeting quickly after that and made plans to touch base later in the day after Hooper and Trobaugh met with Francesca at the Italian law enforcement offices in town.

Parker and Maeve headed to the lot where the military vehicles were kept to pick up the car that had been assigned to Parker.

"So, are you the lead investigator on this case?" Maeve asked, squinting in the sunlight as they walked out of the building.

"Technically, yes, but Trobaugh and Hooper are doing the majority of the heavy lifting here, and they're working more closely with local law enforcement than I am. I'm in the field following every lead that comes in. We just want to get this solved before anyone else gets killed."

"And you have an informant?"

Parker looked over at her, surprised. "You must be talking about what I was telling Trobaugh this morning." She paused as they both flashed their IDs to the guard at the lot entrance. "I'm getting some information from a private citizen at the moment, yes."

Maeve was quiet as they started the drive out of the base. When they finally pulled onto the main road, the sunlight was intense and glinting off the windshield. She pulled a pair of aviator sunglasses out of her pocket and turned to Parker.

"That's pretty specific information she gave you," Maeve said. "How could she possibly know that if she doesn't have firsthand knowledge?"

"That," Parker said, veering a little too sharply to the right as she took the exit that led to the airport, "is exactly what I want to know."

Chapter Thirteen

As they neared the airport, Parker's phone rang and she glanced at the number before she accepted the call.

"Alessia? Are you okay?"

"I'm fine," Alessia said, her voice rushed and louder than usual. "But I may need your help with something."

Parker clicked the call over to speakerphone. "Where are you?"

"I'm at the cathedral two blocks down from the café at the moment, but I'm driving to the Palazzo Aulenti on the north side of town. You've seen it—it's the only skyscraper in the city, in the financial district."

A sudden horn blared over the speaker followed by loud cursing in Italian. Parker glanced at Maeve while she waited for a chance to speak.

"What's going on?"

Alessia hesitated and Parker heard her shift and grind through the gears in her father's Jeep.

"I don't know how much I can tell you. But I remembered what you told me about your work, that you help women who are in dangerous situations…" Her voice trailed off, and Parker pulled to the side of the road.

"That's right," Parker said. "Is someone in trouble?"

"I'm going to tell you only what I have to tell you." Alessia paused. "I'm breaking a confidence to do it, but I might not be able to handle this myself, and someone's life is in danger."

Parker met Maeve's eyes. "I'm listening."

"I got a call a few minutes ago from Declan, the priest at my mother's church. He knows enough"—Alessia paused again, as if she was choosing her words one by one—"about me to know I might be able to help with this, and there's no time to find anyone else." Alessia took a breath. "A thirteen-year-old girl came to confession this morning and told him she was going to jump off the Palazzo Aulenti. She said it was her last sin and she needed to confess it before she died."

Maeve made a writing motion with her hand, and Parker handed her the pen she kept in a loop on her sleeve. Maeve scribbled the name of the building and basic directions on a scrap of paper and handed it to Parker.

"Did the girl say when?"

"No, that was all she said, but Declan said he feels like she's headed there now. He was afraid if he involved the authorities, it would make the situation worse."

Parker put the car into gear and headed back toward town.

"Do we know anything about this girl?"

"He doesn't know much about her, except that she's only been in Salerno for about a year. Her family is from France. Declan studied there, so they speak French to each other. I don't know if she even speaks English, I forgot to ask."

Parker glanced from the road to Maeve. "Don't worry about that, I've got that covered. How far is the cathedral from that building?"

"She could walk to it in fifteen or twenty minutes."

"And how long ago did this happen?"

"About an hour ago."

Maeve gestured to the exit they'd almost passed, and Parker whipped the car around just in time to slide sideways into it.

"Will you meet me there?" Alessia asked, her voice faltering. "I have a bad feeling about this."

"Of course, I'll be there in…" Parker glanced at Maeve, who held up five fingers. "Four minutes."

"Good. Meet me in the lobby by the elevators."

The phone clicked off and Parker glanced at Maeve, who was staring straight ahead toward town.

"Are you okay with this?"

"Of course." Maeve didn't take her eyes from the road.

"Provided you stop driving like a bloody American for once and get us there."

Parker shifted into high gear and smiled. "Yes, ma'am."

When they finally got to the lobby of the massive building, Parker saw Alessia waiting by the elevators. The space was still eerily quiet. Even the sounds of their footsteps on the marble floors were muffled by their military boots.

Alessia looked up as they approached and started to press the button for the elevator but stopped, her finger frozen in the air.

"Who is she?"

"Alessia, this is Sergeant Maeve Waterbury. She's a linguistics specialist with the British Armed Forces at NATO."

Maeve reached over her shoulder to push the elevator button. The door opened immediately and they stepped in. Alessia pressed the top button.

"What's the girl's name?" Maeve asked, her eyes locked onto Alessia.

"Sophie, I think."

The elevator shuddered as it rocketed to the top at an alarming rate. Parker leaned back against the mirrored wall and closed her eyes.

"This all may be for nothing. I don't even know if she's here," Alessia said, watching the numbers flash above the door as the elevator passed floor after floor. The air around them seemed heavier than it should be; Parker could feel it filling the space between them as Alessia continued. "But I know Declan. And he would never reveal a confession unless he had to."

The elevator stopped at the top floor and they turned left, looking on both sides of the hall for a door to the staircase that led to the roof. They broke into a run at the same time, their footsteps the only sound in the cavernous hall. Maeve finally found the door at the end of the last hall. It was locked. Parker pulled out her knife and tried to trip the mechanism inside, but it wouldn't budge. Maeve sank to her knee, pulled a multi-tool off her belt, and looked into the keyhole. She selected a thin steel bar from the tool and inserted it, turning it slightly to the left, then again in an upward direction. The door clicked open.

They raced up the short staircase to a heavy steel door at the top and stepped out onto the roof. The sun was blinding, ricocheting off the white rooftop and back into their eyes. The soft hum of the HVAC systems perched on the rooftop was a strange contrast to the cacophony of traffic horns and raised voices below. A pigeon swooped across the roof and glided to a stop on a nearby electrical wire, its call piercing and shrill. Time seemed to slow, and it struck Parker what a lonely place this would be to die.

Alessia rounded the corner of the staircase housing, but it was deserted, even as they walked to the third wall. Finally, they stepped around the final corner and scanned the desert-like surface, guarded from the din of the city below by a safety wall. A pile of abandoned roofing tiles sat in the corner, white pigeon dung dripping from the edges, but the roof was deserted. They walked around for a minute, until Alessia peered over the edge holding her hair back against the wind.

"Maybe she changed her mind. I hope that's it." Alessia looked around at the rooftop, dotted with murky skylights and yellowed pools of rainwater. She looked up to the sky and ran her hands through her hair, lacing her fingers behind her head and looking at Parker and Maeve.

"But that's crazy, because I know Declan. I heard the panic in his voice." She shoved her hands into her pockets, her eyes scanning the surface again. "I know if he was worried enough to tell me, it was already a life-or-death situation."

"Well, she's obviously not here," Maeve said in a flat voice, heading back toward the entrance to the rooftop staircase. "Let's just go."

Alessia's shoulders slumped, and she and Parker scanned the rooftop one more time before they rounded the corner toward the access door. Maeve was standing beside it with her finger to her lips, her other hand flying through the laces to her boots. She took one off, then the other, then opened the rooftop door and slammed it shut.

She locked eyes with Parker and Alessia and mouthed *Stay* before she walked carefully to the corner in the opposite direction, paused, then stepped around it. Parker kept her back glued to the wall behind her and listened. The second Alessia heard someone speaking, she started toward the corner, but Parker silently grabbed her and pulled Alessia back against her body, her arm strong across Alessia's chest.

"Don't." The word was the barest whisper, shattered instantly by the city sounds from below.

Alessia struggled against Parker's iron hold. "She's there. I hear them talking. I have to go."

Parker held her arm steady, her voice calm and low. "You don't know Maeve yet, but I'm telling you, she's got this. You have to trust her."

"No." The word tumbled out of Alessia's mouth in a rushed whisper, tears building in her eyes. "I'd never forgive myself if she died and I didn't at least try."

Parker hesitated, then relented and led them silently to the corner. Alessia slipped past it before Parker could stop her.

A thin girl with dark hair and a plaid Catholic school uniform was standing on the ledge, looking out at the sky. The wind whipped at her white button-down shirt, flattening it against her body from the side and loosening strands of hair from her ponytail, blowing them in the same direction. Maeve was a few steps ahead of them, halfway between the ledge and the corner Parker and Alessia had just stepped around. She didn't acknowledge their presence, just kept her eyes on the girl in front of her—the one balanced on the six-inch-wide wall of concrete that stood between her and death.

The girl on the ledge looked over her shoulder and spotted Alessia and Parker.

"Why are they here?" Her voice was desperate, pleading, and Maeve took one step toward her.

"They don't matter," Maeve said simply, her voice casual and calm.

"They do matter! I'm supposed to be alone." The wind whipped more strands of hair around the girl's face as she looked over her shoulder. "Nobody come even one step closer!"

"They won't, Sophie." Maeve didn't look at Parker or Alessia, just kept her eyes locked on the girl. "In fact, they're going to sit down now where they are, so you don't have to worry about them."

Parker sat down slowly, and Alessia followed reluctantly a few seconds later.

"See?" Maeve said without looking back. "Just forget them. It's just you and me talking."

A tear fell from Sophie's cheek and dropped off her chin. She wiped her eyes hard with the heel of her hand and looked at Maeve.

"You don't know me." Her voice had the shrill finish of someone who knew desperation was all they had left. "You don't know why I have to do this."

Maeve looked down, shoving her hands into the pockets of her uniform pants, then took a step back.

"You're right, I don't. Only you know." She looked back to the ledge, the sun glinting off her blond hair as she took off her cap and dropped it on the ground, easing the elastic out of her hair and shaking it out around her shoulders. "But I'm listening."

The girl turned toward the sky, her toes of her black Chuck Taylors already past the chipped concrete edge, and Parker watched her take in a long, slow breath. It was surreal to see Maeve here, shoeless on the roof with her hair blowing around her face, but she'd seen it before—the night in Greece when she'd left her boots on the beach and walked into the sea toward the dolphins.

Parker watched Sophie's shoulders rise and fall with every breath. She closed her eyes against the vivid memory of how it felt to have your breath be the only thing that's yours.

"It doesn't matter," the girl said to the sky, the wind whipping the words from her mouth and scattering them across the ledge before she could grab them back. "I'm going to be splattered all over that sidewalk soon. It doesn't matter now who knows the truth."

"I'm here." Maeve paused, squinting into the sun. "Tell me the truth."

The girl didn't look at her, just focused her gaze on the horizon and stretched out her arms like an eagle. She stayed there for a long moment. Parker and Alessia were stone-still, too frozen to exhale.

"She loves him, I know she does," Sophie said as her arms fell to her sides. "And I can't take that away from my mom. I won't."

Maeve nodded slowly, pushing her hair back from her face. "You're keeping something from her to protect her."

To anyone else it would have been a question, but to the two of them, it wasn't. Sophie looked back at Maeve and slowly turned around to face her, the wind pushing her slightly off balance.

"It's the first time I've seen her happy since my dad left. And I thought I could just deal with it."

Maeve was silent for a moment. "So she's with someone new now?"

Sophie shifted her weight from one foot to the other on the ledge.

"They got together about two years ago. That's why we moved to Salerno."

Parker saw Maeve choose not to speak. She watched her press her lips together and wait, giving Sophie the space to tell her story.

"And at first it was great. He was cool and treated me like an adult. He even let me drink with him when Mom was at work."

Maeve shaded her eyes with her hand. "When did it change?"

"A few months ago, I guess." Sophie looked back to the sky as a jet left a white trail through the expanse of pale watercolor blue above their heads. Her balance faltered and she looked back down at her feet to steady herself. "He and Mom had a fight one night, and Mom got drunk and passed out on the couch." She paused, squeezing her eyes shut against the memory. "And then he came into my room and got into bed with me."

Maeve didn't say anything, but nodded. Alessia squeezed Parker's arm as a long moment passed before Maeve locked eyes with Sophie. "And you didn't have anywhere else to go."

Sophie didn't answer, just turned back around and looked toward the rooftops in the distance. A long stretch of silence followed. Maeve's eyes never left Sophie's back.

"Look," Maeve said finally, as casually as if she were speaking to someone on a bus. "Do you mind if I sit down?"

Sophie glanced back over her shoulder. "Whatever. But go down there, don't come any closer. I know you think you're going to stop me from jumping, but you can't."

"I know that," Maeve said as she climbed onto the ledge about fifteen feet away from where Sophie stood, casually, as if it weren't the only barrier between her and a hundred-sixty-foot drop to the concrete below. She straddled it like playground equipment, one leg on either side, bare feet dangling against the side of the wall. Her voice was softer than her words. "You're in control. If you decide to do it, I can't stop you."

"Why do you care, anyway? I don't even know who you are."

Maeve looked out over the horizon and didn't speak for so long Parker wasn't sure she'd say anything at all.

"You're right, we don't know each other." Maeve paused, then looked at Sophie until she turned and met her eyes. "But I know exactly what it's like to have no control over something that's happening to you."

A tear ran down Sophie's cheek and into the corner of her mouth. She wiped it with the back of her hand and turned back toward Maeve. "Are you just saying that?"

"No," Maeve said, slowing her words. "No one else can know exactly how you feel right now." Parker watched her take a deep breath and look out over the city. "But I know how it feels to be trapped."

Alessia's breath caught as Sophie turned slowly and sat down on the ledge in the same position as Maeve, her Chuck Taylor sneakers unlaced in a way that made her look even younger than she was.

"He said if I just let him do it once, he would stop," Sophie said, her soft French accent sanding the words to velvet. She shook her head, pulling at a thin string bracelet on her wrist. Parker watched it dig into her skin as she pulled harder and harder, until she finally wound it around her fingers and jerked. It snapped and fell over the edge. She watched it until she couldn't see it anymore, then took a deep breath and looked back at Maeve.

"But he didn't." She looked up. "He never stopped."

Maeve nodded. They sat there, their memories dense between them, solid and fixed against the wind.

"Did you ever tell your mom?"

Sophie shook her head.

"Why not?"

Sophie held her hair back from her face and swiped at her cheeks with the sleeve of her shirt. "Because I thought I could just forget it." She looked up at Maeve. "You know, deal with it. And I guess I didn't want her to not believe me. That would be worse…"

She stopped and looked down over the ledge at the crooked lines of tiny cars below. "Than this."

"I get it," Maeve said as a tear dropped onto her cheek. She wiped it away. "If you don't ever say it out loud, then it doesn't really exist."

Sophie nodded as she looked toward the thin blue line of the sea in the distance. "So what happened to you?"

Maeve glanced at Parker and Alessia, then straightened her shoulders and spoke. "When I was eleven, someone took me."

"Like, kidnapped you?"

Maeve nodded, her mouth a thin, tense line. A seagull screeched in the distance and she jumped, then lifted her chin and kept talking.

"He kept me in a room in his house for nine months. I never saw one other person the whole time."

"How did you get away?"

"I ran. I saw my opportunity one day and I just decided that anything was better than what was happening. So I ran toward it."

Sophie nodded. They sat there in silence for a few moments, both looking down at the ledge until Sophie finally raised her head to look at Maeve.

"But you were running back to your family." She paused. "I can't do that."

Maeve tucked a wave of windswept hair behind her ear. "Only because you haven't started running. If you do, your mom will be there, I promise. You just have to tell her."

"I can't." Sophie's words twisted into a sob that stuck in her throat. "What if she thinks it's my fault? That something about me made him do it?"

"Why would you think that?"

"Because he said that." Sophie spat out the words as if she couldn't bear to have them inside her another second. "He said if I ever tell my mom, she'll know that I made him do it."

Her shoulders shook with the force of her sobs, and Parker saw Maeve tense against the urge to go to her. But she didn't; she waited, her gaze soft and constant.

When Sophie finally spoke, she didn't raise her head. "That's why I have to do this. There's no other way."

"Do you think what happened to me was my fault?"

Sophie's head jerked up and she looked at Maeve.

"Of course not. He took you. You were trapped."

Maeve nodded, a sudden gust of wind blowing her hair forward, concealing her face as she spoke. "And how did you feel that night, when he got in bed with you?"

Parker watched as Maeve waited for her words to sink in.

Sophie's shoulders slumped and she stared over the edge again. Another gust of wind swept over the rooftop, strong enough to shift one of the roofing tiles in the pile and scrape it across the ground.

"I can't tell her. And if I just jump, it will all go away," Sophie said, her eyes still focused on the ground. "I'm not brave like you were."

"Sophie," Maeve said softly. "I wasn't brave for a long time. When I got back home, I didn't talk about it, either. I felt like it was my fault that my parents had to go through all of it. I didn't want them to hurt anymore."

Sophie started to say something, then paused, picking at the hem of her white shirt where the stitching had come undone. "What made you finally tell them?"

"I guess I finally figured out that by not talking about it I was helping him, not my parents. I just wasn't willing to do it anymore." She wiped her cheek with the back of her hand. "It was just time, I guess."

Sophie watched as Maeve jumped down off the ledge. "I want to show you something," Maeve said.

"What is it?"

"It's a tattoo." Maeve touched her shoulders, hands crossed over her chest. "And you're one of the few people in the world that knows why I have it. So I think you should get to see it."

Sophie hesitated, then nodded.

"It's across my shoulders, so I have to raise my shirt for you to see it, but I have a vest on underneath," Maeve said, untucking her shirt from her uniform pants. "Is that okay with you?"

Sophie nodded, then turned around on the ledge to face Maeve.

Maeve turned and lifted the back of her shirt. Parker watched Sophie's lips move as she slowly read the words. When Maeve turned back around, Sophie slid down off the ledge. Shards of brilliant sunlight shimmered between them, and Sophie tucked a stray lock of hair behind her ear.

"Do you think I'm as brave as you?"

Maeve's words were soft and deliberate.

"I think you're braver."

CHAPTER FOURTEEN

Alessia elbowed Parker as the wind whipped around the corner and across the rooftop, then held up her phone. It was a text from Declan.

I'm downstairs. I won't leave until I hear from you. Please let me know she's okay.

Parker cleared her throat, and Maeve and Sophie turned together to look at her.

"I just wanted to let you know that Declan is downstairs."

Sophie turned back to Maeve. "Will you go with me to talk to my mom?"

"Let's go." Maeve smiled and held out her hand. "We'll do this thing together."

Parker waited and let them leave on their own. As soon as the steel door swung shut behind them, Alessia walked over to the sun-warmed ledge and leaned against it, her hair blowing in the wind. Parker walked over and pulled her into her arms.

"Are you okay?"

Alessia reached up and kissed her, then slid her hands warm and soft around the back of Parker's neck. "Thank you."

Parker smiled, pulling Alessia's body tighter into hers. "For what?"

"For this. I couldn't have handled this alone."

"I did exactly nothing," Parker said, laughing. "Unless you count nearly having a heart attack every time she looked over that edge."

"Maeve was amazing," Alessia said, shaking her head thoughtfully. "I've never seen anyone handle something that intense so…calmly." She paused and looked up at Parker. "What does her tattoo say, by the way?"

Parker looked back at the door Maeve had walked through a moment before. For the first time, she felt like she might cry. She spoke without turning around.

"It says, 'Your silence will not protect you.'"

❖

Later that afternoon, Parker was in her office in front of a whiteboard writing down the sparse leads they had to work with and drawing lines between any connections. She usually did this with suspects, not leads, but they didn't have any of those to work with.

"Not a goddamn one," Parker muttered to herself as she erased the entire upper half of the board.

"Talking to yourself already?"

Hooper looked around the half-open door, closing it behind her as she stepped in and claimed a chair.

"I'm beyond that stage," Parker said. "I've moved past it to making up imaginary suspects just to have one."

"Did anything pan out from the details your informant gave us?"

"Not yet." Parker stared at the board and ran the marker through her fingers. "I know the information is relevant, I just don't know how."

She finally put the marker down on the desk a little too hard and walked behind it to the chair, massaging the back of her neck with one hand. Hooper dug around in her bag and came up with two cans of Coke, oddly still cold, and tossed one to Parker.

Parker popped the top and it immediately foamed over the side and onto the desk. She grabbed tissues from the bookcase behind her and mopped it up, then lobbed them into the trash can behind her. She leaned onto her elbows and looked at Hooper, one eyebrow raised.

"Okay, give it to me."

Hooper smiled. "Give you what?"

"There's something you're here to say."

Hooper leaned forward and popped her can open over Parker's desk. A slightly smaller stream of Coke foam spewed out and formed a river headed rapidly in Parker's direction.

"Hooper!" Parker jumped up and out of the way of the spillage headed for the edge of the desk just in time. "Are you shitting me with this?"

Parker shook her head as she mopped up the mess and threatened to toss the soggy tissues in the direction of Hooper's jacket, but dropped them in the trash out of self-preservation when she clocked the look of horror that flashed across her face. If Hooper got a Coke stain on her uniform, she'd be useless for the rest of the day. She'd already told the story of her pen exploding in her jacket pocket the previous year like she had PTSD.

Hooper sat back in her chair and grinned at Parker.

"You're fucking her, aren't you?"

Parker closed her eyes, leaning her forehead into the heels of her hands on the desk. "Why would you even think that?"

"Well, aside from the women on base looking far more well rested in the last month or so, it doesn't take a genius to figure out that you're stressed the hell out about this case because you're all wrapped up in this girl."

Parker could deny it, but that took a lot of effort, and frankly she wasn't getting enough sleep to come up with on-the-spot bullshit.

"Okay. You're right," she said, leaning back in her chair. "I'm fucking her. And it seems to be getting more complicated by the minute."

Hooper punched the air. "I knew it." She grinned. "Trobaugh voted no, but only because she's jealous of your Little Black NATO Book."

"Who knows about this?" Parker said. "Seriously, this can't get out."

Hooper covered her heart with her hand and pretended to be wounded, then saw Parker's face and sobered up.

"Parker, you know I'd never say anything. No one knows but us. They don't call me 'The Vault' for nothing."

That was true. Both Trobaugh and Hooper had excellent reputations on base, but Hooper had a definite air of power. If she didn't know you, she kept her mouth shut and her cards close to her vest. Parker suspected that for the few people who did know her, it was a whole different ball game.

Parker pulled her phone out of her pocket and brought up the picture she'd taken the day before of Alessia in the vineyards. She was looking out over the trellises, her hair floating around her face in the wind. Her mouth was a deep, sensual pink, and the last of the sunlight shimmered in her eyes. Parker held up the phone, and Hooper took one look and dove for it.

"Holy God," she said not quite under her breath, scrolling through the rest of the pictures, including one of a naked Alessia tangled in the bedsheets, laughing and holding her hand up to block the picture. Nothing was exposed except the gentle curve of her breast from the side, but that was enough. "How you held out for longer than five minutes is beyond me. Assuming you did, of course."

"I'm pretty sure it was six or seven."

Hooper scrolled back through the pictures. "Do women like this even exist? She's tiny, but those breasts—"

"And...we're done," Parker said with a wink, grabbing back the phone and dropping it into her pocket. "But you're not wrong. That body is insane."

Parker leaned back in her chair, tapping her pen on the desktop. Hooper waited, stretching her legs out in front of her and leaning back in her chair, fingers laced behind her head.

"I know this is fucked up, but there's no getting out of it now," Parker said, meeting her eyes.

"Because you're falling for her?"

"Fallen."

"Damn." Hooper smiled. "Well, slap my ass and call me Martha. I didn't see that coming." She paused, the smile fading into a look of concern. "And of course the immediate problem is where the other women on base will get their cardio, but we'll deal with that later."

Parker laughed despite herself. "I sense a 'but' coming."

"And you'd be correct." Hooper lifted Parker's Coke can that she'd forgotten to drink, then switched it with her empty one. "I think you're worried that your feelings for her are clouding your judgment on her possible involvement here."

"What makes you think that?"

Hooper got up and locked Parker's office door, then erased the rest of what was on the whiteboard. "Honestly, I thought she might be involved even before I knew you were taking her to O-Town." She paused, looking at her watch. "I mean, you are actually taking her to O-Town, right? Because I had a lunch meeting that canceled, and I have some free time this afternoon."

Parker launched the dry erase marker at her and hit her square on the side of the head.

"Damn, Parker. All right, I get it, you're taking care of business." Hooper picked up the marker and poised it over the board at the top. "And what shall we call the lovely lady in question?" One eyebrow shot up. "Just first name, phone number, and directions to her house will be fine."

Parker shook her head. She was suddenly grateful for her friend, who, instead of tearing her a richly deserved new one, was unexpectedly setting aside the judgment and trying to help. While being a huge smartass.

"Just the initial *A* will be fine, smartass."

"Fine." Hooper shook her head. "You can give me her measurements later."

Hooper wrote *A* at the top of the board, followed by *#1* underneath.

"Okay, let's list the shit that's worrying you about this girl and take it apart. Maybe it's nothing."

Parker leaned back and smiled until she realized Hooper was serious.

"Really?"

Hooper nodded. "Look, it may be that she has nothing to do with this, and the only thing she's guilty of is being insanely hot. Or maybe she is involved. Either way, we need to deal with it sooner rather than later."

Parker rubbed her temples and looked at the board.

"I guess the first thing that's worrying me is how she knows the things she knows."

"Like?"

"Like how she knew that John Haley was an American the day after the shooting when no details had been released to the press. Or how she knew the Paris victim's name before I did."

Hooper paused, her hand poised over the whiteboard. She finally shook her head and wrote *Shady shit she shouldn't know* beside the first number and looked back at Parker.

"Go on."

"And last week, I bumped into her while I was in Greece and we had dinner." Parker paused, trying to think of how to explain it. "Let's just say it was a tight fit in that booth with me, her, and the Glock strapped to her side."

Hooper dropped the marker to her side. "You're kidding me, right?"

"Nope."

"Jesus, Mary, and Joseph," Hooper muttered, writing *#2 Strapped on and ready to rumble.* She turned to Parker, a more serious look suddenly settling onto her face. "What details have you given her about the case?"

"As few as possible," Parker said. "I want to know what she's holding back, but I haven't told her anything that compromises our investigation."

"I'm almost afraid to ask what number three might be."

"This one I can't really figure out," Parker said, turning her pen through her fingers. "She has someone following her. And it's clear he means business—he ran her off the road a few days ago and she totaled her car." She looked up at Hooper. "Before that we were in Greece, talking on the patio of her aunt's home in Santorini, and when we came in there was a Polaroid of us on the arm of a living room chair. Someone had taken it maybe twenty minutes before from inside the house while we were sitting outside. The weird thing was there was a knife through it, but very deliberately through her face, not mine or in a random spot in the photo."

"But if she's the one doing target practice on these guys, why is there someone else after her? And it sounds like whoever has a hard-on for her could have offed her a while ago if he was serious."

"He's serious," Parker muttered. "I just don't know why."

"Anything else?"

"I don't know," Parker said. "I guess what has me fucked up about this is that I've spent a lot of time with her at this point." She paused, letting out a long, slow breath, and tried to ease the tension building in her shoulders. "And I just don't feel like she's behind this. I know she's involved, but I just can't figure out how."

Hooper turned and wrote something else on the whiteboard, then sank back down in her seat.

#3 You're fucked, my friend.

Parker shook her head and leaned back in her chair. Hooper's phone pinged and she picked it up, nodding at Parker's laptop on the desk.

"Trobaugh finally got the enhanced Lexus footage from our buddy in Cali, and she says this one is way more clear, just due to proximity. It should be in your inbox now."

Parker opened her computer and pulled up her email, sliding it around so Hooper could see it, too. Hooper dragged her chair up and they both leaned forward as the video started. The shooter started to come around the side of the car toward the camera, and Parker slowed the video. Not enough of the face was visible for an identification, but Hooper replayed it anyway, then nodded at Parker's phone.

"Can you bring up that first picture you showed me, the side view?"

Parker's stomach dropped. Whatever Hooper had to say, she was fairly sure she didn't want to hear it. Scratch that. She was positive she didn't want to hear it.

She handed Hooper her phone, and Hooper set it up by the computer.

"See that beauty mark?"

Parker shrugged. "I don't know. What the hell is a beauty mark?"

"A mole." Hooper pulled a pen from her jacket to point at the small, dark mole above Alessia's mouth on Parker's phone. "Sorry, buddy, but it looks your girl and our shooter have some things in common."

Parker looked, then sat back in her chair and rubbed her forehead.

"Listen," Hooper said. "Obviously there are other women with a beauty mark in the same spot, and some even draw one on for God knows what reason. I had a girlfriend once that did that. But keep your eyes open." She paused. "Wide open."

Parker nodded, her eyes landing on what Hooper had written on the whiteboard. *You're fucked, my friend.*

❖

Alessia drove into town early to have breakfast with her mother after she was done baking. Every morning, Giada woke at 4:00 a.m. to "start the bread," which meant baking the café's bread using dough that her baker, Carlos, had made and set out the night before. They'd worked together for the last forty years, but Carlos had always flatly refused to get out of bed before dawn, so Giada would start the dough in the ovens while it was still dark, then line up the steaming loaves to rest on the counters. Carlos took over at the dot of sunrise, after he'd downed the three shots of espresso Giada left for him on the counter in one gulp, chewing the grounds in the bottom of his cup as he pushed through the swinging double doors of the kitchen.

When Alessia arrived, Giada had her favorite brown-butter crepes already steaming on the table. She was behind the counter finishing up making change for a customer, and when she was done handed her apron to Celia, the part-time employee she'd hired recently.

"Alessia." She kissed both of her cheeks and pulled her into a hug when she got to the table with her coffee. She dumped four cubes of sugar into it and stirred it with a silver baby spoon she pulled from her shirt pocket. "Have you met Celia?"

"I did meet her. You hired her to replace Lexie?"

"Just temporarily. Your sister will be back soon, I know it. Father Declan told me yesterday he saw her at mass."

Alessia nodded, her shoulders tensing at the mention of her sister.

"I'm sure she'll be back soon, Ma," Alessia said, reaching for her knife and fork. "But when that happens, do not try to get me in the same room with her. We're done. You know that."

"Alessia, she is your flesh and blood." Giada covered Alessia's hand with her own. "She made a mistake."

Alessia squeezed her hand, then pushed the brown-butter-and-sugar sauce onto her bit of crepe with her fork and said nothing. It was more than the fact that her sister slept with her fiancée; it was that she still felt the weight of the humiliation that had dropped over her like ice water that night. The knowledge that she'd fallen for Liz's lies, actually believed that they'd be family and trusted her when she said she wanted to build a life together, was almost too much to bear. She'd lain in bed for a week—even laughing once at the irony of where she was, having not slept in days—and refused to eat. That is, until she found Giada outside her bedroom door, holding a currant scone, her face wet with tears. She'd started to eat again for her, used her wedding invitations for target practice with her father, then launched herself into running the Underground with him. She hadn't lifted her head since then.

"Oh, I forgot." Giada held up one finger, then scurried over to the register, reaching to the shelf underneath and bringing back a sealed envelope.

"What's this?" Alessia asked, folding the last of her crepe into her mouth. "Where did you get it?"

The small white envelope was nondescript, except for one neatly typed letter stamped on the front: *A*.

"Someone must have slipped it under the door last night. It was here when I opened up this morning."

Giada hurried back behind the counter to help with a sudden influx of customers, and Alessia laid the envelope on the table, pushing aside her plate. It was too plain, too innocuous looking to be anything innocent. Ripping open the package containing the audiotape at her wedding reception flashed though her mind, and she shoved the envelope into the inner pocket of her leather jacket, half hoping it was a bomb that would go off randomly before she had a chance to open it.

"Bye, Ma," she said, leaning over the counter to kiss her mother and hand Celia her plate. "I have an appointment I have to get to."

"Think about what I said about your sister," Giada whispered, wiping her hands on her apron and holding her daughter to her for another second before she turned to help another customer.

Alessia stepped out on the sidewalk into the morning sun and put her bag on her shoulder as she ducked into her father's jewelry store. He was behind the counter with a jeweler's loupe attached to his head, wild gray hair sticking out in every possible direction as if he were caught in a constant wind swooping up from under his feet.

"Thank God you're here," he said as her saw her, lifting things out from behind the counter and piling them on the glass showcases. "Help me find my loupe, will you? I just had it, but I went to help a customer and when I got back it was gone."

Alessia smiled and set her bag down behind the counter.

"I mean," Sal continued, muttering under his breath as he bent down to look toward the very back of the storage space behind the counter, "I don't know who walks right past the diamonds and steals a jeweler's loupe, but there you have it."

"Da," Alessia said, bending to repack the things he'd placed on the showcase to look for his loupe. "It's on your head."

"What?" Sal furrowed his brow and felt his forehead with a smile. "Who put it there?"

He took off the loupe and stashed it under the register. "Flip the sign for me. I have something for you in my office."

Alessia sighed and felt her pocket for the envelope. She hadn't decided if she should open it in front of her father. He worried too much about her being a part of the Underground now. And common sense told her whatever was in it was guaranteed bad news.

She flipped the sign and followed her father to the back, where he motioned for her to sit on the couch. She took off her jacket and settled in, rubbing her eyes with the heels of her hands. She didn't know what it was about being hunted that drained the energy from her body, but it was starting to wear on her. Staying up until all hours with Parker wasn't the smartest either, for a few different reasons, but something about being in her arms made her feel safe enough to sleep, if only for a couple of hours.

"All right, Flower," Sal said, placing a small paper bag on the coffee table in front of them. "I walked to the chocolatier this morning before they opened and got you the rosewater truffle you love. That diet club meeting is next door to them today, and you know they always sell out in five minutes when that lets out."

Ridiculous tears burned the back of her eyes, and Alessia blinked them away as she opened the bag and pulled out the truffle, topped with white chocolate shavings and sugared hibiscus flowers. Sal leaned over and tried to peer into the bag. Alessia handed him the enormous dark chocolate and wild mint truffle he loved.

"Thank you, Da," Alessia said. "Although I might have done better with a whiskey-filled one today."

"What's wrong, my girl?"

Sal bit into his truffle, dark chocolate melting instantly onto his fingers, which he licked off with gusto, peering over at his daughter.

"Did you by any chance leave me an envelope at the café sometime last night?"

Sal shook his head, his mouth full of the smooth mint filling, which Alessia knew was his favorite part. Alessia pulled the envelope out of her pocket and dropped it on the table.

"I went to have breakfast with Ma, and she said it was on the floor of the café when she came down to start the bread. That's four a.m., so whoever it was must have slid it under the door last night."

"Do you want me to open it?"

"We probably need to, but I need to tell you something first."

"Nothing good ever starts with that sentence."

"That's probably true." Alessia picked up her truffle and set it back down. "You remember the last case I worked in Greece?"

"That's the one where John Haley got shot at the airport afterward? That's a hard one to forget."

"Right. Well, the last night I was there, after I'd put Olivia in a cab to her safehouse, I ran into Parker on my way back up to Lucia's place."

"Why was Parker there?"

"Some military conference, apparently. She actually saw me put Olivia and her son in the cab, but she didn't realize what was going on and didn't ask any questions. We had dinner and I decided to show her Lucia's house—"

"Interesting," Sal cut in. "I've never heard of you taking anyone there, even Liz."

"Anyway, we were sitting out back on the patio for a while, then I showed her the pool room. When we came out, there was a Polaroid of us on the patio stuck through the rose print armchair with a knife." She sighed, remembering the slash in the photo paper. "Specifically, the knife blade went through my face in the photo."

"Did Parker know what it was about?"

"No, but since then there have been other things happening, like someone trying to run me off the road a few days ago, so she knows something is up."

Sal set the rest of his truffle down and rubbed his hands together. "I know you didn't tell me so I wouldn't worry, but I knew there had to be something else going on lately. You haven't been yourself." He sighed. "We've talked about this before, and you're as stubborn as Lucia, but I worry that someday one of these guys won't stop until they get to you."

Alessia nodded. She loved working with her father. The fact that she was sought after as a wine consultant, sometimes booked a year in advance, allowed her to do two or three consulting appointments a month with vintners and devote the rest of her time to the Underground. The only part of it she didn't love was the fact that her parents worried about her, although Giada had wordlessly decided a long time ago that it was better for her not to know the details. That request remained unspoken, but it was one that both husband and daughter respected.

"And now there's this." Alessia and her father looked down at the envelope. Finally, Sal scooped it up.

"Let's see what fresh hell they've dumped in our laps this time. No time like the present."

Sal slid his thumb under the seal and pulled out a plain, folded sheet of paper. He read it, the color draining from his face, and handed it to Alessia.

It's been almost a year since you stole my wife from me.
Happy anniversary, bitch.
This will be one you'll never forget.

CHAPTER FIFTEEN

Alessia dropped the paper onto the table like it had caught fire in her hand. Her father glanced at the calendar, then got up and started pilfering through his file cabinet, brows pushed together in concentration.

"Do you have an idea who sent this, Da?"

"I might." Sal flipped through the files at lightning speed and opened another drawer with a thud. "If I can find the damn file."

Alessia sat back into the couch and rubbed her temples. Sudden images of Parker and the previous night crowded into her mind, and she reluctantly pushed them to the back. She needed to be careful. Surrender had not ever been a concept she considered, in any situation, but something about the way Parker handled her made her crave it.

Her father held up a file and slammed the cabinet door shut, jarring her out of her thoughts.

"I've got it," he said, slapping the file down on the table.

Alessia picked it up and looked at the name. *Matteo.*

"Why didn't I think of that? He's the only one on that list we made that hasn't turned up dead."

She thumbed through his file.

"Da, that case wrapped July twenty-seventh of last year." She picked up the note and read it again, then put it and the file back down. "It's July twenty-sixth. He's been looking for me for a year."

"Alessia, my love." Sal leaned forward, his hands on his knees. "You need to get out of town. Now."

"Then what?" Alessia asked. "Just hope he doesn't hang around and wait until I get back?"

They sat in silence, Alessia's fingertips brushing over the gun in her holster.

Matteo had come home early and intercepted Alessia and his wife as they left his home. His wife had tried to escape on at least three other occasions, but the last time he'd caught her as she left the house in the middle of the night and beat her unconscious. Someone in the Underground had received an anonymous call the next morning, and the case had been transferred to her.

"I remember his eyes," Alessia said, her voice soft, as if she were speaking only to herself in an empty room. "He swore he'd find me."

"Well," Sal said. "Someone's already taken out two of the three men who've threatened your life. Maybe they'll get to him before he gets to you, but you need to get the hell out of town until well after this *anniversary* he seems so set on."

"Da, I'm not leaving. If he wants me, he'll find me. I need to deal with it."

Sal shook his head and let out a slow breath. "At least come stay with us for a while."

"That would be the first place he'd look for me. He dropped off the note at the café, for fuck's sake."

Alessia sighed and dropped her head into her hands. Sal walked over and sat by his daughter, pulling her into his arms.

"Don't ever tell your mother I said this, but I understand why you want to stay and deal with this."

"You do?"

"I know you well enough to know that you're not going to want to back down from this fight, and you've got the training you need to handle it." He paused, holding her eyes. "Promise me one thing?"

"I will if I can."

"Keep Parker as close as possible. I know you can't tell her why you need her, but I'd feel better knowing she'll be with you as much as possible for the next few days."

"Da, I can do this myself. Besides, what makes you even think Parker and I are that close?"

Sal leaned back and looked at his daughter, one wild eyebrow raised.

"Okay," Alessia said, smiling despite herself. "I'll try."

"And bring her to Sunday dinner this week. I like her. And I never said that about Liz."

Alessia kissed his cheek and popped the truffle into her mouth. "No promises, Da."

❖

That evening, Parker stood in front of her whiteboard, the marker between her teeth.

She needed a new set of eyes on this, but it was late in the day and they'd all been keeping long hours. Trobaugh and Hooper had already gone for the night, and Maeve had been working in town with Francesca going over the details of the case.

"Everybody has to eat," Parker muttered. She made a mental note that she'd started talking to herself as she picked up her phone to text Maeve.

Hey, want to grab some dinner and go over the case?

She went back to staring aimlessly at her whiteboard. A few seconds later, her phone pinged and Parker picked it up.

Sorry, got a better offer.

Parker smiled.

A better offer than me and a plate of pasta? I'm positive that doesn't exist.

She smiled and sat down at her desk. Clearly she wasn't going to get anywhere tonight, and the mention of food had made her stomach start to rumble. A few seconds later, the phone pinged again.

I'm meeting Francesca for dinner at seven.

Damn girl, you win, Parker typed back. *I want details tomorrow.*

Parker pulled on her jacket and slid her bag on her shoulder. On her way out the door, another text flashed across her screen.

Good luck with that, Captain.

She smirked at Maeve's sarcastic evasiveness, then turned her attention back to her empty stomach. Unfortunately, she was going to have to solve the dinner dilemma by herself. She'd just left the MP Administration building when her phone rang. Parker fished it out of her jacket pocket while she crossed the base on her way to the DFAC. She'd remembered it was fried chicken night, so at least she'd get some bonding time with Petra and some kickass fried chicken.

"Hey," Alessia said when Parker picked up the phone. "What are your plans for dinner tonight?"

"Army cafeteria," Parker said, smiling. "Don't be jealous."

"I'm not sure I can beat that, but if you want to risk it, I might have something here you'll like."

Parker realized suddenly she was walking around the base smiling like an idiot.

"When do you want me?"

"Start driving."

The phone clicked off, and Parker slid it back in her pocket. *Even Petra would give up fried chicken for an offer like that.* She reconsidered quickly. *Okay, maybe not Petra, but almost anyone else.*

As Parker drove up to Alessia's house, she saw her already on the porch, waiting with a wicker basket in her lap. When she saw the car, Alessia got up and locked the doors, then climbed into the car with the basket in her lap. Parker leaned over to kiss her and felt Alessia melt into her, her hands warm around the back of Parker's neck.

"Please tell me you have food in that basket," Parker said, attempting to lift the lid to peek inside. "I'm starving."

Alessia slapped her hand and crossed her arms over the basket. "Don't you dare. You're just going to have to wait." She flashed Parker a smile. "It's good for you."

"Well, that's probably true," Parker said, leaning over for one more kiss. "Now, where are we going?"

Alessia directed Parker to the main road leading away from town and leaned back in her seat, kicking off her sandals to prop her bare feet on the dash and rolling down the window on her side. Parker looked over at her in the afternoon light, her hair blowing around her face in the breeze, her eyes soft and far away. Parker watched as she closed her eyes and drew in a breath, gathering the scents in the air.

"What do you smell?"

"Evening," Alessia said, eyes still closed, the late afternoon sun falling across her lashes. "And bergamot trees. The scent is like razors, sharp raw citrus, but it's tempered by the woody resins in the tree itself as the temperature drops in the evening. It sort of…rounds out the corners of the scent."

She drew in another breath, this one through her mouth, then out through her nose. "They only grow in Italy." She paused and opened her eyes. "Well, you can force them to grow in other countries, but they don't like it, and the scent is different."

Parker smiled, settling her hand on Alessia's thigh. "Where are we going, by the way?"

"The mountains. The base of the mountains, anyway. I want to show you something."

The road out of town wound slowly upward toward the massive snowcapped ridges in the distance, and the handmade rock fences lining the vineyards next to the road slowly started to look more like history than money. After a few minutes, Alessia directed her to take a sharp right turn onto a dirt road leading through trees so dense there were only tiny slivers of sky through the swaying tops of them. Boulders rose around them on both sides, then turned into cliffs dotted with gnarled trees hanging on the edges with wizened tenacity. The air was warm and still, like a liquid summer evening in the South, and the noise of the main road had long since fallen away. The road eventually wound into an endless upward turn that resembled a corkscrew, then ended abruptly at a small gravel lot. Parker shifted into Park and looked over at Alessia, who was putting her shoes back on around the basket in her lap.

"Now do I get the basket?"

"What makes you think the basket is for you, Captain Haven?"

"Just a hunch."

Alessia tipped her head to the side. "What's the 'hunch'?"

Parker pulled her cap down and nodded toward the basket. "It refers to the official clearance I have to access the contents of that basket, ma'am."

Parker made a half-hearted attempt to lift the lid again, and Alessia handed it to her.

"You can't look, but you can carry it for me."

Parker smiled, shaking her head as she got out of the car and locked it. The basket was straining at the handle as she walked around to the front of the car.

"What do you have in this thing, anyway?" Parker said, lifting it to examine it more closely. "It must weigh forty pounds."

"Which is exactly why you're carrying it," Alessia said. "And I'm not."

She winked at Parker and led them to a narrow path between the trees, marked by stones lining the edges.

"Do I hear water?" Parker stopped to listen to the faint sound that was either falling water or the wind shifting the treetops.

Alessia smiled, looking farther up the trail and winding her hair into a loose bun on the top of her head. "I'm not telling you, just keep walking."

The trail was unmarked and steep, until it suddenly opened up into a small clearing surrounded by enormous boulders so close that they turned into a terraced cliff surrounded by clusters of deep green pines. A waterfall tumbled down the stones and across the landings into a collection of small pools, each overflowing into the next at different heights, with steam rising like a hazy cover of fog from each one. The pools near the bottom were the largest, shaped like a bowl, and about ten feet across. The slow fall of the water from every direction was surreal, and it echoed off the boulders, a forgotten fountain in an abandoned stone temple.

"This is gorgeous," Parker said, setting the basket down and pulling Alessia into her arms. "Is that hot water?"

Alessia nodded. "It's a hot spring. There are several around Salerno, but this is my favorite. Not many people even know it's here. I thought you'd like it because you loved my aunt's hot spring pool."

Parker walked over to the closest pool and dipped her hand into it, running her hand across the stone. The basins had been sanded by centuries of flowing water; even the worn stone felt silky under her fingertips.

"It feels like bathwater," she said, turning to Alessia with her hand still in the water up to her elbow.

She stood, watching Alessia as she chose a long, low boulder covered in dense, velvety moss to open the basket. She lifted a brown paper box out of it first, which she set carefully to the side, then a small, insulated pouch.

"Basket is open," she said, tossing a look over her shoulder at Parker. Alessia opened the insulated bag and gave her a small plate as she sat across from her, then handed over a steamy, warm hot dog.

"A hot dog?" Parker laughed, peering into her basket where she saw squeeze bottles of American Heinz ketchup, mustard, and relish lined up. "How in the world did you get this? Do they even have this stuff over here?"

"It wasn't as easy as I thought it was going to be," Alessia said, pulling out the condiments and a tiny plastic container full of chopped onion. "I had to order some of it. We have sausages, but these are the different Ball Park." She hesitated. "That is the name, right? Ball Park?"

Parker squeezed ketchup onto her hot dog and reached over to give Alessia a kiss. Alessia pulled out Lay's potato chips next, and another small container that turned out to be ranch dip. Parker didn't have the heart to tell her those two things might not go together, but once she'd tried them, she realized she'd been wrong.

"What's in the box?" Parker nodded toward the brown paper container she'd set to the side.

"That's for after dinner," Alessia said. "How's the hot dog?"

"Amazing," Parker said, finishing the first one and reaching for the second. From the looks of the bag, Alessia had made ten or so, which would be a challenge without Petra around. "What made you want to do this?"

"I thought you might be missing some American things, so I looked for them online."

Parker watched Alessia place her hot dog and bun carefully on her plate and cut into it with an antique sterling knife and fork.

"What are you doing?"

Alessia looked up, confused. "Eating the dog."

"Oh, my God." Parker laughed, picking it up and putting it in her hand. "I might consider not telling anyone you did that if you promise never to do it again."

Alessia smiled and bit into the hot dog like a pro, even adjusting her hand to mimic the way Parker held hers. Parker leaned over and swiped at a bit of ketchup at the corner of Alessia's mouth.

"Thank you for this," Parker said, kissing her forehead. "It's amazing. I needed this today."

They ate in silence for a while, Alessia pulling out two Cokes in glass bottles from a separate cold compartment in the bottom of the basket. Parker popped the tops and basked in the last of the evening sun, just before it dipped behind the trees.

"That was amazing, you know." Alessia leaned back on the rock, letting the warmth of the sun melt onto her face. "What you did to me the last time you came to my house."

The comment startled Parker out of her thoughts and replaced them with entirely different ones. Memories flashed through her head: her scent like sun-warmed skin, the arch of Alessia's neck as she came, how she felt inside, like liquid silk... Parker shook her head and looked back at Alessia.

"I was lucky to be there," Parker said simply, tipping Alessia's chin up with her finger and kissing her, pulling away with a soft bite to her lower lip. "Now, tell me what's in that box or I'll never do it again."

Alessia laughed and picked up a new plate for both of them.

"Close your eyes."

"What?"

"Close your eyes until I tell you to open them."

Parker smiled. "Yes, ma'am."

She shut her eyes tight and heard some rustling as Alessia opened the box, then the flick of a lighter.

"Okay. Open."

Five candles flickered on the top of a decadent, although slightly lopsided, chocolate cake. Uneven swirls of fudge icing held three layers together, each with its own tilt in a slightly different direction, with rainbow confetti sprinkles dotting the top.

"Happy birthday."

Parker looked up at her, trying to ignore the tears behind her eyes. "How did you know it's my birthday today?"

"I can't reveal my sources." Alessia leaned forward to give her a sweet kiss on the cheek. "But I'm sorry about the cake. I've just never been a good cook. I completely missed that gene, apparently."

"Thank you." Parker pulled her close, touching her forehead to Alessia's. "This is the sweetest thing anyone has ever done for me."

Parker closed her eyes as she blew out the candles and had started cutting the cake when she saw Alessia holding up her fork with a quizzical look on her face.

"You can use a fork for this one." Parker laughed, looking around them in the dusk. "But there's no one here to notice anyway."

"I'm glad," Alessia said, somehow managing to get a tiny dollop of frosting on the tip of her nose despite the fork.

"And why is that?"

"Because we're getting in the water."

Parker feigned concern. "Can I take my cake with me?"

"Yes," Alessia said with a serious look, crunching rainbow sprinkles. "It's your birthday, you get anything you want."

Alessia ate a few more bites, then passed the rest to Parker and started unbuttoning her shirt. Parker watched as she let it fall off her shoulders, then slid her shorts off her hips and folded them neatly into a pile beside her.

"No weapon this time?"

Alessia smiled, one delicate bra strap falling off her shoulder.

"It's in the basket."

"Of course it is." Parker laughed, reaching over to slide the other strap off her shoulder. "I should have known."

Parker finished her own cake and popped the remainder of Alessia's into her mouth as Alessia pulled a small paper bag out of the bottom of the bag and tucked it under her arm. They packed up the remainder of the food and dishes, then set the basket under a nearby tree, Parker tucking Alessia's gun into the waistband of her pants. Alessia stepped carefully onto the ledge of the first pool, dipping her toe in to test the temperature.

Parker watched as she shook out her hair and swept it back into a higher bun, balancing with her bare feet on the narrow ledge at the side of the pool. She was wearing black lace underwear and a sheer black lace bra, cut straight across, a sexy contrast to the lush full breasts above it.

"Are you coming?"

Alessia's voice reminded Parker she was staring, and she followed as Alessia stepped through the pools to the main waterfall. The air was warmed by the steam, and Parker watched as Alessia sat on the edge, her feet in the water, and unrolled the top of the paper bag she still had under her arm. She pulled out a handful of small ivory candles and lit them, dripping a few drops of wax onto the rock beneath each one to secure it, spacing them out around the edge of the water. Dusk was falling into darkness, but the trees were scattered father apart here, clearing a path for the rising moon.

Parker pulled off her T-shirt and boots, tucking Alessia's gun under her uniform pants and underwear, then slipped into the water naked, finding a spot on the smooth rock to sit where the swirling water stopped at her shoulders. Alessia slid her bra and panties off, dangling them on a low-hanging branch to the side of the pool, and slid in across from Parker.

"I almost wish I hadn't seen that," Alessia said, glancing over at Parker's bare chest. "Now I'm not going to be able to get your body out of my head, and the last thing I need is to be distracted right now."

"And why is that?" Parker ran her wet hands over her face and back through her hair, looking up at her with a wink.

Alessia smiled. "That's not helping."

Parker stretched her arms out on both sides of the ledge. "Oh, I'm definitely not trying to help."

Alessia laughed, then held Parker's eyes through the steam. Parker's case was still there, shimmering between them, but she hadn't asked Alessia any more questions, which made her more uneasy than if she had. Alessia moved through the water to sit by Parker, who lowered her arm around her and pulled her close. She was quiet, the water shifting into ripples as she moved her fingertips over the surface.

"When do you have to go back to America?"

Parker laughed. "Thankfully, not for a while yet." She looked over at Alessia, her gaze dropping to her mouth. "But it's possible they'd extend my deployment if I asked."

Alessia nodded, hesitated, then looked up at Parker. "Do you have someone waiting for you at home?"

Parker shook her head, reaching out to trace the line of Alessia's jaw with her thumb. "I wouldn't be here with you if I did."

"Good answer," Alessia said as Parker pulled her over to sit across her hips. She wrapped her hands around Alessia's ass and captured her nipple, stroking it with her tongue. Alessia leaned back in the swirling steam, her hair dropping into the water.

Her nipples tensed as Parker pulled them hard into her mouth, one hand firm against Alessia's back, the other wrapped warm around the back of her neck. Alessia pressed her hips into Parker, then rested her forehead on her shoulder as Parker slid her hand between them and started gently stroking Alessia's clit.

"God, Parker..." Alessia's voice trailed off and the steam rose around them, blocking out the rest of the world. Alessia rolled Parker's nipple in her fingers and Parker knew from the way she was moving that she wanted her inside, but she didn't go there yet, just stroked her clit until Alessia was begging her for it, her words wet and urgent against her neck.

"I need you inside," Alessia said, guiding Parker's hand lower.

"Soon," Parker whispered, her hand slipping from Alessia's grasp and returning to her clit. "But not until you come for me like this."

She lightened her touch until just the tip of her middle finger glided over her clit and Alessia bit down lightly on her shoulder. She stroked her slowly, enjoying how tense Alessia's clit was, almost trembling under her touch.

"Are you ready to come, baby?"

"Yes," Alessia whispered breathlessly against her neck, her thighs tightening around Parker's hips, rocking to meet every touch.

"If I let you, will you come again for me?"

Alessia nodded. Her breath was hard, her muscles tight, waiting for Parker to push her over the edge.

"Good girl," Parker whispered, giving her the pressure she wanted, gliding her fingers over Alessia's clit in strong strokes as she pulled her nipple again into her mouth and let it fall back through her teeth. Alessia bit her lip as she rocked against Parker's hand, her breath warm and urgent against Parker's neck. Parker leaned into her chest and worked her clit, moving it through her fingers like water until Alessia threw back her head and an orgasm rocketed through her, her fingers locked onto Parker's shoulders as if they were her only anchor in a hazy underwater world.

Her hips slowed gradually as her head dropped to Parker's

shoulder, a slow shudder running through her suddenly that raised goose bumps on her arms.

"I'm going to take that as a good sign?"

"Jesus Christ," Alessia said, slowly finding her voice. "I didn't even know it was possible to come so hard."

Parker turned Alessia's head and kissed her, her hands soft, holding her face.

"Then that's a good place to start."

Alessia smiled, then stood and pulled herself out of the water and lay naked on the ledge, the moonlight falling like liquid smoke over the planes of her body.

"Hot?"

"Actually," Alessia said, her eyes closed, "I feel like my body might be what's causing all the steam, thanks to you."

Parker shifted to the opposite side of the pool and drank in the glistening length of Alessia's body. She'd been lucky enough to date some beautiful women over the years, always using her job as an excuse to move on when they got too close, but Alessia was different. Everything about her, from the shape of her lips to the way she walked, was deeply sensual and unflinchingly honest. Everything about Alessia was perfect for Parker. Except, of course, for the fact that she was slowly emerging as the only suspect in her murder investigation.

When she looked up again, Alessia was lying on her side, watching her through the steam. Parker pulled herself out of the water, walked around to where she was, and lowered her body on top of Alessia's, one slick thigh between hers.

"I'm dying to get all over you," she said, "But you're lying naked on bare rock. Let's get you somewhere more comfortable."

Parker leaned into her hips, her words falling down the slope of Alessia's neck as she spoke. She sat up slowly, bringing Alessia with her, and edged them closer to the slow waterfall that fell onto the rock ledge beside the pool they'd just been in. The water flowed across higher, terraced layers of rock above their heads before it flowed down onto the ledge, and there was a small open area behind the waterfall.

Parker moved behind her, resting Alessia's head on her lap as the water splashed gently at her feet. She leaned down and whispered into her ear, as if the words were a secret.

"Move your body under the water."

Alessia inched closer, until the water fell at the tops of her thighs.

"Lie back, baby."

Parker rested Alessia's head on her lap again, running the flat of her palm over her nipples. The flow from the waterfall hesitated around them on the ledge before it slipped into the pool, surrounding them with steam as the evening air cooled.

"A little closer."

Alessia moved under the water until it fell onto her clit, then brought her thighs together and looked up at Parker. She took a sharp breath as Parker watched her thighs slowly start to open again under the water.

Alessia closed her eyes. "That's…intense."

Parker smiled, holding her until she relaxed back against her body again. "Just find what feels good and stay there." She slicked over Alessia's wet nipples with her fingers. "Take your time. It may be something you're not expecting."

Alessia shifted her hips, slowly letting her thighs fall open where the water ran lighter and slower.

"Take a breath, baby," Parker said softly, just above her ear, rolling her nipples gently in her fingers. Alessia relaxed under her touch, her thighs open, water falling languidly onto her clit.

"This feels…" Alessia's hips rose off the rock slightly as her voice trailed off. "Oh, my God."

Parker whispered in her ear. "I'll be back. Just lie back and keep your eyes closed."

She stood, laying Alessia's head carefully back down on the ledge, and sat in the small open space behind the waterfall. Alessia found the pressure she needed, and Parker watched her thighs start to tremble in the candlelight, her breath hard and fast.

From the other side of the falling water, Parker slid inside her, finding the spot that was already tense and pressing back against her fingers. Parker worked her, adding another finger and turning them slowly inside her, one direction and then the other, varying the pressure, until Alessia's back arched and she moaned, shifting her hips toward a heavier stream of water. Parker closed her eyes and kept her own breath deep and slow, tensing against the orgasm she was on the edge of just watching Alessia's slick breasts rise and fall through the candlelight and steam, surrounded by black velvet night.

She felt Alessia getting close. She was slick and warm inside, rocking her hips harder against Parker's hand on the other side of the water.

"Don't stop."

Alessia's words were barely more than a whisper, just loud enough to hear over the falling water, and Parker slowed and intensified her touch as she felt Alessia start to come. Her body rose in a sharp arch under the water, thighs shaking around Parker's wrist as her orgasm moved through her like an ocean wave, turning her, lifting her, shaking the breath from her lungs, then leaving her limp and breathless on the shore as it faded slowly away.

Parker moved through the waterfall to cover Alessia's body with hers, sliding a hand under her back and moving them away from the falling water. Alessia's breath was still ragged, her arms tight around Parker's shoulders, face buried in Parker's neck. Parker held her, breathing in the scent of her skin and the cold night air, until she felt Alessia relax against her. Wind sifted through the trees around them as Alessia rolled them over and sat across Parker's hips, her slick, bare skin sliding across Parker's center.

Parker laid her hand between Alessia's breasts and Alessia covered it with hers, sliding her clit across Parker's, her wetness slicked between them. She watched as Parker's abs and arms flexed, the candlelight flickering over the hard lines of her body until Parker groaned and wrapped her hands fiercely around Alessia's ass to slide her back and forth in the rhythm she needed, rocking her against her, every muscle tense as an orgasm rocketed through her, taking her breath with it.

Alessia lowered herself slowly down to Parker, who wrapped her arms around her and held every inch of Alessia's body to hers. A gust of wind blew out one of the candles on the ledge, leaving a thin wisp of smoke rising from the wick in the suddenly still air.

"So, what did you wish for?" Alessia pulled away slightly to meet her eyes. "When you blew out your candles?"

Parker pulled her back into her arms, her words as soft as love. "You."

CHAPTER SIXTEEN

Parker rose at dawn the next morning, pulling the duvet over Alessia before she left. As she departed, she saw Luna peek around the corner of the winery, watching as she got into her car and pulled out onto the road.

She raced into the barracks and showered, throwing on her uniform before she'd even dried off completely. She smoothed her hair back into an elastic and grabbed her cap and jacket on the way out the door.

Someone opened the door to the DFAC as she passed, and Parker breathed in the aroma of fresh coffee and something else with an insane amount of cinnamon in it, but there was no time. Just before she got to the administration building, she remembered she'd forgotten her bag. With all her notes in it. For the case she was supposed to be working on when all she could think about was the way Alessia's bare ass felt in her hands.

The next thing she knew, she'd smacked directly into someone coming the opposite direction. Someone tall.

"Where the hell are you going so fast?"

It was Hooper, who switched her gym bag to the other shoulder and looked her up and down.

"You do realize it's Saturday, right?"

Parker just stared, the fog of sleep deprivation starting to clear.

"And that we got the day off because Colonel Williams is at that conference in Rome until tomorrow night?"

"I totally forgot," Parker said, taking off her jacket with a sigh of relief. Suddenly, she wasn't late for anything, and there was no need to dash into her boss's office with wet hair and no coffee. "Where are you going so early, anyway?"

"Where I go every Saturday morning," Hooper said, brushing something invisible off the sleeve of her hoodie. "Country Sunrise Yoga."

Parker searched her face for a sign she was joking. "Are you making that shit up?"

Hooper nodded toward the grassy field to the left of the barracks reserved for PT tests and training drills. There were about fifteen people wandering around with water bottles, lining up yoga mats, and stretching.

"It's yoga. And Kenny Chesney." She paused, as if Parker might be a little slow. "It's hard to beat that combination."

Parker coughed into her arm, doing her best to stifle a laugh. "I'll walk over there with you since I'm headed back to the barracks."

"That's a good idea," Hooper said, glancing over at her. "You need to go back to bed. You look like a hot-ass mess."

"Don't hold back, Hooper," Parker said, smacking her with her jacket. "Tell me how you really feel."

"Hey, it's not my fault you look like you just rolled out of a sorority house and landed on the lawn." She waved to the yoga geeks on the grass as they approached. "But you're welcome to tell me any details you feel the need to share. Start when the clothes hit the floor."

"Well," Parker said. "It started outside. She took me to this hot springs waterfall in the mountains. We're outside, no one around, and she just started taking off her clothes to get into one of the pools."

Hooper stopped in her tracks. "Holy shit."

"I know, right?" Parker said, dropping her voice to a low, conspiratorial tone. "And when she was taking off that tiny lace bra, her breasts just—" Parker stopped suddenly and looked at her watch, then gestured to the same yogi in tie-dye waving wildly for Hooper to join them. "Oh, gosh darn it—look at the time. You're late for Kenny Sunrise or whatever the hell that is down there."

Hooper rolled her eyes and started down the hill, her fuchsia yoga mat slung over her shoulder. "Very funny, asshat. You'd better not be lying because I need the rest of that damn story the next time I see you."

Parker somehow made it back to the barracks and into her room without falling asleep, then managed to work on the case for the next few hours, going over the evidence again and again, looking for a suspect that never emerged. She finally fell into bed with the files on her chest, and didn't wake again until her phone rang.

❖

"Alessia, are you there?"

Alessia blinked, then fell back into the pillows, the phone to her ear. She looked over at the small copper clock on the landing wall.

"Ma, it's almost midnight. I'm here, what do you need?"

She closed her eyes again as her mother started speaking.

"Have you been in the café today?"

"No," Alessia said, shaking the fog from her head. "I haven't been there since yesterday when I came to see you."

"Someone's been here."

"What do you mean?" Alessia said, sitting up in bed. "Are you okay? Where's Da?"

"He's asleep in his chair upstairs," Giada said, worry creeping into her voice. "But when I came down a few minutes ago to make sure the ovens were off, you know Carlos leaves them on sometimes and I just—"

"Ma, I love you," Alessia said, rubbing her forehead. "But get to the point."

"Well, I thought I'd get the deposit out of the register while I was down there, but when I looked in the bag, the note was gone."

"What note?" Alessia paused, a sinking feeling rushing over her. "You gave the note to me, remember? When we had breakfast yesterday."

"No," Giada said. "There was another note slipped under the door this morning. It had the same *A* initial on the front, so I just put it in the register to give to you later." She took a deep breath. "But when I went to look for it tonight, it was gone. I found it ripped open on one of the tables by the front door."

"Ma," Alessia said, jumping out of bed and clicking over to speakerphone. She pulled on a pair of jeans and her gun holster, checking that the Glock was loaded and strapping it to her hip in a matter of seconds. She grabbed a sweater she'd left on the landing and laced up her boots. "Just read me what the note says. Word for word."

"Well, I tossed it in the trash," her mother said, her voice growing father away as Alessia heard her dig into the trash. "I just figured you'd already read it, but then something didn't seem right." She paused. "You're always so tidy, you'd never just leave it on the table."

"Ma, it wasn't me." Alessia struggled to keep her voice steady. "But I need to know what it says. Can you read it to me?"

Alessia ran down the stairs, hugging the wall, and grabbed her keys as she stepped out the door in the pitch dark, locking it behind her. The stars glittered overhead and the gravel crunched under her feet as she unlocked the Jeep.

"I didn't bring my glasses, and it sounds like it's important. I don't want to get it wrong." Alessia could hear her rattling around behind the counter, searching for her spare pair.

"Your glasses are under the register, Ma," Alessia said, revving the engine and flooring the gas pedal as she turned out of the winery.

"Ah! So they are." Alessia forced herself to be patient as her mother searched the trash for the note. "It's here. Do you want me to read it?"

Alessia took a breath, forcing herself to answer in a calm voice. "Yes, please. Just how it's written."

"Well, there's not much on it, but let's see…" Her mother's voice picked back up as Alessia silently rounded the corner into town at felony speed. "It says, 'Our anniversary is finally here.'" She paused. "What anniversary is that, dear? It's not Liz, is it?"

"No, Ma, it's not Liz." She shifted into fifth gear as the road straightened out in front of her. She could see the lights of town. "Can you read me the rest?"

"After that it just says, 'Christchurch Cathedral, midnight.'"

Alessia dropped her speed as she got closer, making a quick left turn into the downtown area, the streets damp from the gray mist sweeping in from the sea and hanging in the air.

"Okay, Ma, just go upstairs with Da and stay inside tonight, okay?"

Alessia tried to keep her voice calm and even like there was nothing wrong, but even as she listened to it come out of her mouth, she guessed she only had about a fifty percent chance her mother would actually buy it. But that wasn't her priority at the moment. Alessia searched frantically for parking before wedging the Jeep onto a sidewalk two blocks from the café.

"Do you promise me? And don't tell Da."

Alessia knew her father had become increasingly worried about her safety, and that he'd trade his life for hers in a heartbeat. She didn't want to worry about him making that decision.

Giada's voice was hesitant. "I promise."

Alessia hurried down the darkened sidewalk, darting into alleyways and side streets on her way to the cathedral. She listened through the phone to the familiar sounds of her mother switching off the café lights and locking the door as she started up the stairs.

"But is everything all right, Alessia?"

"Everything's fine, but I need to go now, okay?"

Alessia switched off her phone before her mother could ask any more questions, then dropped it in her back pocket, turning down a damp cobblestone alley one block from the cathedral entrance.

❖

Parker felt for her phone in the dark, trying to follow the sound through the tangle of blankets, only to hear it hit the floor the moment her fingers found it. She glanced up at Petra's bed but it was still empty, which meant she wasn't home from her date. She picked up the phone and clicked to answer the call on the last ring.

"Hello?"

"Parker?" Giada's words fell out of her mouth in a rush. "I know you gave me your numbers for the phone in case of the espresso machine to break, but I am scared for Alessia, and she made me promise not to tell her father, so I can't, but something's not right and I didn't know who to call, so I call you."

Parker shook her head to clear it, focusing slowly in on Giada's voice, her usually proficient English jumbled with panic.

"And now she turned the phone dead and I can't reach her but I think she is in trouble and I—"

Parker stopped her there in what she hoped was a soothing voice. "You think something is wrong with Alessia? Why?"

"Because the notes, and the meeting at midnight…"

"The meeting at midnight?" Parker sat up and switched on her lamp, looking around for her clothes. "What meeting? Tonight?" She glanced at the clock. "Now?"

"Yes, now." Giada's words tumbled over each other. "She think I don't hear when she's driving like a maniac, but I hear, and I know she's going now to the cathedral, but there is no reason. Nothing good happens after midnight, and now my baby is out there in the dark and—"

"Giada," Parker said, pulling on her jacket. "I'm leaving the base now and coming into town. I'm going to find her for you, okay?" Her hand hit the glass exit door to the barracks, and it swung open and hit the side of the building as she raced out, taking the steps two at a time. "Where is the meeting?"

"In the cathedral."

"The one just down from the café?"

"Yes." Giada started to cry, although Parker could hear her trying to hold it back.

"I've got this, Giada, okay? I promise you, I'll take care of her." Parker flashed her ID at the soldier at the transportation lot and sprinted to her car. "Just stay where you are, and I'll call you as soon as I can."

Time seemed to stop as Parker turned onto the road leading into town, pressing the gas pedal so hard she heard it slam against the floor as she burned through the gears one after another. She racked her brain as she drove.

What meeting is Giada talking about? Notes? And who the fuck is Alessia meeting?

Parker took a turn that skidded the car almost off the road, her hands wrapped so tightly around the steering wheel that her knuckles shone white in the dark. Alessia hadn't given her a heads-up about the situation, which meant it was either illegal or dangerous, and she knew from experience that going into either situation blind could be deadly.

❖

Alessia ran up the dark cathedral steps and looked at her watch: 12:12 a.m. The Gothic-style door seemed immense in the dark with its enormous hammered iron hinges and curved top, and Alessia held her breath as it swung silently open. She stepped in and shut the door behind her, drawing her gun as she crossed the vestibule and flattening her body against the wall beside the sanctuary doors.

She heard voices on the other side of the doors, dampened and scattered by the soaring ceilings and marble floors of the cathedral. She leaned her head against the wall and tried to concentrate on what she knew going in, which wasn't much. The notes had to be from Matteo. Based on the mention of the anniversary date, it was the only thing that made sense, and her father was right—he was the last man left alive of the three who'd threatened to kill her. But if Matteo was inside the sanctuary and she was outside, who the hell was he talking to?

She crept to the center of the double doors and leaned carefully against one of them with her shoulder. It was heavy, made of carved teak, and she pushed it open just enough to see the candles lit in the iron sconces that lined the walls of the sanctuary. The amber candlelight flickered like memory against the limestone walls, and she opened the door just another inch to see rows of glowing prayer candles in red glass holders in front of the altar. She stepped back and slowly eased the door shut.

She stepped back into the vestibule where she'd been, her back against the wall, sifting through the library of scents diffused through the cathedral. The air was intense, heavy, and dominated by the smells of the centuries-old stone walls that caged it. She exhaled through her nose, filtering through and discarding the scents of the airy dust settled at the tops of the marble columns and the aging paper in the prayer books behind each pew. She was searching for something else, something she'd smelled a trace of as she raced up the steps outside. Something that shouldn't be there.

Matteo's volume had amped up and started to ricochet off the upstairs choir lofts that framed the sanctuary on both sides. The second voice had quieted, but Alessia suddenly didn't need to hear it to know who it was. Her heart dropped as she recognized the scent of skin as familiar as her own.

Lexie.

Alessia holstered her gun, then stepped into the sanctuary and let the door swing shut behind her as Matteo swung around and stopped cold.

❖

Parker raced up the twenty-seven stone steps leading to the cathedral door. It was slightly ajar, and she stepped carefully inside the vestibule, scanning the area quickly for anyone waiting inside, then lowered her weapon, listening. There were voices, at least two, maybe three, coming from the sanctuary behind the double doors, but she couldn't hear them well enough to identify the words. But she didn't need to; there was an electric charge to the air that she recognized. Fear had its own sound, smell, and heartbeat.

She looked around the dimly lit vestibule, weighing her options. The doors to the sanctuary lay straight ahead, and there were two smaller unmarked doors to the left and right of where she was standing just inside the main entrance. She stepped sideways through the door to her left, her gun trained on the sanctuary doors ahead, where the muffled voices leaking through the cracks were gaining volume.

She climbed a steep, curved staircase up to the choir loft that opened over the main area of the church. She silently lowered herself to the floor, moving in a low army crawl down the narrow loft area, stopping at what she guessed to be the midway point between the sanctuary doors in the back and the altar at the front. She flattened her body to the stone floor, concentrating on the voices floating upward. She knew Alessia's voice. It was clear and strong, but Parker heard the soft floor of fear give beneath it. The other was a male voice she didn't recognize, but what she did hear was the lilt of desperation in it, hidden beneath uncontrolled rage. His voice had a razor edge, and he was using it to slice Alessia to ribbons.

Parker knew she couldn't stay on the floor; she had to move to where she could assess the situation. She raised her eyes just far enough above the loft wall to see a man, his arms covered in tattoos, standing with his back to Parker, facing the altar. He had a stocky Greek build and a receding hairline, the same height as the woman he had pinned in front of him like a shield, one arm tight and straining across her neck. Beads of perspiration on the bald center of his head glittered in the candlelight.

Facing them at the altar was Alessia.

The second Alessia slipped through the doors of the sanctuary, Matteo froze, then dragged Lexie over in front of him, the barrel of his gun at her temple, shoving her head to the side.

"Matteo, you don't want her," Alessia said, putting her hands up as she started to walk down the aisle toward them. "You want me."

"Stay where you are," he screamed, looking from Alessia to Lexie, white spittle gathering at the corners of his mouth. Blue-gray veins shimmered under the layer of sweat gathering on his forehead. "What kind of mindfuck is this?"

"I'm the one who was at your house that day," Alessia said, glancing down at her sister. "I'm the one you want. Let her go."

He continued to look from one to the other, then jammed his gun harder into Lexie's skull.

"I'll tell you what," he said, his shock slowly morphing into a plan. "I'll just shoot both of you, and it won't matter which one of you is the bitch who stole my wife."

Alessia locked eyes with Lexie, who was gasping for air against the beefy arm slung over her windpipe, her head shoved into a grotesque angle by the gun. Alessia heard Matteo continuing to shout, but it seemed to be from a distance. All that mattered now was her twin, the other half of her heart. The space between them melted away. She nodded slightly at Lexie and felt her relax just enough to draw a breath. Matteo's voice started to penetrate, and Alessia turned back to him.

"I said," Matteo screamed, "which one of you cunts wants to die first?"

"We're twins, Matteo." Alessia tempered her voice to a low, soothing tone. "She looks like me, but she has nothing to do with this. You only want me."

"I don't give a fuck at this point." Matteo's voice cracked as a drop of sweat rolled off his cheek onto Lexie's forehead.

"Actually, you do." Alessia took a step in their direction and Matteo jerked Lexie backward, her heels dragging the ground. "One of us was there that night, and only she knows where your wife is now. If you kill both of us, or just shoot the wrong one, you'll never find her."

Alessia turned and walked through one of the rows of pews to her left, turning at the wall and walking casually to the front. Sometimes, the only choice was to call someone's bluff, and this was one of those times. It was that or stand frozen in one place and watch this animal choke her sister to death.

"What the fuck are you doing?" His voice had a shrill edge.

"It's dark back here," Alessia said. "So I'm walking to the front where I can see you better."

She resisted the urge to look back at him until she reached the altar at the front, and when she did turn to face him, she saw that her instinct had been right. His body language told her he was unsure of his next move, his eyes darting in every direction as if he was suddenly off balance. But Alessia also knew she was pushing him to the breaking point. She shoved down the panic threatening to explode in her chest. Lexie wasn't going to die. Not on her watch.

❖

Parker positioned herself so her eyes and weapon were just above the choir loft wall, then angled her gun at the edge of it until she had a clear shot down to the man in the aisle. He was standing about two yards in front of the midpoint, facing toward the altar and away from Parker. To see her, he'd have to both turn around and look up to where she was.

"Someone needs to tell me where my fucking wife is." Anger shook his words as he spoke. "Or I'm going to shoot you both right now."

He tightened his arm around the girl in front of him. A quick glance at Alessia told Parker two things: Alessia was carrying a gun under her clothes, and the target hadn't stopped to notice.

"It's me you want, so why don't you just let her go and I'll tell you anything you want to know?" Alessia said.

Parker watched as the girl squirmed in his grasp, trying to get her words out over his arm across her throat. "She's lying, Matteo. You sent the note to me. Why do you think I'm here?" Her voice cracked as she met Alessia's eyes. "Just tell her to get the hell out of here."

She made a sudden attempt to slip out of his grasp but failed miserably. He yanked her back and jerked his arm even tighter around her windpipe. Alessia looked quickly up to the loft and locked eyes with Parker for a split second, then just as quickly focused back on the man in the aisle. Parker kept her gunsight trained at the back center of the target's head. If she had to shoot and she was off by an inch, the bullet might take out the girl instead, and whoever it was, it was obvious she and Alessia knew each other. It was also obvious that Alessia and the man she'd called Matteo had history. Parker felt like she was watching the last five minutes of a movie she'd never seen.

A maniacal laugh rocketed off the walls, then ended abruptly as if the end of it had been sliced off with a machete and dropped to the ground.

"I found out what you do, you know," Matteo shouted at Alessia. "This fucking Underground, or whatever the hell you call it."

He waited for a response and got nothing.

"So you people just steal our wives behind our backs and make them disappear?" His voice pitched up an octave as Parker watched a single blue vein throb on the side of his neck. "That woman belonged to me. What happened in our house was our business."

"The last time you beat her, you almost killed her, Matteo," Alessia said. "She has permanent nerve damage and had to have her jaw pinned back together."

"That's none of your fucking business." He was so angry now his body seemed to vibrate where he stood. Parker drew in a slow breath, steadied her hand, and focused on the target. "She was none of your fucking business!"

The sanctuary went eerily silent, his last words echoing off the limestone walls and falling to the floor. When he spoke again, his voice was low and controlled.

"You're never going to tell me, are you?"

"Let her go, Matteo," Alessia said, looking at the girl under his arm, still struggling for breath. "I'm not talking to you until you let her walk out of here."

He grabbed her by the hair and forced the girl to her knees, facing Alessia. Parker saw Alessia look down to her, and saw the tear that fell off her chin as she tore her eyes away to focus on Matteo again.

"Let's just give you some motivation, then." He pressed the cold steel of the gun barrel to her skull. "I'm going to count to three. And if you start talking before I get to three, I'll let her go. If you don't, you can watch her brains blow out all over the floor."

Parker held her breath. She knew what Alessia was thinking, and she was right. Her weapon was in a holster under her sweater; she could never reach it in time to kill him before he shot her. The girl started crying softly in a keening rhythm, almost as if she were praying. Her shoulders slumped, and when she opened her mouth to say something, he slammed the butt of the gun into the back of her head, knocking her face-first onto the floor. Without taking his eyes off Alessia, he reached for the girl's hair and yanked her back up to her knees, winding his fist around it, her blood dripping slowly from her temple to the stone floor.

He smiled at Alessia. "Ready to talk, bitch?"

Alessia didn't answer. She was pale, standing as still as stone, her eyes focused on the girl as she struggled to get back on her knees in front of Matteo.

"One."

The sound of his voice hung in the air, as if begging Alessia to talk. He waited until it faded completely before he spoke again.

"Two."

He cocked the hammer, then pressed the weapon into the side of her head. He was shaking, the muscles in his jaw contracting and twitching, the gun vibrating against her skull.

"Three."

A gunshot rang out, so loud it seemed to crack the stone walls, and Parker watched as Matteo jerked forward, then slumped over the girl on the floor.

"No!" Alessia screamed, the word cracking and falling away as she dropped to her knees and buried her face in her hands. She rocked back and forth where she was, still screaming as Francesca walked up the center aisle, gun drawn, and placed two fingers on Matteo's neck.

Parker holstered her weapon and ran down the stairs, just in time to see Francesca pull Matteo's body off the girl, who sat up slowly, the blood that had been flowing across her forehead now changing directions and inching down her face. Francesca looked up from Matteo and nodded toward Alessia, still in a crumpled pile on the floor in front of the altar.

"Go get her. I've got this."

Parker ran past them and gathered Alessia into her arms, pulling her face up to look into her eyes.

"Alessia," Parker said. "She's alive, baby. Look."

She raised her head slowly to look toward Lexie, who struggled to her feet and ran to her sister. Alessia jumped up and wrapped her in her arms, whispering into her hair. After a long moment, Alessia let her go enough to cradle her face in her hands.

"Are you okay?" she whispered. "Really?"

She nodded, her head falling onto Alessia's shoulder, tears streaming down her cheeks.

Alessia looked over at Parker. "You shot him?"

"No," Francesca said, pulling her cell phone out of her pocket. She clicked it on and pressed it to her face. "I shot him."

She stepped away toward the back of the church, speaking softly into the phone.

Alessia smiled at the girl, then took a step back to stand beside her.

"Parker," she said. "This is my twin sister, Lexie."

❖

An ambulance arrived not long after to take Lexie to the hospital, and the paramedics allowed Alessia to ride with her. Parker said a quick goodbye as they climbed in, promising to meet them there, then walked back in and pulled Francesca aside. Italian law enforcement was already starting to arrive, and the area was being taped off as a crime scene.

"How in the world did you know he was here?"

"I've been following him for three days. We think he was behind the sniper attacks."

"But the shooter was a woman," Parker said slowly, shaking her head. "We have it on tape."

"He may have gotten someone else to do his dirty work, but we're pretty sure he was the force behind it."

"So who the hell was the woman?"

"To be honest, I don't think we'll ever know, and if this guy is who we think he is, I don't care. Whoever she was, she was a professional; she left nothing behind but a single shell casing, and that was clearly an unusual mistake. We have no full visual on her face, no fingerprints or DNA, no details on the car she was driving, and not one single person saw her commit the crimes." She paused, looking back at the doors as law enforcement and CSIs started streaming into the church. "She left us nothing to go on."

"And you think he was behind it?"

"I do," Francesca said, dropping her voice. "He has direct ties to the other two victims based on their shared history of domestic violence, and a string of arrests for violent crimes. And his first wife left him five years ago and married our second victim, Anton, so I think it's safe to say there was bad blood between them. He also had a direct motive to go after Alessia after the Underground helped his wife escape."

"I heard him say something about the Underground," Parker said. "What the hell is that?"

"Officially, I don't know." She searched Parker's face and hesitated before she went on, leaning closer. "But unofficially, it's a known network of volunteers across five European countries that help victims of domestic violence escape and start their lives over."

She straightened up. "I can't say more than that, and if you tell anyone I said anything at all, I'll deny it." She smiled, looking over her shoulder and holding up one finger to an officer who was motioning her over. "But I can tell you this. Your girlfriend is a badass."

Parker ran her hand through her hair, trying to piece back together the shards of information that lay shattered around her feet. She shook her head, then looked up.

"Hey, Detective," she said to Francesca, checking no one else was within earshot. "How was dinner the other night?"

"Excellent," Francesca said with a wink, glancing at her watch. "In fact, I'm late for our next one now."

Chapter Seventeen

A week later, Alessia and Parker walked into Giada's kitchen and were enveloped instantly by the scent of the bubbling red sauce almost overflowing on her stovetop. Giada came over to hug them both, then hugged them again together as Alessia laughed.

"Ma, you can let go of us. We're staying for dinner."

The sauce pot decided to boil over at that second, and Parker moved it to the sink for Giada, who hovered over it with a spoon then scooped up a taste, blowing on it for a moment before she handed it to Parker.

"Giada," she said after she'd put the bite in her mouth and closed her eyes to savor it. "What do you put in this stuff? I'm going to have to take that whole pot with me. It's addictive."

Parker reached for the spoon and tasted it one more time, and a beaming Giada clasped Parker's face in her hands and kissed both her cheeks.

"Ma," Alessia said, looking around the kitchen. "Where's Da? I have that bottle of Chilean white he wanted."

"Parker can take it to him, love. Why don't you go and check on your sister?" She ignored the look Alessia gave her and nodded in the direction of the hall. "I think she's in her room."

Parker took the bottle from Alessia, and Giada pointed her toward the patio, where Sal was sitting outside at the long table, tearing hunks from a round loaf of bread.

"Parker," Sal said with a wide smile, looking up at her and then over to the kitchen windows. "Just in time to help feed my little angels."

Parker took a seat beside him as a swirl of doves and seagulls clamored at his feet.

"My wife pretends not to notice when yesterday's bread goes missing, but I think it's because she secretly likes them. They're finally starting to grow on her after almost fifty years."

Parker laughed, tossing a chunk of bread to a smaller dove the color of ash in the back of the group. "You and Giada have been married for fifty years?"

"Our anniversary is October fifteenth of this year." Sal turned the wide gold band on his finger. "I asked her to marry me on our third date, but between you and me, I knew she was the one before the first. I saw her working in her parents' cafe downstairs. Now the girls look just like she did that day."

"So, what's the secret?"

"The secret to a happy marriage?"

Parker nodded, tearing the last of the loaf into chunks.

"The magic combination," Sal said, "is to choose a woman with a kind heart. Then put her happiness above your own. Always."

He turned to look at Parker, brushing off his hands and sweeping the last of the crumbs off the end of the table to the birds.

"What about you? Do you want to marry someday?"

"Yes, sir," Parker said, turning to meet his eyes. "I'd like to marry your daughter someday if she'll have me."

Sal paused, then walked over to the wine rack by the door and opened the cabinet, pulling out an unlabeled, dusty bottle and two tiny glasses.

"What's this?" Parker asked as he sat back down and handed her a glass, filling it almost to the rim.

"This," Sal said, raising his glass to Parker. "Is a toast." He paused, meeting Parker's gaze with a warm smile and clinking his glass to hers. "To welcome you to the family."

❖

Lexie's room was the last one on the right, with a huge picture window framed in whitewashed wood that looked out over the turquoise sea in the distance. Alessia hadn't seen her sister since that night, although she'd called Giada every day for updates on her recovery. She loved her, she just wasn't at the point where forgiveness was an option, and she wasn't sure she ever wanted to be.

"Hey, Lex," she said as she rounded the corner and walked through the open door. "Are you coming out for Sunday dinner? I brought some sauvignon blanc for Da, which means we'll be able to get a head start on the syrah."

Lexie was sitting on the window seat, looking out over the expanse of half-moon terra-cotta tiles that made the houses below look like square stairsteps as they led down to the sea.

"Hi, Ally," she said without looking up. "I don't think I'm coming to dinner tonight. I'm not hungry."

Alessia sat beside her on the window seat, one eyebrow raised.

"Really? You think that's an option with our mother?" Alessia nodded toward the door. "If you think she's not going to come through that door to get you in about three minutes, you really have been gone too long."

"I know." Lexie smiled and pulled her legs up underneath her on the ledge. "She keeps trying to treat my concussion with pasta."

There was a moment of quiet and Alessia looked down, taking the time to choose her words, then looked back up at her sister.

"Lex, I need to know why you did it," she said, bracing against the tears already threatening to spill over in her eyes. "We don't have to talk about it again after this, but I need to know why you tried that hard to hurt me."

Lexie ran her hand through her hair and shook her head. "I slept with Liz because I was a jealous idiot who never let myself think about how it would break your heart." She looked up at her sister, her dark brown eyes a mirrored reflection of her own. "I don't have an excuse, Ally. And I don't deserve to be forgiven."

"Why did you have that audio tape delivered to me at the rehearsal dinner? Why not just let me find it somehow or give it to me privately?" Alessia paused, her voice trembling. "Why did you have to humiliate me in front of everyone we knew?"

A tear slipped down Alessia's cheek, and her sister leaned over to her desk for a tissue and handed it to her. "What are you talking about?"

"The tape with you and Liz. It was delivered to me just as the speeches were starting. I thought it was from someone who couldn't be there, so I played it. Everyone listened to you and Liz talking about how you'd been sleeping together behind my back."

"Ally, what I did with Liz was unforgivable, but I didn't have that tape delivered to you. I didn't even know there was a tape until just a few weeks ago."

"Don't lie to me, Lexie. I came back here after I left the dinner. I think the envelope is still in my desk in my room."

"I'm not lying." Lexie leaned forward and took one of Alessia's hands in both of hers. "Go get it."

Alessia stayed still, her eyes filled with tears.

"Alessia, please. I didn't even know what happened that night until Declan told me, and I still don't know how someone taped us and set me up, but that's what happened, I swear."

Alessia got up and went to her room across the hall, then returned, still staring at the envelope in her hands. She finally leaned against the doorframe and looked up at Lexie. "My name is written on it," she said. "But it's not your handwriting."

"Whose handwriting is it?"

Alessia walked back to the window seat and handed the envelope to her sister. Lexie turned it over, then looked again at her sister's name written in pencil across the front.

"I honestly don't know whose handwriting that is." Lexie looked up at Alessia, her eyes filling with tears that threatened to spill over. "I didn't do this, Ally, I swear."

This time Alessia reached over to Lexie's desk for a tissue, then handed it to her sister.

"I know whose it is. It's Liz's handwriting. She tried to disguise it, but I know that weird A she makes, and it's right here." She took a breath, rubbing the back of her neck with her hand. "I'm so stupid. I can't believe I was so angry that I didn't notice it."

Lexie dried her eyes and leaned over again to look at the envelope. "But that doesn't make any sense. Why would she do that?"

"She told me a week before the wedding she wanted to postpone it so she could travel alone in Australia indefinitely, and I told her no." She paused. "So I guess this was her way of getting out of marrying me and shifting most of the blame onto you at the same time."

"Has anyone seen her since?"

"Someone told me a few months ago they'd gotten a postcard. But I don't think she'd be stupid enough to contact me again."

"So you thought this whole time I set this all up?"

Alessia nodded.

"Ally, I would never do that to you." Lexie shook her head and looked out over the sea, the whitecaps starting to break at the shore as the tide came in. "I don't expect you to forgive me for what happened, but please know I had nothing to do with that."

Alessia pulled her in and held her as long and tight as she had after the shooting.

"I know."

"You do?" Lexie pulled away slightly to look in her eyes. "Really?"

"I know you, Lex. I know you're telling me the truth." She looked down, twisting the tissue in her hand, then balling it up and squeezing it in her fist. "I think the part that broke my heart wasn't Liz, it was that I felt like I suddenly didn't know you. I never would have thought you'd do something like that, and I couldn't figure it out." She looked back up at her sister. "I felt…blindsided."

"I can't imagine how terrible that must have been for you." Lexie wiped the tears from her cheeks with the back of her hand. "Can you ever forgive me?"

"For sleeping with Liz?"

Lexie nodded.

"Already forgiven." Alessia smiled, squeezing her sister's hand. "Neither of us knew it at the time, but you definitely helped me dodge a bullet, so I actually owe you a thank you."

They both looked up just then as Sal rounded the corner carefully carrying a small saucer holding three shot glasses of his special grappa and set it between them on the window seat.

"Girls," he said, looking over their heads as if trying to remember what he'd planned to say. "You're part of each other's souls, and even if you think you can never get past this, I—"

They looked at each other and fell into giggles.

"What?" Sal said, looking around. "I feel like I've missed something."

"Da," Alessia said, smiling. "If we've already made up, do we still get the grappa?"

"Thank Baby Jesus." Sal clapped his hands together, beaming and grabbing a glass. "You can have the whole damn bottle!"

He joined his daughters in a drink as Alessia and Lexie downed their shots and set their glasses down on the window seat with a single thud.

"You didn't give this to Parker, did you, Da?" Alessia asked, handing him back the glasses.

"Yes, she and I had a drink just before I came in here with these."

"Da! She's an American."

"Yeah," Lexie said, tilting her head to the side with an identical look of concern. "You can't just start them out with this stuff."

"Excellent point." Sal ran his hand over his shock of wavy gray hair, standing most of it on end. "I'd better go supervise."

He crossed the room in two long strides and paused, looking back at his daughters.

"You two are the most beautiful part of my life," he said, his voice thick with emotion. "But even more beautiful back together."

Alessia crossed the room and handed him the saucer he'd forgotten, kissing him on the cheek.

"Da," Lexie said from the window seat, trying not to laugh. "The American!"

He remembered Parker suddenly and scurried off down the hall. Alessia came back to sit by her sister.

"So how did you get mixed up with Matteo?" she asked, stealing a swig of Pellegrino from Lexie's open bottle on the desk. "I about fainted when I figured out it was you in the sanctuary."

"I came back a few weeks ago. I knew I had to make an appearance at some point or Ma would go crazy—"

"You definitely missed that window," Alessia said, smiling.

"And I'd just walked from the train station and let myself into the café when I saw you and Da at the door."

Alessia looked puzzled. "What were we doing?"

"You both came in and sat down at one of the tables near the counter. You were making that list of the men who'd threatened to kill you."

"You were there?" Alessia asked, shaking her head. "Wow. I was clueless."

"Well, at that point, I wasn't ready for anyone to know I was back in town, so I just sat there and listened."

Alessia nodded. "So that's how you found out about Matteo."

"Yeah." Lexie collected their tissues and tossed them in the trash. "And when you left, I went next door and let myself into the jewelry store to see if I could find his information in the files." She paused, shaking her head. "And I use the term 'files' loosely. I actually found it in a pile of crumpled sticky notes in his desk drawer. But there was enough info to find him."

"Why did you want to do that?" Alessia shrugged off her jacket and laid it over the bed. The late afternoon sun was the color of warmth and intensified by the glass as the sun started to set over the ocean.

"Because you talked to Da about how you'd been less careful since your breakup with Liz, and some of them had been able to track your identity. That was my fault, and I had to at least try to fix it, even if you never spoke to me again." She paused, her eyes shimmering with emotion. "And I would never let anyone hurt you, you know that."

"But it wasn't your fault," Alessia said. "It could have just been bad luck."

Lexie smiled. "It was my fault."

"Okay, maybe a little."

They laughed and leaned against the window, both of them stretching their legs out on the bed across from the window seat.

"What was your plan for Matteo?"

"I didn't have one. In fact, I waited a while before I even contacted him," Lexie said. "But that's where it got complicated, because he saw you the day after in Santorini while you were wrapping up a job."

"And followed me and Parker to Lucia's house."

"How did you know that?"

"He left a little hint," Alessia said. "He took a picture of us sitting out on the patio and left it in the house with a knife blade through my face."

"Subtle." Lexie laughed, rolling the sleeves up on her shirt. "Anyway, so by the time I contacted him, he was already following you here."

"He did try to run me off the road, and a couple of other things, but he wasn't much of a stalker." Alessia dug her lip balm out of her pocket and handed it to her sister after she was done with it. "You must have been keeping him busy."

"That was the plan. But it started going south pretty quickly, and when I saw that note in the café that he'd left for you, I knew that was my chance."

There was a long pause.

"I'm tempted to ask what you mean, but I'm afraid you'll tell me." Alessia ran her hand through her hair. "What about the other two on the list? John and Anton?"

Parker stuck her head around the corner. "Sorry to interrupt, but Giada sent me in here to tell you something about the bread, but I think she really just wants to know how it's going." She stopped, looking from Alessia to Lexie. "What should I tell her?"

The sisters looked at each other and smiled, then turned back to Parker.

"We were just starting that way anyway," Lexie said. "I'll go see if she'll let me get away with giving her the short version." She stood and pulled her sister up as Parker left to go back to the kitchen. Lexie peered quickly into the mirror to swipe a bit of mascara under her eyes.

"I'll get out there first and let her know everything's fine," Lexie said, rounding the corner and leaning back into the room. "Take your time."

Alessia nodded and looked around Lexie's room, remembering all the sunlit afternoons they'd spent playing there when they were growing up, scanning the photos of the two of them covered in mud as toddlers, playing in the sea, and on holiday with their parents that lined every wall.

Except for one.

As she left, she looked up at the numerous awards, medals,

and trophies mounted on the wall by the door, glinting in the last of the afternoon sun. At the center were five framed gold medals, each mounted with a photo of Lexie accepting the top prize for Italy. Framed magazine articles from around the world hung above them, calling Alexa Cavalii a "shooting prodigy along the lines of Mozart" and "Italy's secret weapon in the 2016 Summer Olympics."

Alessia reached out and traced the edge of the closest frame with her finger, then turned out the lights and went to join her family, closing the door softly behind her.

About the Author

Patricia Evans is currently writing your new favorite novel in her hand-built tiny house, nestled deep in the forest, where she's surrounded by a bevy of raccoons and a sleepy brown bear named Waddles.

She travels to Ireland and Scotland several times a year in search of the perfect whiskey and cigar combination and spends most of her time trying to ignore the characters from her books that boss her around as she writes by the fire.

Follow her adventures:
www.tomboyinkslinger.com
@tomboyinkslinger on Instagram
patricia@tomboyinkslinger.com

Books Available From Bold Strokes Books

The First Kiss by Patricia Evans. As the intrigue surrounding her latest case spins dangerously out of control, military police detective Parker Haven must choose between her career and the woman she's falling in love with. (978-1-63679-775-5)

Language Lessons by Sage Donnell. Grace and Lenka never expected to fall in love. Is home really where the heart is if it means giving up your dreams? (978-1-63679-725-0)

New Horizons by Shia Woods. When Quinn Collins meets Alex Anders, Horizon Theater's enigmatic managing director, a passionate connection ignites, but amidst the complex backdrop of theater politics, their budding romance faces a formidable challenge. (978-1-63679-683-3)

Scrambled: A Tuesday Night Book Club Mystery by Jaime Maddox. Avery Hutchins makes a discovery about her father's death that will force her to face an impossible choice between doing what is right and finally finding a way to regain a part of herself she had lost. (978-1-63679-703-8)

Stolen Hearts by Michele Castleman. Finding the thief who stole a precious heirloom will become Ella's first move in a dangerous game of wits that exposes family secrets and could lead to her family's financial ruin. (978-1-63679-733-5)

Synchronicity by J.J. Hale. Dance, destiny, and undeniable passion collide at a summer camp as Haley and Cal navigate a love story that intertwines past scars with present desires. (978-1-63679-677-2)

Wild Fire by Radclyffe & Julie Cannon. When Olivia returns to the Red Sky Ranch, Riley's carefully crafted safe world goes up in flames. Can they take a risk and cross the fire line to find love? (978-1-63679-727-4)

Writ of Love by Cassidy Crane. Kelly and Jillian struggle to navigate the ruthless battleground of Big Law, grappling with desire, ambition, and the thin line between success and surrender. (978-1-63679-738-0)

Back to Belfast by Emma L. McGeown. Two colleagues are asked to trade jobs. Claire moves to Vancouver and Stacie moves to Belfast, and though they've never met in person, they can't seem to escape a growing attraction from afar. (978-1-63679-731-1)

The Breakdown by Ronica Black. Vaughn and Natalie have chemistry, but the outside world keeps knocking at the door, threatening more trouble, making the love and the life they want together impossible. (978-1-63679-675-8)

The Curse by Alexandra Riley. Can Diana Dillon and her daughter, Ryder, survive the cursed farm with the help of Deputy Mel Defoe? Or will the land choose them to be the next victims? (978-1-63679-611-6)

Exposure by Nicole Disney & Kimberly Cooper Griffin. For photographer Jax Bailey and delivery driver Trace Logan, keeping it casual is a matter of perspective. (978-1-63679-697-0)

Hunt of Her Own by Elena Abbott. Finding forever won't be easy, but together Danaan's and Ashly's paths lead back to the supernatural sanctuary of Terabend. (978-1-63679-685-7)

Perfect by Kris Bryant. They say opposites attract, but Alix and Marianna have totally different dreams. No Hollywood love story is perfect, right? (978-1-63679-601-7)

Royal Expectations by Jenny Frame. When childhood sweethearts Princess Teddy Buckingham and Summer Fisher reunite, their feelings resurface and so does the public scrutiny that tore them apart. (978-1-63679-591-1)

Shadow Rider by Gina L. Dartt. In the Shadows, one can easily find death, but can Shay and Keagan find love as they fight to save the Five Nations? (978-1-63679-691-8)

Tribute by L.M. Rose. To save her people, Fiona will be the tribute in a treaty marriage to the Tipruii princess, Simaala, and spend the rest of her days on the other side of the wall between their races. (978-1-63679-693-2)

Wild Wales by Patricia Evans. When Finn and Aisling fall in love, they must decide whether to return to the safety of the lives they had, or take a chance on wild love in windswept Wales. (978-1-63679-771-7

Can't Buy Me Love by Georgia Beers. London and Kayla are perfect for one another, but if London reveals she's in a fake relationship with Kayla's ex, she risks not only the opportunity of her career, but Kayla's trust as well. (978-1-63679-665-9)

Chance Encounter by Renee Roman. Little did Sky Roberts know when she bought the raffle ticket for charity that she would also be taking a chance on love with the egotistical Drew Mitchell. (978-1-63679-619-2)

Comes in Waves by Ana Hartnett. For Tanya Brees, love in small-town Coral Bay comes in waves, but can she make it stay for good this time? (978-1-63679-597-3)

Dancing With Dahlia by Julia Underwood. How is Piper Fernley supposed to survive six weeks with the most controlling, uptight boss on earth? Because sometimes when you stop looking, your heart finds exactly what it needs. (978-1-63679-663-5)

The Heart Wants by Krystina Rivers. Fifteen years after they first meet, Army Major Reagan Jennings realizes she has one last chance to win the heart of the woman she's always loved. If only she can make Sydney see she's worth risking everything for. (978-1-63679-595-9)

Skyscraper by Gun Brooke. Attempting to save the life of an injured boy brings Rayne and Kaelyn together. As they strive for justice against corrupt Celestial authorities, they're unable to foresee how intertwined their fates will become. (978-1-63679-657-4)

Untethered by Shelley Thrasher. Helen Rogers, in her eighties, meets much younger Grace on a lengthy cruise to Bali, and their intense relationship yields surprising insights and unexpected growth. (978-1-63679-636-9)

You Can't Go Home Again by Jeanette Bears. After their military career ends abruptly, Raegan Holcolm is forced back to their hometown to confront their past and discover where the road to recovery will lead them, or if it already led them home. (978-1-636790644-4)